THE WILDS

The Wilds Book One

Donna Augustine

For Jon,
Thanks for being such a great friend!

ISBN: 978-0692522882

Edited by Devilinthedetailsediting.com
&
720Editing

Chapter One

Have you ever wanted to be someone else so desperately that you wished for it with everything you had? Closed your eyes at night and prayed you would wake up as someone else? Would sacrifice anything to just not be you for another day? That's how I used to feel when I first came here, fourteen years ago a screaming child of four, crying as my parents walked out of this place without me.

I stayed like that for a long time, too, a black hole of emotion. I'd destroy any light that came too close. I cursed the world and everyone that dwelled upon it.

It was six years ago that I was lying in my private cell in The Holy Sanctuary for the Criminally Insane—or the Cement Giant as me and the other inmates called it—and had one of those moments, the kind where I could see beyond the confines I'd erected in my mind. The bars that had kept my mind in this dark place, as surely as the cement walls kept my body, weakened and rusted away.

I don't know why it happened. Maybe it was simply age or maturity, but the anger that had been pouring out of me like a spigot on full blast started to slow. I realized that this was it, the only life I was going to get. I could either let myself rot here in misery or I could find a way out. I'd already gotten one second chance. I'd survived when so many others hadn't. Was I really going to waste it here?

See the thing is, I'm a Plaguer, one who's had the Bloody Death and lived. That's not something many can say. When the Bloody Death hit the world a hundred and fifty years ago, it had a zero percent rate of survival. From what I've heard and read, one day no one had ever heard of the Bloody Death, and the next it ripped through the human population like a forest fire after a six-month drought. And just like a fire, it killed fast and painfully. People would be up walking around fine, only to fall bleeding on the street one moment, and gripped in agony and dead the next.

From the records left behind of that time, ninety-five percent of the population contracted the Bloody Death and all of them died during the initial outbreak. Not to mention that it didn't spring up and then disappear. No, it's been coming back every ten or twenty years. You don't have to be a math genius to know those odds suck. I guess it's a good thing there were so many humans to start with or we might have gone the way of the dinosaurs.

Everyone is fearful of when the next wave might hit. Maybe that outbreak will be the one to end us all. It's not like anyone knew where the Bloody Death came from, or why it still mysteriously showed back up from time to time, which added to the fear. The unknown and all that? Some people have a real hang-up about not knowing things. I don't understand that fear, but maybe it was because as a Plaguer, I've always known more than I wanted.

When rumors started creeping up about how a teeny tiny percent of the population, something like less than .001%, was surviving, most people thought it was a lie. Plaguers are so rare you can go your whole life never meeting one, but I'm living proof they exist.

The first couple of days after I'd survived the Bloody Death, I'd thought I was the luckiest girl to walk the Earth. I was young when it happened, only four and so full of childish delusions. Children can be like that before life teaches them better.

I still regard myself as lucky, but now I know survival comes at a cost. The Bloody Death changes you, makes you see things. They say these things aren't true, but I know better. They say all Plaguers are psychotic, contaminated and ruined, need to be locked away to protect society from the evil they spew about monsters.

I say they're blind. But maybe willfully so. I know what the Plaguers before me have said. I've seen the things they've seen. There's a reason no one wanted to believe them. I understand why they hide us in places like this.

The people here, they tell me that this is the only safe place for me. That I would be killed if I'd been born somewhere else, like the Wilds, which encompasses the vast majority of what used to be the United States now except for the small slivers pieced out to form the few smaller countries that exist.

I'd prefer to take my chances. I didn't survive the Bloody Death to only go on and live as if I were truly dead. If I was meant to be alive, I didn't want to walk this Earth—I wanted to truly live it, dance and revel in everything it had to offer, feel every sensation and emotion open to the human psyche. I would. Even if it took me until I was a hundred and I only had one single day of freedom, I would not die here; I would die living.

The door to my cell opened and startled me. It wasn't time for the daily release yet. I looked up from my bed, already dressed for the day in the simple white dresses we were given, to the guard.

"You're getting a visitor."

I let out a sigh. It was going to be one of those days.

Chapter Two

I sat on a metal folding chair in the bleak visiting room of painted cement, among a handful of other "patients" sitting with their parents or other family members who hadn't given up on their kin yet. It was only a matter of time. They all threw in the towel eventually.

It was almost understandable. I had a pretty thick callous built up over my heart from hearing the crying and pleading all the time, and it still clawed at me. Seeing it once a month or so when you had that fresh heart meat all tender like? Brutal.

Plus, no one ever got out. Once you were here, there was no release. You died here. But not me. That wouldn't be my end.

Out of the corner of my eye, I caught sight of the woman across the room watching me. She was one of the nurses, or at least that's what she pretended to be. Like the Plaguers before me, I knew better. A dark haze clung to her like a storm cloud she couldn't shake or maybe didn't want to. There was a name for them. Dark Walkers, the Plaguers had called them. Even before I'd come here, before I'd gotten sick, I remembered the tales spread by the Plaguers. I'd thought they were ghost stories. My mother had told me Dark Walkers didn't exist. Of course I believed her. My parents had been my entire world—until they weren't.

As the Dark Walker stared at me, I worried another knot in a head already full of red ones, never breaking from the act that helped keep me alive. Once upon a time, behaving as crazy as they said I was had been an act. I'd watched some of the other inhabitants of the Cement Giant and learned it all from them, the actions that would deem me mentally unstable. I'd embraced the facade because it was better to have your enemy think you were crazy and weak than having them know you were just waiting for your moment.

The nurse's attention was fine-tuned on me worse than normal today, but I was always on their radar. The Dark Walkers knew, or at least suspected, that I could see them for what they were. They ran test after test, each more painful than the last, but I never gave them what they wanted. It was ironic that my hunters were the only ones that wanted the truth and the last ones I'd ever tell it to.

I switched gears from forming knots to chewing on the stub of a thumbnail worn down to almost nothing, while I wondered who was going to walk through that door, the one that led out of this place.

At exactly nine, my visitor made his entrance. He had to be here for me, as I was the only one left sitting alone across from an empty seat. But even though it had to be him, I doubted what my eyes were seeing. He looked nothing like the others the Dark Walkers had sent, trying to trick me in to divulging my secrets in the past.

He was late twenties or maybe a very well aged early thirties. Even dressed up in his suit, he didn't look like a pencil pusher or a government worker. There was an edge to him that had nothing to do with his dark coloring or deep-set eyes. He scanned the room, like I did when I was sizing up which guards were on duty.

I'd thought I was going to sit here, spew the normal bullshit about how everything was just grand while the Dark Walker's spy tried to find a way to trip me up. After the first ten or twenty of these visits, I'd gotten the role I was playing down to the point I could nap through it, but this visit had just become interesting.

He handed his badge over to a nurse of the normal human variety. She made a show of flipping it over like she had some clue, clearly not viewing him as the threat I saw him to be. Sometimes I found it shocking how easily people believed what they were told. I wanted to shake her and tell her to wake the hell up. I'd tried doing that in my younger years. It never worked. People believed what they wanted.

Most of the time it's the things they find most beneficial to their situation, and they do all sorts of mental gymnastics to make it fit neatly into their reality.

I never understood that. The truth was so much easier to deal with, no mental backflips or cartwheels required.

The Dark Walker in the room with us noticed, though. They didn't miss much and didn't seem to have the same aversion to reality that humans sometimes had. This one had been here for a few years and she was even savvier than most of the ones I'd met. I watched her watching him. She seemed to be at full alert, as if she was viewing him as a threat.

She didn't wait long before she turned and left the room, probably to get reinforcements. This morning might turn out to be the most action I'd seen in years, or at least since Piggy Iggy, one of the other inmates, had gone nuclear all over the cafeteria after eating bad food out of the garbage.

The stupid human nurse handed him back his ID. She pulled out something for him to sign, but his attention had already settled on me.

I didn't break eye contact. After all, I could only play meek so much, and I didn't see a reason here for the charade. This wasn't a Dark Walker or one of their spies that I needed to hide my true self from. I shot him my *what the hell do you want* stare. It was a particular favorite of mine and handled quite a versatile amount of situations with little effort. It was also something that flew under the radar if a guard wasn't looking at your face at the time. It ranked even higher than my *you've got to be fucking kidding me with this shit* stare, which usually needed more information about what was happening before it could be used.

There was a subtle movement of his head that may or may not have been a nod, a picking up of the gauntlet—challenge accepted? I'd like to think I was right, but every so often I did wonder if perhaps I was as crazy as they said. How the hell would I know, anyway? It's hard to be objective about one's own sanity. What if the guy just had a crick in his neck?

He turned away to sign the paper and then the nurse pointed him in my direction, even though it was clear he knew exactly where to go. He wasn't getting any credit for knowing. I was the only person sitting alone. He could have the IQ of a rock and have figured that out.

He walked over toward the table in a sluggish manner, completely at odds with the physique his ill-fitting suit tried to hide. He pulled out the chair and sat down across from me, again with the stilted movements of someone fifty years older and horribly out of shape. I couldn't believe this act actually worked on some people.

There was something hard about his pale eyes but I wasn't afraid of him. Most people probably were when he wasn't playing dress-up. I should've been too, but it was difficult to dredge up fear for a human when you lived your life next to monsters.

Now that he was in range, generally within five feet of me, I waited for some of my "Plaguer Delusions" to hit. The information I got from people was never delivered in the same way but there were usually certain similarities. Sometimes the memories hit hard and fast and other times they leaked out in a small trickle.

I waited for something to come to me, a snippet of history so traumatic that it was burned into their mind, just waiting to be seen and heard, relived. Occasionally they didn't come at all, which was looking like it would be the case with him as he bent over paperwork that I suspected was nothing more than a prop.

It wasn't like I'd never drawn a blank before; it just wasn't often. Figured it would be him who would leave a big fat blank. Most of the time, I didn't want to see the things people shared. The flashes of a person's history, the stuff from the darkest corners of their mind, no matter how short, told me a lot. It always seemed to be the bad stuff too, never the good, only experiences so bad they cut out their own niche in the human psyche.

With a Plaguer, it was almost impossible to put your best foot forward. A good first impression meant that you didn't kill your brother last week or rape the neighbor's daughter. Because the truth of it is, in times like these, there wasn't anyone who was squeaky clean. I judged people on a sliding scale and a body count. I usually gave them the first murder for free and didn't knock serious points off until the third.

Still, I didn't need a red flag in my face to know this guy was on the hunt right now; maybe he always was. I hadn't survived this long without learning how to identify the threats. But what would he want with me? I had nothing to take.

"Your name is Dahlia Franks?" he asked, finally looking up from his notepad.

I didn't bother answering, just continued to sit and play the crazy part. This was one of the perks of being nuts. No one expected you to behave in accordance to the general population's playbook, and I enjoyed being a nonconformist.

He already knew who I was anyway. It made me wonder why people asked unnecessary questions.

He continued on, not missing a beat. "I'm here on behalf of our government of Newco. My name is Samuel Right. I'm doing randomized interviews to assess the living conditions in the Newco's various government-run facilities. Quality control, you could say."

I nodded as I swapped my thumbnail out for the pinky. It was my least favorite nail and, as such, had a decent stub left on it. In the last fourteen years I'd been here, not once had I ever heard of quality control interviews. No, this guy was a spy of some sort, but for who? For what? Not the Dark Walkers.

The Dark Walkers had sent in plenty of spies over the years, trying to trick me into telling them I knew they were different. They always posed as visiting experts that might be able to help me. They'd even sent in a supposed aunt I didn't know of, who could take me home with her if I just told her the truth. That one had almost gotten me snagged. It had mentally fucked me for weeks, too. But I never did tell, and I had a feeling that was why I was the only Plaguer left standing in this compound.

I didn't know how, even then at the young age of four, I knew instinctively to hide my knowledge of them, but I had. Just shows self-preservation is hard-wired into us. After all, I'd never seen a mouse sit back and wait for the cat to eat it, no matter how tiny and young it was.

"May I ask you some questions?" he asked, and I thought I caught a glimpse of something in those light eyes before they shuttered closed. It wasn't from fear. No, this guy didn't seem timid, and he certainly wasn't worried about me. He was hiding something, and if I had to guess, he'd heard enough about Plaguers to know something about what we could do but not enough to be accurate or to know how much.

He was playing a part but not well enough, and yet I still didn't think he was working for the Dark Walkers. That didn't mean he could be trusted.

"Just to get some background, you were brought here at age four after you killed your teacher. Is that correct?"

I leaned back in my chair and dropped the nervous nail-chewing act. I set my gaze on him, barely blinking. I said, "That is what the records say."

One of the things I hated most was thinking of the past, in particular that time after I'd gotten sick. My parents had told me I'd never had the Bloody Death. I'd just had a bad flu.

They sent me to school like nothing had changed, warning me to say nothing of any sickness. It might have worked if there hadn't been monsters there, just like they were here. This Dark Walker had been pretending to be a teacher.

I'd told my parents but they'd said monsters didn't exist. That I shouldn't speak of such things and that I was bad.

I'd gone back to school the next day and I saw the monster watching my friend. He was going to do something to him. I just knew it. Even then, I'd known that just because the people around me were stupid, didn't mean they should die.

So I lay in wait at recess. While the monster was eating his sandwich, I snuck up behind him and stabbed the monster in the neck repeatedly with my pencil until there was nothing but gurgling noises. The monster was defeated. They should've thanked me. They didn't.

There was a lot of chaos after that. They talked to my parents. I don't know what was said but I'd like to think they'd fought for me, that they hadn't had a choice. The next day I'd thought we were going to the beach. They drove me here instead.

That was when I'd become the hunted. There were monsters here as well but I never got the opportunity to kill another. That didn't mean I wouldn't in the future.

As if he sensed my agitation with the subject, he switched gears. "Do you like your accommodations here?" he asked, pencil poised over paper.

Now this was the perfect opportunity to use my *you've got to be fucking kidding me with this shit* stare.

No reaction from him. He shot off more

questions. "And the food? Would you say the meals are acceptable?"

It was hard not to laugh in his face. I was a walking stick figure of almost comical proportions. We were all thin here, but not like me. My friends called me Olive Oyl after some cartoon they'd found a while back.

The powers that be said I needed to be on a restricted diet, that the plague would return if I were at full strength. I couldn't say whether they were right or wrong. It wasn't my choice and I hadn't been given the opportunity to test the theory. I'd like to think that there were easier ways to kill me if that was what they were after. "I eat like a queen," I replied. "Can't you tell?"

I waited to see how he'd take that answer. He didn't even blink. "You *are* a Plaguer? Is that correct?"

I fisted my right hand where it was resting on my lap underneath the table. "Isn't that in your records, too?"

I watched his expression close enough that I could see his pupils dilate against the light background of his irises. Why would this be good news to him when most were disgusted by this fact and almost all were frightened that contact with me was lethal?

I wondered what any of this had to do with quality control. Did he not realize he'd gone way off script, or did he not care?

"And you're prone to delusions?" he asked.

Why was he asking this? It was common knowledge that Plaguers had them. We were insane. We spread lies and talked of monsters. Everyone knew it.

"Delusions?" I asked, pretending to have no idea what he was saying. Maybe he *was* with the Dark Walkers. This was more in line with what they would send people out to ask. Normal humans didn't like to hear what Plaguers said, let alone give it any merit. There was a reason lines like *don't shoot the messenger* came about. People didn't like to hear bad things. If they could deny them, more than nine out of ten people would. I know, the math is a little funny there because what's more than nine out of ten? Yeah, you got it. Pretty much everybody.

He leaned across the expanse of metal table. "Yes. Do you see things like most Plaguers?"

"I don't know any other Plaguers— anymore. I can't answer what most see," I said. My calm was starting to be rattled. I wanted to know who this guy was. Government worker? That was total bull. Spy for the Dark Walkers? No, I still didn't think so.

His eyes were still dead set on me. "Do you see delusions?"

For some reason I thought he wanted me to say yes. Like it meant a great deal to him. That this was what he had been hunting down. Part of me wanted to speak the truth to him that I denied so often. It wasn't about making him happy or not. I was tired of pretending. Eighteen years old but I felt like I was a hundred.

We openly stared at each other, sizing the other up. He finally broke the standoff by the slightest softening of his tone as he said, "You want to answer this."

It felt like something was left hanging off the end of that sentence. I didn't know what I saw in him, why I felt like he wanted this or why his slight softening undid me, but for some reason, I spoke and gave him what I knew he wanted. "Yes. I see things."

He leaned back in his chair, and for the first time since he'd walked in the door, he openly showed me a tiny glimpse of who he really was as he smiled like he'd just had a bloody meal of raw meat. There was someone brutal hiding behind this act. Whoever he really was, he was happy that I was a Plaguer who "had delusions." Who the hell was this?

I wouldn't get to find out, though. The door to the visiting room opened and I knew who it was immediately. Not only did the Dark Walkers have a cloud that clung to them, but they also had a smell. It was like a sickly sweet perfume that repelled instead of attracted. The woman who just walked in was the worst and also the one in charge.

Ms. Edith, as we were told to address her, walked over to our table. Black suit, white shirt and hair pulled back without a single stray in sight. She was one of them, the dark haze clinging to her. I forced myself to sit still even though my body tensed. I hated being near them, couldn't breathe through the smell. Luckily there weren't too many that I came in close contact with. There were others here, but only her and the other nurse came within a few feet of me.

"How are things going over here, Mr. Right? We hadn't expected a visit," she said, looking at him and then me. My fingers started knotting into my hair, reflexively going into the crazy act. I hadn't even thought of the action until Mr. Right's eyes flickered to my hand in my hair and then back to her.

"Last minute. Sorry for the abrupt arrival."

Her smell was stronger than normal, and I'd been around her enough times to know it happened when she was irritated. So he wasn't working for them? I looked up through lowered lashes to watch the interaction now that I knew for sure she hadn't been aware of this visit. His eyes darted to me a few times and I had the strangest feeling he sensed how much I hated to be around her.

He stood and smiled. "We're just finishing up."

"And how did things go?" she asked, her normally shrill voice sweetened unnaturally.

"Splendid. I'll send this report back to headquarters and I'm sure everyone will be very pleased."

Boy, this guy was just oozing with lies today. He looked down at his notebook and then back to her and that was when the fun really started. He softened his smile, leaned in closer to her and then offered up his arm to her. He was dialing up the sex appeal until even my inexperienced little heart was doing flip-flops, and I wasn't even the target. Nothing of the raw brutality I sensed was showing through now, or the earlier awkward act. Seemed my visitor was quite the chameleon.

"If I could get a quick tour, I'll be out of your hair."

Whatever Dark Walkers were, which I'd bet my ass wasn't human, they apparently still liked human men. She smiled back and locked her hand down on him in a way that made me imagine claws hidden under that flesh. "I have a free moment. I can show you around."

They walked off and he didn't even glance back at me. I wasn't sure where I'd gotten the crazy feeling that being truthful with him was going to set something in motion, but I had. Watching him disappear with one of the monsters made me feel a little heavier in my chair, and the adrenaline that had coursed through my veins while I'd been squaring off with him was now receding.

This was turning into one really strange day.

Chapter Three

I was still watching their backs from my metal chair when the nurse, the human one, motioned for me to get up and go to the cafeteria. Lunch was in progress. I caught what would probably be my last glimpse of him and then moved on with the business of surviving.

The cafeteria was in full swing as I made my way over to where they distributed the meals. A lady in a white outfit and hair net handed me my special fare over the food counter and I headed toward the table where the handful of other girls I considered friends sat at.

There had been a point in my life where I'd never thought I'd have friends. I had this crazy idea that the only reason any of them had come around me in the first place was in part due to their own suicidal tendencies. This place could do that to the best of people, and well, looking around, I wasn't sure any of us fell into the upper echelon of the human race.

Not that I was in a place to cast judgment, though. At the time, it was just nice to have a human being to talk to, clinically depressed or not, I hadn't been too choosy. I'd tried to counsel them to the best of my abilities for my own selfish reasons, hoping they would hold on for a bit. Surprisingly, some of them did. Three of them had become the glue that kept what was left of me together.

Looking over at the plates of my co-survivors, no one had a gourmet meal in front of them, but they were still more appealing than my own Plaguer fare of broth and bread. They had yellow stuff and a round meat-type thing. The only similarity was the roll.

I watched as Margo ripped open hers and then placed a piece of mystery meat inside it before laying it back on her tray.

"Check for clearance," she said. On cue, Margo, Patty Cindy and myself all searched out our particular corners and the guards who stood at them. When we all gave the okay, her roll was swapped with the one on my tray.

These three girls had made life bearable here. They alternated who gave up part of their meal for me every day. They listened to me when I had no one else to talk to. They were my sanity and my motivation. I wouldn't get out of here just for myself but for them, because if I didn't get out, no one would. I was the best shot we had. It wasn't because I was the strongest or smartest, but because I was the only one fearless enough to grab the opening if it came.

"I swear, I think they mean to starve us out sometimes," Patty said, her dark hair sticking up every which way after we'd gotten hold of a pair of scissors last week. She'd wanted a pixie cut.

It wasn't like any of us had pretended to have a clue on how to cut hair. Luckily there weren't any mirrors in this place. We were each other's mirrors, so Patty currently thought she looked smoking hot.

"Or at least starve Dahlia," Margo, who still had a normal head of brown hair, said.

"Who was the visitor?" Cindy, the only blonde among us, asked.

We'd all been in for a while and none of us got visitors anymore. It was always a big deal when someone came. I got more than anyone and it was never somebody I wanted to see. For the others, the last visit had been for Margo about five years ago, before her mother eventually stopped coming.

None of these girls were Plaguers, but that was the least common ticket into this place. In truth, there were lots of ways to be deemed criminally insane. Like in Margo's case, when she claimed her father was molesting her. Margo's father was a government employee. You didn't say bad things about government employees, even if you were their daughter. You either took what they dished out and ate it up with a smile or this was where you ended.

"Said he was government quality control, but he sure didn't look like he worked for any government we know," I said between a large bite of bread and meat.

23

Margo's head tilted downward. "I was really hoping maybe… I knew it was a long shot, but a visitor? I just figured…"

I knew who she had hoped it was; who she thought it might've been. I was glad she didn't finish her sentence. Just like Margo's father, mine had worked for the government, but higher up. The last thing I'd heard about my parents was that my father had died. I'd thought briefly afterward that maybe my mother would try and get me. She had been the softer-hearted of the two. That was three years ago.

"What did he look like?" Cindy asked, breaking the tension and always looking for a little entertainment.

I was still chewing the same bite—I liked to really make the most of meals—which bought me some time to get my head around a good description. And it had to be good. Visitor stories were big entertainment for us.

"He was in this drab gray baggy suit but it didn't matter. You could see the muscles underneath when he moved, like he was a gladiator of old or something." I tried to emphasize every word and give my retelling as much suspense and intrigue as I could. Most of us could retell the most mundane happenings as if they were absolutely riveting. "He had this way of looking at you through steely eyes." I squinted my eyes and tried to make them deeper and intense like his had been, and shot each of them a second or two stare. "It made you think he might pounce on you at any second." I paused now for effect before I added, "And you wanted him to!"

"So he was hot?" Cindy asked, gripping my arm in excitement.

"Steaming," I said, and realized my story was actually true this time. I hadn't lied, although I would've just to perk them up.

Margo let out a sad little sigh. "He had to have been good if you thought he was hot. You don't like anyone. To see prime male meat." She jolted up suddenly. "Oh, talking about hot, drop something. I just got a new Moobie in hot off the presses. Already read it last night."

I immediately dropped my napkin to the ground. I leaned down to retrieve it and grabbed the book from Margo under the table. I had it stashed and adjusted it up my dress in under two seconds flat. Moobie was much better reading than the short list of approved books we could get from our classes once a week.

Moobie spy books were banned reading, and we lived for them. One day I was going to get out of here and be just like Moobie. He went to elegant parties, traveled the world, and had the coolest lines. He always knew exactly what to do in any situation. The best thing about him, though, was he didn't take shit and no one pushed him around. Ever. He generally kicked ass.

If it weren't for Margo, I'd never know about Moobie. She was sleeping with Ben, one of the guards, and he sneaked them in for her. It was like the dysfunctional compound version of bringing flowers to a date.

As far as the guards went, Ben wasn't that bad, at least judged by my sliding scale. Margo figured it was better to choose one guard she could stand than waiting for them to all have a go at her. Patty and Cindy followed suit shortly after. There seemed to be an unspoken thing—or maybe it was said in the guardroom, or wherever they went, for all we knew—that once you had a guard boyfriend, the other guards backed off.

I seemed to be the only one who the guards avoided of their own accord, and I was thankful for it. If that meant that maybe I was too ugly to bother with, than *hear, hear* for ugly. Winning a beauty pageant wasn't going to get us out of here and I wasn't in the market for a soul mate; all I wanted was freedom.

A chair clattering to the ground drew our attention to the front of the room. Hagger, another of the guards and one I held in particularly high disgust, was standing over Piggy Iggy laughing. He'd tripped her. That was one of his favorite pastimes. He'd probably watched her heading toward the garbage—she had serious tunnel vision for garbage—and instead of telling her she couldn't dig though it, he'd tripped her instead.

Instinct drove me to my feet. Hagger's eyes met mine. We'd had run-ins before. I'd like to say I'd won some of these confrontations, that I hadn't gotten my ass kicked and bad, but that outcome only happened in my dreams. And to be precise, I'm talking daydreams. He'd kicked my ass in a couple of nightmares, too, not that I'd openly fess up to that. I just couldn't win with that bastard.

Patty's hand stalled me when I would've moved forward, holding me in place, silently encouraging me to sit.

"This isn't a fight you can win," Margo said. "Don't land yourself in the hole again. You almost didn't make it last time."

I looked at Margo and saw the desperation on her face. I felt the bite of Patty's nails in my skin, because she was gripping me so tightly, and the watery look to Cindy's downcast eyes. As much as they kept me going, I knew I was their emotional crutch here too, and no matter what they said I was the only one left with any hope we'd get out. One by one, they'd given up and accepted this place as the end of the line for them. I was the only one that truly believed we would all eventually have a life beyond here.

And if I had to carry that torch and see it done, I would do it. These girls were my family. I'd chop off my limbs for them.

I broke eye contact with Hagger. Margo was right. I'd come down with pneumonia last time I'd been tossed in the hole.

Piggy Iggy wasn't my favorite person, but it was hard to stand back and watch—but that was what I did. Iggy finally got to her feet and I relaxed enough to sit down again. One day I wouldn't have to sit. I'd walk right up to Hagger and let him have it. I'd bide my time now, but that day would come.

"We'll all be getting out. You'll see. Just remember, if I get out, I'll send you the sign and be ready." I'd had lots of time to think on what I'd do when I got out. How I'd bust them out as well, and I knew exactly how I was going to do it.

"Dal, I don't think it's ever going to happen," Margo said, and I could see that the disappointment of my last visit not being what she'd hoped was weighing her down more than normal. "Maybe you should just face it. It's easier to live without the disappointment."

She leaned back in her chair, not eating anymore. Her face was drawn and there was a sadness in her eyes that was there more often than not lately, like she was mentally hitting the wall of the Cement Giant until it robbed her of

28

who she was. I saw so clearly what this place was doing to her, doing to all of us, and I refused to believe that this was what the entirety of our lives would be. My eyes shot to some of the tables where the old-timers were. They were like zombies at this point, no sparkle left in their eyes.

I wasn't giving up and I wouldn't let them either. "I'll get out. Just make sure when I send you the sign, you're ready."

***

The fifty-by-fifty yard was empty today as I lay down on the bench so that all I could see was the sky, not the dreary cement building or the depressing cement wall that enclosed the space and made it hard to take a deep breath. With my face raised to the sky, I let the drizzle land on my skin. I liked when it rained, but I was the only one. Everyone else had stayed inside. The rain wouldn't stop me from getting the small taste of the outdoors. Without the noises of other people that would destroy my illusion, I could pretend I was in a huge field with nothing but trees surrounding it.

It was nice alone. This was what it would be like when I left here. I'd run until I couldn't breathe hard enough to pump my muscles, and not because I hit a gray cement wall. There wouldn't be any cement or white clothing or ugly ponchos like I wore now. I'd surround myself with bright colors, polka dots and stripes in every shade from purple to yellow. And flowers, I'd have flowers everywhere, like the ones I remembered from the garden growing up.

I'd pick flowers and bring them into the house every day and hang yellow curtains, the color of sunshine, over a sink where I'd wash sky blue plates.

"Time." The guard's deep voice from near the building called out the word. It was Tim, another one of the many guards here. He did the outside duty, and although he didn't have a bad voice, I dreaded hearing him from the second I stepped out here.

I didn't move, pretending I didn't hear the call.

"I said 'time.'" Tim was getting mad. If I didn't move soon, I knew what would come next. Tim wasn't the worst. He didn't throw punches for fun, but he did have a short temper.

I hesitated. If they weren't coming for me soon, and without the girls tempering my instincts, I'd risk the beating. Why? Because sometimes it was worth the pain just to remember who you were. But they *would* be coming after the visitor this morning, and I needed to be as healthy as possible. I took a final look at the sky.

I wouldn't die here. No, that wouldn't be my end. I didn't know if I'd go out in a blaze of glory like some of the characters in the Moobie books, but there was no way I'd give them my final day.

I dragged myself back toward the door, past the rusted swing set that looked like it had been here for a century, the same one that was all shiny and new in the pamphlets they handed out to the visitors.

I walked back toward my room for final head count, past the other girls in the place, most of who avoided me, and with a few coconspirator winks to the ones who kept me going.

I spotted a new girl on my way to my cell. She must have gotten here this afternoon sometime. She'd looked only four or five, and I caught a quick glance down at her hand. No brand. I wasn't sure if I was relieved for her or not.

She was three rooms away, which meant I'd be able to hear her tonight when the crying started. I wished I could help her, but there isn't anything that can speed up some processes. No soothing words that can wipe away the pain. Unfortunately, she'd have to live through this on her own until the tears finally stopped.

Kevin and Rob, two more guards, walked down the hall doing head count and shutting us in our rooms as they went. They'd double back to whoever they were sleeping with after everyone was locked away.

They got to me, made a check on their clipboard and my metal door slammed, shutting me into the eight-by-eight room for the next sixteen hours, unless she called for me tonight like I expected.

There was a single window in my gray cell, ten inches by ten inches, but it didn't open. There was a bed, a table and a chair. A bedpan was underneath every bunk for those who couldn't hold it until morning. There were some pens and papers on the table but that was it. There were always pens and papers around. They encouraged me to put down my horrible thoughts but I'd never done it. I kept it all inside, locked up tight.

I flopped down on my bed and pulled out my new Moobie. My fingers ran over the leather cover as I opened it. I'd escape into Moobie's world while I waited for the footsteps to come down the hall and drag me back into this world again.

Chapter Four

An hour after lockdown, the sound of feet hitting concrete as they walked in the otherwise silence of the hall reached me. It was Ms. Edith's personal guards. I knew the visitor today would pique the Dark Walker's interest. A sickness that had been building exploded in my stomach as I heard them getting closer.

I always prayed I was wrong, that they'd walk past, but the footsteps were always followed by the sound of a key in the lock. They opened the door to my room and stood there. They didn't need to say anything and I didn't fight them. I got up from my bed without any hint of how I dreaded what was to come, shoulders square.

We walked down the corridor, one guard in front of me and one behind. I didn't know their names. Her guards didn't last too long. I wasn't sure what happened to them and didn't really care either. They only had one work detail and that was handling the Dark Walker's business.

I used to resist but it hadn't made any difference. I actually thought some of the guards enjoyed the struggle. I hadn't for the last year, not since it had dawned on me that as much as I dreaded what was to come, my opportunity to escape might also lie in these moments.

The less I fought, the more and more lax they were becoming. One of these times, I'd get my opening.

We walked across the compound through the maze of halls and I was always amazed in these moments just how massive this place really was, what lay down some of these other hallways. We made it to the other side of the building to a set of doors that led to her dominion.

This was where the bile would start to rise in my throat, not that I'd let on to the guards. No matter how many times I'd been through this, I still dreaded it. When I was being honest about it, I knew it was fear I felt. I might have hated that most of all, being afraid. No matter how I tried to talk myself down in my head, diminish it as just a short period of pain, I could never totally get rid of the feelings.

The guard in front opened the doors and we walked through into the part of the compound that was off limits to most. I heard the guard behind me lock them after us.

This was when it got the toughest. When I wanted to turn to them and beg them to let me leave. I bit the inside of my cheek to stop the words that wanted to come.

I'd done it when I was younger. Begged. Groveled. Humiliated myself to them, on my knees with a mixture of tears and snot running down my face.

It hadn't mattered. Had somehow made it worse afterward. Now it wasn't just the pain I faced when I came here but humiliation as well. I'd always remember how pathetic I'd been. I've heard pride is a sin. In my book, begging is worse.

But that was a long time ago. I hadn't begged for help in years and wouldn't. It didn't matter what they did to me. I could get past the pain but I'd never forget grabbing on to a guard's leg and the embarrassment of getting backhanded for messing his pants with a mixture of my tears and snot. Or the laughter that followed when I'd peed myself in fear.

We came to the room, the heavy metal door gliding open silently. This one was always well oiled. A single wooden chair sat in the center with straps attached to it. It reminded me of the electric chair I remembered seeing a picture of once.

I wasn't the first Plaguer to sit in this chair. I knew they'd killed my kind here. Some of the guards talked, especially to the girls they were sleeping with. Ben, Margo's guard, had even warned her in a weak moment. He'd said to tell me to give them whatever they wanted when they brought me here. That they'd kill me if I didn't.

He was wrong. I'd already be dead.

I crossed to it of my own accord and sat in the chair, not fussing at all as they bound my wrists and legs with thick leather straps with buckles. This was where the Dark Walker would interrogate me.

I'd endure what was to come and I'd survive it. Hopefully, an opportunity might present itself afterward. As much as this part of the compound didn't look that different than the rest, just more painted cement, there was one very important difference. There was a window in here, large enough for a body to squeeze out of, and it opened. I'd seen the latch. There were no bars in front of this one like all the rest, or anything else to impede my escape.

Six months ago, after I'd awoken from what she'd done to me, I'd found myself alone in this room but I'd been unprepared for the opportunity. I wouldn't be again. If I'd acted quick enough, I might have gotten out of here. But I'd sat too stunned to even try and escape the chair before they walked back in.

After I was strapped in, they hooked up the device that would send shocks through my body. They were just finishing as Ms. Edith entered. She wore her dark hair in the same bun but had switched her jacket to a white lab coat, as if she were some sort of doctor. God, I hated her most of all.

One of the guards placed a chair several feet

in front of mine and she walked over and sat upon it as if it were a throne. Then she smiled. She always did, as if we were old and dear friends. I couldn't get memories from Dark Walkers but I didn't need them. She enjoyed these sessions.

"Hello, Dal," she greeted me, using my nickname. I wasn't sure why that burned me worse than anything else. One day I'd punch her in that same mouth that she used to speak to me as if she really knew me.

"Hello," I greeted in response, holding back my own anger.

The guard finished attaching the torture device to me and handed her a small box with a wire that ran to where I sat. It had a dial on it and a button. It was simple but effective. I knew the higher that dial went, the more likely I was to die.

"Leave," she said to the guards. We both watched them walking out, her with enthusiasm and me with dread.

I knew what came next.

"You had a visitor today," she said as she toyed with the dial.

I didn't answer. She wasn't asking, just stating the topic of today's interrogation.

The thing was, I knew there was no way to escape the pain today, even if I told her everything she wanted to hear, but my mind still scrambled for a way out. I hated it. It made me feel like an animal.

Her fingers toyed with the dial again. I didn't look directly at it, knowing she wanted me to. She wanted to see the fear I withheld from her.

It didn't matter where she'd dialed it up to anyway. The lower settings would be more bearable but last longer. The higher settings would bring oblivion quicker, but eventually, it always came. I'd almost never left this room on my own two feet. There were only a handful of times that I had in the years I'd been here, and those were only due to outside interruptions. Now these sessions were held at night. There was nothing like a pesky work call to disrupt a good torture.

My eyes flickered to the dial before I could stop myself. She looked at me, smiling.

"So, let's start with what you said to your visitor today." She leaned back in her chair and crossed her legs while I was nearly immobile. The gesture wasn't lost on me.

I relayed the conversation verbatim to her, seeing no point in bothering to withhold any of it. The visiting room was rigged for sound, another Ben tip. Plus, she didn't want to know what was said. She wanted to know what I'd seen.

"Was there anything else?" she asked. "Did

you get one of your hallucinations?"

That was the thing about Plaguers; even though I hadn't heard anything else, which was the truth in the visitor's case, no one believed me anyway. I debated when to feed her the lie. I needed to survive this session and how ever many more it took to get out. But if I made it too easy, she wouldn't believe my made-up story. I'd made that mistake before.

"No," I said.

The pain shot through me and my body jerked with it. I didn't cry out. Maybe I should've but I fought against it. I could only give them so much of myself before I'd have nothing. The hurt stopped and I slumped against the straps that held me in place, my breathing louder than it had been.

"Dal, you know holding back just prolongs this. Why do you want to make it harder on yourself?" Her fingers went to the dial, creeping it up until I knew it had to be near the danger zone.

"You're right." I knew she was getting close to hitting the button again. Time to lie. She was more impatient today than normal.

"So why don't you tell me what you saw? You need to tell me about the delusions you have so that I can help you." Her voice was soft and pleading, as if that was all she ever wanted to do.

I blurted out the lie I'd come up with earlier, about him killing his coworker. It was a joke, since I didn't even believe he worked for the government. By time I was done, she seemed pleased with herself.

She leaned forward, her hand coming to rest on my knee like a concerned guardian. "You know these are delusions, right? They don't mean anything."

"Yes," I said, placating her.

"So let's talk about what you see when you look at me. Do you have any visions of me? Do you see anything differently?" She leaned back again in the chair, hand on the dial.

She knew I did, or highly suspected. This was all a game with her and the winner was predetermined. Sometimes I wondered what would happen if I told her the truth, but that survival instinct that I relied on so heavily always stopped me.

"I see nothing."

The smile came and the knob turned. "You're sure? Nothing at all?"

I shook my head.

"Now, Dal, I know you're lying. You could stop this if you'd just be honest with me. You need to tell me so I can help you. I don't want to hurt you. But you're only giving me one option."

Even if I got out of here tomorrow and lived

a thousand years, the hate I had in my heart for her would never dim. Sometimes in these moments, it swelled so large I feared the hate might one day take over everything I was. "I see nothing."

Her hand went to the control and the pain shot through me.

I must have been wavering in and out of awareness for a while, but when I finally came to, it was only me and one guard in the room. She was gone and so was the other one.

He stepped in front of me and our eyes met. As far as mental scars, he wasn't the worst I'd ever experienced, a bad beat-down before leaving the person to die. At least I could feel the remorse with this guard.

He put a finger to his lips. "Don't say anything and close your eyes. I'm supposed to call her when you come around."

"Let me go," I said, sensing the opportunity that came from this man's inner conflict. "Just loosen a strap and leave the room. That's all I need."

He hesitated just long enough for a tiny flare of hope to flicker within me before he shook his head and snuffed it out. "Can't do that. I let you go and I'll be the one sitting in that chair tomorrow," he said, getting angry at the request.

"You just need to loosen it. That's all," I said, weighing the chance of pressing him to further anger against the potential of getting to him to help. "No one has to know you did anything."

"She's up?" the other guard said as he appeared in the door, and I knew the possibility of enlisting any aid had gone from struggling to drowning. The guard who'd just arrived had some ugly shit in his head and not a drop of remorse to be found.

"Yes. Was just going to go get her," the guard said, referring to Ms. Edith.

"She's going to need a few minutes. She's on a call." The recent arrival walked farther into the room and took the seat Ms. Edith had left open. He reached down and picked up the control box that sat by the foot of the chair.

"Mark, we aren't allowed to touch that," the nice-ish guard said.

"Chill out, Bruce. Who's going to know?" Mark played with the dial, bringing it up to where I knew one quick press of the button would kill me.

"Stop playing with that. She dies and Ms. Edith is going to be pissed. This is the last one we have left," Bruce said.

He had to mean Plaguers. It was true. I was the last Plaguer left in the compound. Larissa had disappeared two years ago, probably died in the chair I now sat in. I often forced the thought of her from my mind, like I did now, because we all had a limit on what we could tolerate before we broke. I couldn't break.

"But why does that bitch get to have all the fun?" Mark was leaning back, holding the control and looking at me like I was a treat to eat.

If I showed fear, it would egg him on. That was what happened to the others he'd killed. His corrupt spirit fed on fear and he'd gotten carried away. One murder had turned into five. I couldn't panic. I'd gotten so close; there was no way I could die now. Not here.

The other guard made a reach for the box but the asshole yanked it backward and away.

"Stop fucking around with that. You can't do it full blast. You'll kill her for sure," Bruce said when he'd been unable to get the control from him.

"I don't know about that. She's taken more than any of the others and she's still alive."

"How do you know what she's taken?" Bruce asked.

"Just because you don't like to listen in doesn't mean I can't."

"Doesn't mean she'll be able to this time. You answering for her death? 'Cause I ain't." Bruce eyed the control, looking for an opening to snatch it away.

"Stop being such a mouse and grow some balls." Mark turned away from his coworker and all attention landed squarely back on me. "Ms. Edith has a real hard-on for Plaguers. Let's play a game, me and you. What does she think you see? Is it true what the Plaguers have said? About there being Dark Walkers?" He made an exaggerated shudder but I could tell he really wanted to know.

He wouldn't believe it if I told him. He brought the control in front of him and stared at me. "You going to answer me?" he asked. "Or are you going to need some encouragement?"

Just as I started fearing I wouldn't have a chance to escape tonight, or any other night, that I might really die in this hellhole of cement, the lights above my head started flickering, drawing all of our attention. They made a buzzing noise and then they were out. The room was cast in utter darkness.

I heard one of the guards move and the door swung open. The hall was unlit as well. From the intensity of the darkness, the whole place might have gone out.

"The generators died. That asshole Paul probably didn't fuel them," Mark said.

"Go check it out. I'll stay here, since we aren't supposed to leave any of the inmates alone out of their cells in a lights-out situation,"

Bruce suggested, and I prayed I'd get another opportunity alone with him.

"We aren't under attack. It's Paul."

"Then you go."

"No, you go," the other guard yelled as they argued in the dark.

I heard noises in the far distance as the situation was probably causing alarm. Footsteps echoed down the hall beyond our area as others went to go investigate the outage.

My two guards were currently arguing. I'd gotten the sense there wasn't much respect there, and the discussion quickly digressed into insults.

I didn't care what they were saying. They couldn't see me and they were distracted. If I could get out of this chair, I might be able to get to the window and out of here before they stopped arguing.

I yanked at my hand, willing to sacrifice some layers of skin or break my thumb if needed. Last time I checked, thumbs weren't necessary to run.

They were still arguing when a slight breeze trickled over my skin and fresh air wafted by my nose. That window hadn't been open when I'd first gotten here. Maybe they opened it while I was knocked out, but I would've noticed a breeze before now.

It was a new moon so there wasn't a drop of

light to see even if I could turn around, but I took a deep breath. That was *definitely* fresh air. Was the place under attack? Had someone cut the power to the generator? I wanted to hop up and down in the chair.

This wasn't necessarily anything good for me, but anything bad for them had potential. The guards were still arguing and had decided to move on to rehashing every wrong the other ever committed, if the "you stole my soda a month ago" was any indication. Did neither of them realize the window was open and we were probably no longer alone?

I yanked harder on my right hand, the one that had more give in the strap. There was another strap around my chest, holding my back firm to the chair and stopping me from using my teeth on the buckle. I had to get my wrists out. I'd been tensing my arms when they buckled me in to give me some leverage and room, but I needed more. If I could get one free, I could unbuckle myself.

I froze as I felt the draft of something, or more likely someone, moving past me. Then I went back to my struggles. This was my opportunity and I wasn't going to lose it. Whoever was busting in here could go about their business while I went about mine.

I yanked at my hand violently, more than willing to rip it from my wrist if that was the cost of freedom, when there were shuffling noises in front of me, approximately where I'd heard the guards standing. There was a grunt and then the sound of someone falling before another body sounded like it hit the floor.

This couldn't have been going better for me. Who knew how much time the stranger had just bought me by taking out my guards? I briefly contemplated asking for some help before the intruder disappeared off to their target, but didn't have to make that choice. Fingers were at the straps of my chair before I could contemplate what was happening. I started to struggle violently, expecting some of what the guards had gotten.

"Stop," a male voice said. "If you dislocate something it's going to be harder to get you out of here."

I immediately knew the husky male voice. "You?" The fake government worker was breaking me out? I *knew* something had been wrong with him. "What the—"

"Not now," he said. "Let's get out of here first."

That last sentence stopped the flow of questions about to gush out of me. It didn't matter. I'd take whatever help I could getting out of here and worry about the source later. If he was worried about me dislocating something then he certainly wasn't planning to kill me.

Good enough in my book!

I went perfectly still as he worked the straps at my wrists. As soon as they were free, I undid the one around my chest. I yanked off the electrical leads in a quick swipe as he undid my ankles. It didn't matter to me who he was or why he was here. I was getting out! That was all I cared about. I could die a foot from that cement wall and I'd still not regret it.

Chapter Five

The second I was free, I bolted toward the window. There was no hesitation. I didn't bother asking him who he was or why he was here. I didn't care anymore. I had a single preoccupation. This was my chance to escape.

My fingers gripped the waist-high sill, getting ready to launch myself onto it when his hands came to my waist and gave me a boost. I was startled by the touch.

People avoided touching me. He'd helped me out of the chair but with the straps it had been unavoidable. Now he was touching me again when he didn't have to. I would've made it through the window, albeit a bit slower, on my own. I didn't bother asking him about that either.

It was a fleeting thought as I saw nothing but fields of grass and forest in the distance. I leapt from the window and my knees groaned as I landed on the dirt six feet below. I looked to my left and saw the huge wall. It was just as ugly from this side. This was the first time I'd been on the outside of the cement giant in fourteen years, and the adrenaline ripped through my system like I was tapped into a geyser.

The lights that normally glowed from the top were out. He, whoever he was, had definitely cut the electricity to the entire compound. He must have gotten to the main generators but I'd been under the impression they were well guarded.

I scanned what I could see of the place, trying to get my bearings, from the outside looking in for once. Margo, I'd try and get her first, but how? The windows were too small in the cells. I eyed the window I'd just come out of, still wide open. If I went back in, would I get back out?

I hesitated for a moment, thinking of the people I was leaving behind: my friends and the young girl who had just come to this place. It was a stupid choice but I took a few steps back toward the building before I was jerked to a halt.

"I have to get my friends," I said, trying to jerk my arm loose.

"You won't get anybody. You'll be dead and I didn't do this to walk away with nothing," he said, his grip still firm.

I had no idea who this man was. Pretty sure his name wasn't Samuel, and I'd bet everything he didn't work for the government. But he was right. I'd already had a plan; I'd had one for years and it would take some work but it was my only shot at helping them.

I nodded, agreeing but not having the heart to say out loud I was leaving them behind, even if only for a short while.

"Put this on," he said, releasing me and handing me a dark sweatshirt.

I turned to see he was dressed all in black as I took the sweatshirt from him. It was three times my size but I gratefully threw it on over my white clothes and then pulled the hoody up over my bright hair.

The second it was on, he grabbed my hand and started tugging me after him. We were making a mad dash for the tree line I hadn't seen in years, not since my parents had brought me here. The guilt was staggering as I took my first step away, but the feeling of the freedom I'd been craving was overwhelming.

I was running through a field of grass and then surrounded by trees as we entered the forest. Leaves and branches whipped at my skin, leaving trails of early evening dew across my skin along with some welts, and I'd never felt anything so wonderful. My lungs couldn't get enough of the smell of wet bark or the feeling of my feet hitting something other than cement. A few deer were startled by our approach and darted across our path as we ran, and I had to force myself to concentrate on not getting distracted.

A couple hundred feet in and I slipped and fell. My cloth moccasins were predictably not conducive to running, just as they'd been designed. Flat on my back and I wanted to laugh for no other reason than the wonderful feeling of looking up at the tree canopy from where I'd fallen.

He stopped instantly and was assessing me while I was already getting to the business of ripping my shoes off.

"Your feet?"

"Will heal if we get the hell out of here. Dead doesn't get better," I said, knowing I would've run on a broken ankle if needed. He nodded an approval I didn't need or care about.

He leaned down and grabbed my hand, yanking me upward faster than I would've moved. I didn't mind. We weren't home free yet and the sirens started blaring in the distance, punctuating that fact. The compound must have gotten their generators back on and also discovered my disappearance. That was the sound of a full alert, all bodies on deck, there's an escaped prisoner. I'd only heard it a handful of times since I'd been there.

"They're going to send out dogs," I said, but I wasn't sure if he was listening to me as we raced through the forest.

I remembered the last girl who had managed to escape, or sort of. She hadn't gotten far, maybe not even out of these same woods. They'd loosed the dogs. The next morning they'd found pieces of her, which they'd carried back and placed in the courtyard. We'd had an afternoon viewing, stuck out with what was left of her in the yard underneath the hot sun. Even if you managed not to look, you couldn't escape the smell of rotting flesh. There wasn't a single girl who didn't know what happened if you ran. I'd never faulted Patty, Margo or Cindy for their fear.

I was built differently, or maybe the Bloody Death really *had* made me insane, because I remembered that afternoon vividly and how I'd thought she'd been the lucky one. She'd died outside the compound. She'd died trying, not withering away until she was a mere shell of flesh, no better than a zombie.

Still, my legs pumped a little harder. I might have more balls than my friends but I still didn't want my story to end as dog food.

"Only a little farther," he said as we ran hand in hand, an instant connection formed with a complete stranger from being in such an intense situation together.

I ran without asking how much was a little bit farther was. Whoever Samuel was, he had some sort of plan and I had none. Plus my lungs weren't quite up for the double duty of keeping my legs moving and speaking at the same time, lungs that were already tiring from their lack of use. I hadn't run like this in, hmmm, maybe ever?

Exercise of any sort had been strongly

discouraged in the most unpleasant of ways. A first offense usually warranted a few meals missed. Subsequent offenses were dealt with in more harsh terms, sometimes broken bones. They'd broken Larissa's leg after she'd been found doing jumping jacks in her room more than once. It had healed wrong afterward, which hadn't been a surprise. They hadn't put a cast on it or set it properly. They'd wanted to cripple her.

I tried not to think of Larissa after she disappeared, but I'd never tried to exercise again. I couldn't if I wanted to be able to escape. It was another piece of life that they'd stolen from us, but I'd decided it was more like I'd put it on a shelf, on hold for the day I needed to be whole. For this day. This was the moment I'd been saving.

I pushed past the burn in my chest as I took great gulping breaths but the weakness in my legs was growing. No matter how I pushed for them to keep pace, no matter how I willed my mind to overcome my physical limitations, I couldn't make them move quicker. It wasn't the pain that started slowing me down. I could take pain, ten times the amount my legs were dishing out, but I couldn't force them to move.

His grip on my hand helped pull me forward to compensate but he couldn't make up for the clumsiness that was coming along with the muscle fatigue. When I tripped, his hand on mine kept me from falling. Then he was pulling my arm upward and giving me his back. "Get on," he said.

"We'll never make it. You can't carry me."

"I know what I can do. Get on my back."

Any resistance was driven away by the sounds of dogs barking in the distance. I jumped on his back and wrapped my arms around his neck, my ankles locked at his waist.

He took off the second I was on. I wondered what he ate to fuel him, since it felt like we were moving even quicker than when I'd been running alongside him. I chalked that up to the strange sensation of riding another human being.

I heard the pack barking in the distance but I couldn't tell if they were getting closer or my adrenaline was making me think they were. I wasn't going to die here. I refused to die here. I'd once thought that I wanted to die a free woman. Now that I had freedom in my grasp, I wanted a chance to live, goddamn it!

He stopped suddenly and I thought it was fatigue as he shrugged me off him and onto the ground. My feet had barely touched dirt when he moved away and I was left swaying, more exhausted than him even though he'd been carrying me the last few minutes. Before I could ask what he was about, he was pulling branches off a metal contraption with two wheels. It was a bike, but a type I'd never seen.

He climbed on top of it, putting a leg on either side, and then held out his hand to me. "Get on. This is quicker," he said, although it did nothing but sit there.

When I didn't move, he reached forward and dragged me behind him. "Hold on tight."

He kicked the thing and it seemed to roar in anger at the affront. I'd read about these things in Moobie's adventures. It was either a motorcycle or dirt bike. I'd never seen either so I couldn't say which one.

I was sure we were dead. There was no way they hadn't heard that great noise, but then we took off at such a pace I had to cling to him to keep from falling. The trees started whipping by at an alarming rate as he steered it onto the dirt road that led away from the compound.

We were going so fast now that there was no way the dogs would catch us. I threw my head back and let delirious laughter bubble out.

"Why are you laughing?" he asked, forced to yell over the noise the bike was making.

"Because I'm free!" I yelled into the air as loud as I could as my hair whipped about my head.

Chapter Six

We traveled on the main road for a while but had veered back off into the forest several hours in, or at least that was how long I'd thought it had been. I had no real way of telling time without the moon in the sky to judge. The bike had a light that shone in front of us that he used to navigate the forest.

He'd steered his loud bike off onto a pathway of sorts, which hadn't been visible from the road but he'd obviously known was there. It made me wonder how many times he'd taken this route, and what for?

I didn't complain or even question where we were going. I didn't know what this man wanted or if I liked him, but I *did* like our current direction. Of course, I wasn't too picky about where we were going as long as it was far enough away from the compound that I wouldn't get caught while I organized a rescue for my friends.

The farther we traveled, the better my chances were of them not finding me, and I was ready to gamble on whoever was willing to help. I'd been ready for a while to take any chance provided, and this man, whoever he was, seemed to know his way around.

The machine we rode on slowed down and

we came to a complete stop in an especially thick part of the forest. I climbed off, slightly stiff from running earlier, and started to make my way to a group of shrubs in the distance, any conversation having to wait until nature was taken care of. I'd been holding it forever and my bladder had been quite put out that I wouldn't take a bathroom break during my big getaway.

I heard him climbing off as well before he spoke. "Where are you going?" he asked.

"It's been hours," I replied, hoping he'd take the hint. He didn't say anything else as I darted behind some shrubbery to take care of my business.

Shielded behind the bushes, I realized I had my first big decision to make. Did I take off now and go solo or did I go back to where he was and use him to get a little farther from the compound before I branched off on my own? I'd never be able to travel as quickly as he could. If I did break off on my own now and they sent people after me, they'd overtake what little distance we'd gained easily if I was on foot and they were on horses. If they took one of the trucks I'd heard they had, it might be even worse.

I didn't know where we were headed but I knew what awaited me back there. Sometimes the devil you know is just that—some asshole to steer clear of.

I stood and straightened out the bottom of my now dirt-streaked white dress that hung below the dark shirt he'd given me, and headed back toward the unknown. I'd go with him willingly but a couple of questions weren't out of order.

"Sam" was waiting by the bike when I got back. We looked at each other in the dark. I still couldn't get a read off him, not even a hint. It would've been so much easier if I could've. Of all people to have to get stonewalled by, why did he have to be the one with a cement wall almost as big and thick as the compound's? The one person I really needed to get a handle on and I was drawing a blank. I let out an aggravated sigh when I realized the only thing left was talking. Talk wasn't my strong point, and cajoling information ranked even lower. I'd never had to do it before and the compound wasn't known for polishing up your social skills. Not to mention, I didn't want to talk. I wanted to just *know* shit like I always did.

I committed myself to having to speak to him and let out a string of curses—that kind of talk I was adequate at.

I stopped, close enough to not be awkward but far enough that I'd have a slight lead—I hoped—if I decided to make a last-minute run for it. "Who are you? It's quite obvious at this point you aren't really a government inspector, or not one that isn't planning on reporting back to work anytime soon if this is any example of your work ethic."

"No. I'm not a government worker." He shook his head once but didn't offer up any details. Way to inspire confidence there, buddy. If it was possible, this guy's social graces might be worse than mine. I never thought I'd see the day.

"Are you going to tell me what your name is? Or should I call you by that bullshit one you gave at the compound?"

He looked about the forest like he could actually see more than five feet into the dark. "I'll tell you after we get about forty miles south of here."

"Forty miles south?" I plotted the geography in my head quickly from my memory of the maps I'd seen. Newco wasn't that big. "So we're heading into the Wilds."

"Exactly."

I needed to get into the Wilds. I could regroup there and prepare to carry out my plan. Now that the immediate adrenaline of being chased was gone, the logic was taking back over. If I was going to help the girls get out, it was going to take some work and preparation, and that couldn't be done if I was still being chased through this country. The Wilds was my best bet.

I closed the gap between us slightly and got a better look at the enigma I'd be riding right across the border with. I could decide what to do about him after he got me where I wanted to go.

"Do you have a problem with going into the Wilds?" he asked.

I shook my head, indicating I didn't have issue with the stated destination. He hadn't busted me out to let me walk, and I doubted I had any real say. I suspected he was trying to measure up the amount of resistance he was going to get. None was the answer he was looking for.

But it was just a guess as to what he was thinking. It was pissing me off that I had no idea what was in his head. Blank. He wasn't giving me even a thread to cling to and let me delude myself into some false understanding.

My mind rushed back to the first meeting with him. I hadn't *caught* glimpses of emotion. He'd *fed* them to me like breadcrumbs down a path into the woods. He'd known exactly what he needed to show to ferret out what he'd ultimately wanted to know, if I was a Plaguer in the full sense. This guy was good. I'd thought I was incapable of being manipulated, but it was like finding out you'd been playing in the little leagues on the day of the big match-up when the real deal walked in.

"What do you know about the Wilds?" he

asked.

"I've heard the stories." Everybody had, even in the loneliest corners of the compound.

"They aren't stories. They're true."

That was a tall order then, because there were a whole lot of stories, beasts that roamed the forests, outlaws and pirates. If you were a historian, from all that I'd heard, the Wilds was like the Wild West, with creatures that walked right out of your nightmares, and some pirates thrown in for good measure.

It was also the brightest beacon of freedom available, if you were tough enough to survive. None of the countries messed around in the Wilds. There was no law. There was no government. If you were stronger and could take it, it was yours. If you were tougher, you were in charge. If you were weak, you begged for citizenship to one of the countries; even with the corruption and flaws, it was still better because the weak didn't survive any life worth living in the Wilds.

In my opinion, the Wilds was the perfect place for me to regroup and start preparing.

"I've got no problem with the destination but I want to know why you broke me out before we go any farther."

"Forty miles." He looked down at my right hand where it was hidden in the folds of the dress. "Let me see your hand," he said, pointing to it.

I knew what he wanted. "My brand is none of your concern."

He was in my space and grabbing my wrist anyway. I tried to tug it away but his hold was solid and resisting was only going to accentuate how weak my position really was. I stopped fighting, as there was no need to broadcast it. I looked over at the bike as he stared at it.

The brand, the ugly, scarred letter P that had been burned onto the top of my hand, was clear to him. Most people were repelled by just the mention of it. The revulsion at the sight of it was usually stronger. I might be out of the compound but I was still marked. There was no outrunning that.

He pulled it closer, only a few inches from his face, as if trying to determine its legitimacy or something.

He dropped my wrist after half a minute or so. "It is my business. In the Wilds, Plaguers are killed. I need you alive."

"There's nothing I can do about it so I guess I'll have to figure out how to stay alive," I said in a flippant tone. I knew what that brand did to me more than anyone. I'd lived with it, year after marked year.

He went to a pack attached to his bike and dug around in it. "Here." He thrust a pair of black leather gloves at me, ones with the fingers cut off. "Put these one."

I took them. He clearly had all the details planned. "Won't this make people suspicious?"

"Maybe, but no one expects to actually ever meet a Plaguer, not with the survival rate. You live in a place that houses them. How many have you met?"

In all the years I'd been there, I could count them on one hand, and I knew I'd met a lot less than the amount of people who survived the Bloody Death.

"If they see it, it's a different story."

"But if they do get suspicious?"

"It doesn't matter. If someone wants you they'll have to get through me first, and they won't." He motioned to the gloves. "This just makes things easier."

I put them on, looking down at my hands and not seeing the ugly scar for the first time since I was four. I looked back at him, not wanting to give any hint of how I hated that thing or how I felt about being able to disguise it. It was just skin, after all.

"You plan on telling me why you busted me out?"

"Like I said, when we cross the border."

"Why?"

"Because if they get you, I don't want you to be able to tell them anything when they try and torture it out of you."

I nodded. It was hard to disagree with that logic. This guy did seem to know a thing or two about the government of Newco and the compound.

He climbed back onto the bike, hands on the bars and feet planted on the ground.

"Get on."

I did without a fight. Who was I kidding? He could've been one of the beasts they talked about that roamed the Wilds and I would've ridden his ass right across the border if that were what it took to get out of here. The bike came awake with a loud growl as we started along a rough pathway that looked like it had only been cleared recently—and roughly at that.

I wasn't sure how long we'd been riding for, but the sky was just starting to get a tinge lighter when I felt one of his hands grip mine where it wrapped around his waist, urging my hold even tighter. I glanced over his shoulder ahead to see what was going on up ahead. A large fence was beyond the trees with a panel removed. In front of it stood twenty-some guards, all in body armor and carrying massive guns, waiting for us.

"Hang on tight," he yelled. "It's going to be a rough ride out of here."

I gripped on to him as the bike picked up even more speed. I kept my gaze on the group we were approaching and couldn't help think that we were already dead. I'd been forced to cower for years and I'd never do it again. I'd meet my death with eyes wide open. I wanted to stare it down and give the reaper the middle finger when I went.

I heard gunfire whizzing by. I recognized it from the drills the guards would do at the compound but I still wouldn't close my eyes. We were flying toward the gate and zigzagging aggressively. I wasn't sure if it was to make us a harder target or to avoid the bodies that kept dropping around us. That was when I realized he had some backup hidden. Newco wasn't killing their people.

As quick as we'd approached the opening, we were through. I looked back at the gate as we drove away, watching as the rest of the guards were running for cover.

We were whizzing past trees again, but this time it wasn't the government of Newco. This forest didn't belong to anyone. It was wild and free, just as I was.

Chapter Seven

We rode the bike down more trails, but these seemed well worn. How many people came in and out of Newco by this route?

The sun had lit the entire sky by time we stopped but still hung low enough for me to judge it hadn't been more than an hour or so. When we did stop, it was only because it looked like the path was ending. Up ahead in between a gap in the trees, I could see water and lots of it. Memories from childhood came to me of sandy shores and vacations with my parents. After so many years in the Cement Giant I'd started to think I'd imagined such sights.

I moved to get off the bike but his hand grabbed my arm, stopping me. I yanked at it out of frustration. This watchdog stuff was getting old fast and my patience was thinning. I was not going to live like a prisoner.

"Don't go past the tree line."

It was a barked-out order. I didn't agree but that didn't seem to matter to him. His grip dropped from my arm anyway, as he apparently didn't expect anything less than me falling in line with what he said. He was right. I'd walk the line, but only because I liked the current direction it was laid out in. Where it fell tomorrow would be another story.

I raced forward to the gap. There was uninterrupted water everywhere, with the exception of a skeleton from the past that marred its perfection. Its iron limbs shot out of the water here and there and broke its surface in no particular order, just chaos. The bridge was all still there but instead of being in its glorious prime of life, most of it had sunk below the water, its bones broken as it exhaled its last breath of life before nature finished erasing its existence. Now it was just another sad remnant of the Glory Years, before the Bloody Plague had had its way.

They say that this planet used to be crawling with buildings and structures like this from a time that seemed more like a thousand years ago than the hundred and fifty it was. There had been so many people and they had made things that were unimaginable today.

I'd seen a picture of one of the great cities they'd called New York. I'd heard there had been other such places. So many that it was almost inconceivable to me if I hadn't seen proof. These places were all uninhabited now, too dangerous to go near once they'd started crumbling. The Bloody Death hadn't just killed our people—it had killed our world.

I looked away from the metal ghost and down the coastline that went on forever. It was a muddy shore that a person could run along and keep going for days with no walls to stop them.

A roar sounded, similar to what our own metal bike let out, and I turned quickly. Samuel didn't seem alarmed, so it was likely the others arriving. I'd known we weren't alone after the guards at the gate had been shot down, but over the roaring bike, I hadn't heard their presence.

He stood in the opening as two riders, another male and a female, pulled up alongside him. That was it? We'd only had two shooters up against all those guards at the gate? I didn't know anything about warfare but I couldn't help but be impressed. I would've thought there were a lot more of them for the damage they'd done to the government's numbers.

The new guy was on the larger side and had scars running everywhere. They were on his arms where they were exposed by the short sleeves of his dark shirt, and there were even small ones crisscrossing his face.

The female didn't look like she'd stand much taller than I did but had a muscular leanness and a cold glint in her eye.

The two of them got off their bikes and they formed a semicircle, all eyes trained on me. It was time to get some answers. I approached the group, waiting to see what I'd find out as I neared. He hadn't offered me up any hints of who he was, but I had fresh meat now. There was no way I'd draw a blank with all of them.

As I got within ten feet, an image of the female killing a teenage boy in combat entered my mind. Not so bad. The kid had been ready to slit her throat and she'd acted in self-defense.

Then I got a read off the scarred man and I started to laugh. It was so shocking I couldn't help myself. That was the memory burned into his brain? He'd gotten caught feeding stray pups? It was a new one for me. I could see how it might have been embarrassing to such a hardened-looking man, but really? Maybe my Plaguer's delusions were losing some of their oomph.

The three of them looked at me as if I were crazy as I laughed aloud at what they thought was nothing. I didn't care. Being a Plaguer, it was something I was accustomed to. If they only knew the truth, we'd see who was crazy and who'd be running for cover.

I continued to march right over to them. When I got within four feet, both of the newcomers took a step back. He'd had me wear gloves but his people were obviously in the loop about what I was. That was something else I was used to, especially from people from the Wilds. Whenever someone from the Wilds had landed in the compound, they'd feared getting near me even worse than the people from Newco. I'd discovered from an early age that people from the Wilds were a very superstitious lot and believed that once you'd had the Bloody Death, you never really got rid of it and could still give it to others.

I was glad they were scared. They weren't going to fight me if they were too scared to touch me. I didn't think they'd shoot me even though they all had guns strapped to their hips. It lowered my possible combatants down to one when I decided I was ready to break off on my own.

But oh what a one. If I had a choice, I'd take my chances on the two newcomers combined instead of him. The way he shut down his emotions, expected to be listened to as if no one ever dared not. When I finally decided not to toe his line—and I was near to positive it would happen, as I had an instinctual aversion to lines—he was going to be a big problem.

"Who are you people and what do you want?" I asked.

"She's haughty for someone who should already be dead," the woman said. "Let's see how tough you are outside your safe little compound."

I eyed her up. Green pants that had leather patches sewn over the knees, a tank top that showed just how lean and muscular she was. Her dark hair was cropped short, only a couple of inches long and probably better for fighting.

Then I thought of how I appeared. Still in

the white dress from the compound but with a dark sweatshirt added on, my limbs were lean but without the muscles she sported, my flaming red hair all a mess. I probably looked like easy pickings to someone like her.

The idea of it made me want to laugh. There wasn't anything in this world that would make me go running back to that compound. If Sam didn't, certainly not some chick dressed for battle. No matter how tough she thought she was, I didn't think she could say the same. I might not look like much but I had a mind honed for conflict, if not a body.

I ignored her. I didn't care what she thought—if she liked me or hated me, it was of no consequence. The same went for the scarred man. They were too scared of the Bloody Death to touch me. I could probably walk away right now without much difficulty. No, my rescuer was the only one who could end up being a problem—especially if he thought he was going to become my new jailor.

He'd appeared cold and methodical in his government outfit. Stripped of it, he was still cold but now looked lethal. I still couldn't pick up anything from him to tell me differently. I didn't care. My first goal in life had been fulfilled. I was outside the Cement Giant. Now I wanted to be completely free so bad I could taste it.

"Well? You said after we got out you'd tell me." I lifted both hands to the forest. "We're out."

He didn't move an inch. "After we cross," he said.

I looked over at the water that I'd been so amazed by until he told me he wanted me to go *on it*. "You want me to go across that?"

"Yes."

"How?"

"On that ship, over there."

He was pointing to a large wooden vessel coming around the bend. It had large sails blowing in the wind and a flag with a strange emblem. I knew what that was. It matched the descriptions in Moobie's adventures. Moobie didn't trust pirates. And just like that, my rescuer moved the line to somewhere I wouldn't toe. That was the issue with other people's lines. Sometimes people drew them in all sorts of crazy places. "You want me to get on a pirate ship?"

"Yes. It's the only way to cross here. They control this water."

People died on ships all the time. Even in the compound, I'd heard about people trying to cross the great waters and dying. I hadn't made it out to drown. Plus, I needed to be able to get back to Newco. That might have been my biggest issue. I couldn't go somewhere I couldn't get back from. "Absolutely not. That wasn't the deal. You said you'd tell me now. I'm not crossing anything," I said, knowing there wasn't anything he could say that would make me get on that boat. If I got on, I might not ever get back. Unacceptable. I was going to have to stall.

"I already hate her. Why do we need this bitch?" the woman said. "She should be shot. She's got that dirty disease running through her and she shouldn't live."

I took a few steps toward her and she retreated. "Come on, do something about it," I said, and then laughed as she tripped on a branch behind her in her urgency to get out of reach.

"I'd shoot you if it weren't for him," she said.

"If you hadn't just fallen on your ass, that might sound a little more threatening." I leaned over her, wagging a finger a few feet from her face and making her scramble backward.

"That's enough," Sam ordered. I wasn't delusional enough to think he was putting an end to our dispute for fear of my feelings. His girl Patches wasn't making a very good showing. The scarred man remained silent, but I had a funny hunch he was enjoying the show.

"Is it enough?" I asked, still looking at the woman below me now, my finger inching closer toward her exposed flesh. I knew I was taunting her. I knew it was childish, but after fourteen years of taking this crap and swallowing it, I'd told myself I'd never take it again. She just happened to have the unique opportunity of being the first one to get in my face since I'd left the Cement Giant. "Well? Tell me."

Every inch she scooted back, I edged forward until a hand wrapped around my arm and started dragging me backward. I looked down at his hand as he continued to tow me away. Why wasn't he afraid of touching me? I was a Plaguer. He was from the Wilds. He had to be. Didn't he understand what that meant? He should be frightened I was going to kill him with my disease, like any goddamn normal person would be. Even country folk, the people that were born and grew up in Newco, took a while before they stopped fearing they'd drop dead from getting anywhere near me.

But there he was, latched on to me nice and tight, towing me a good fifteen feet away from the other two and near the clearance to the beach. I looked down at the offending hand. "What is wrong with you?" I said, almost in disgust. "Why aren't you afraid of touching me?"

He didn't bother responding to my questions, as if it meant nothing to him. He didn't drop his hand until we were away from the other two. "You are going to cross with us."

"I'm not getting on a boat and you won't like what happens if you try and make me." I held up my right hand and pulled off the glove. "You think they're going to take me if they see this? They might not take *any* of you after they see it. I bet they'll think you're all infected, or they will after I make sure and tell them that."

"You are getting on that boat one way or another. I'm trying to do this the nice way and it's in your interest to cooperate." He leaned closer. "But it will happen either way."

"No, what is in my interest is for you to tell me what the hell you want from me and who you people are."

"Don't push me." He was hulking over me.

It was a warning, and I wondered if I was handling things in the best way. But I couldn't get on that boat. What would Moobie do? I thought back quickly to some of his adventures but nothing seemed fitting. I had to stall and he'd have to sleep at some point. Maybe he just needed a reminder of what he was dealing with.

I fell forward slightly until I was leaning almost doubled over with a hand braced on a tree, and coughed like I was trying to evict a lung from my chest.

"Are you sick?" he asked.

Even after that display of weakness, he still didn't back up. Did the man have no common sense?

"I think this has all been too much on my body. I think I'm getting sick." I let out a low moan. Maybe I should bite my cheek and get some blood going on for effect. I didn't really want to gnash up my mouth, though. Maybe I should take a peek at his status first.

Bastard still wasn't backing up. The stone facade looked like it was not only going to crack but completely blow. He knew I was faking.

"You're getting on that boat," he said, although his jaw barely moved.

He really did look like he was going to lose it completely and I wasn't sure that was something I wanted to see. But I couldn't just roll over either. I couldn't get on that boat willingly.

I stood straight up, shaking the fake plague symptoms like I was brushing off a dead leaf from my clothes. "I want everyone's name and where we're heading. I also want an explanation of why you can't tell me. If it sounds plausible, we can discuss the rest of the details and then determine whether or not a boat ride is in order."

I watched him closely. Oh yeah, he was like a dormant volcano ready to blow. I reminded myself that he couldn't kill me. He didn't go through all that trouble for nothing, but he sure looked like he wanted to.

A kernel of fear popped into me and I was

so disgusted by it that it drove my next words. "Would you like a moment to think over your options?"

I wasn't sure what was going to happen next, although him reaching out and strangling me wouldn't have come as a shock. His hands were fisted like he was holding himself back.

He turned and walked away, back toward the other two where they were waiting.

Scarred man was standing looking relatively calm. Patches was off the ground standing again but fidgeting continuously with what looked like repressed anger. Our eyes met and she tilted her head back as if she were sniffing the air and my presence had tainted it with a foul smell, then made a sour face.

I reached a new low I'd never thought I'd stoop to. I stuck out my tongue. Her twitching shifted gears into full speed.

"I say we off the bitch, Dax, and be done with it," she said.

Finally, at least I now had a name for the one who might murder me at any moment.

Dax finished his walk over to her and the scarred man and said a couple of words while I eyed up the beach. This might be it. Why was I waiting? They weren't even paying attention to me. I took a couple of steps toward the shoreline, testing the waters while the body language of the trio seemed to be getting more heated.

"She's a Plaguer," the female said loud enough to make sure I heard. "So what if we leave her."

Dax replied but I couldn't hear what he said.

Dax had his back to me while she kept speaking. The scarred guy was aptly listening and no one was looking at me. What if this was my last chance? I moved slowly to the gap in the trees, not wanting a sudden movement to draw their attention. As soon as I got close enough, I took off down the beach.

I pushed my body past the exhaustion that had already sunk in and sprinted with everything I had left and some that I didn't know existed.

I ran as hard as I could. I shouldn't have looked back to see if they were chasing me. If I hadn't, I wouldn't have seen Dax taking off after me and I wouldn't have been so flustered that I ran right into someone else.

I heard Dax yell, "Hold her," right before a beefy fist connected with my face and I went down for the count.

Chapter Eight

The ground was swaying so hard beneath me that I reached out to grab something before I even opened my eyes. Correction. Eye. I'd had enough shiners in my life to know the left wasn't going to be open for business for at least another day or two.

What I did see out of the one left functioning was clouds rolling in over my head and a large sail flapping in the wind. So much for not toeing the line.

I was on the boat.

"Look at that, you're on the boat."

I heard the distinctive gravelly voice and looked up to realize not only was Dax standing beside me but my hand was wrapped around his calf, with the glove that had somehow gotten back on my hand.

I let go of him quickly and tried to make out his expression where he loomed over me. His face was cast in shadow as he was silhouetted by a mostly sunny sky, making it difficult.

"Thank you, oh wise one. I never would've figured that out."

He squatted down beside me and looked me over, his eyes pausing in the general vicinity of his friend's handiwork. As far as beatings went, this was a one on a scale of twenty. Did he think

I was going to be cowering in fear over something this trivial? I pushed up off the wooden deck just in case he was under the assumption I was beaten on any level that mattered, and got to my feet, ignoring the offered hand.

"You think I'm scared because of a little bruise?" I asked. "You people can do your worst. This is nothing."

"He's not my people. And if I wanted to scare you, you'd be scared."

I lifted my hand, opening and closing my thumb and fingers together, making the message clearer than anything I could've said. He was all talk.

"You might be more trouble than you're worth but at least you're entertaining. Mildly, anyway."

If he was entertained that was news to me. "So glad I can liven up your cruise," I replied, and got to the business of sizing up my new location.

I scanned the boat and saw the man who'd decked me. He was a hulking giant that was securing a sail line at the other end. There were five pirates in view and all seemed quite filthy considering they were surrounded by water.

The three bikes were on the deck as well, and Patches and Scar were at the other end of a boat that looked about forty feet long.

I moved to the rail to get a better view and leaned over as much as I could, looking at the waves that were kicking up along with some winds.

"Don't think of jumping," he said.

I wouldn't ever jump. I looked up at the coast. It was a long ways away, especially for someone who couldn't swim. I'd drown if they didn't come in after me, but hell if I'd tell them that. I hadn't finally gotten out to end up throwing it away drowning, but I wasn't in the habit of broadcasting my weak spots so I kept my mouth shut.

I could feel his eyes on me. "You shouldn't have run."

"And you *should've* done what you'd agreed to, *Dax*."

His head didn't move and his eyes didn't break contact with me. I had this strange idea that he was aware of every single person's location on that deck even when he looked otherwise preoccupied.

"I think they're following us," he said.

I knew who they were, and he didn't mean the pirates. He meant Newco and the friendly staff of the Cement Giant. I gripped the side of the boat to keep from reacting, before telling myself there was no way he knew that for sure.

"Once we get to that land over there, that's when we'll talk."

I looked at the land on the other side nearing us, like I had a choice in the matter. "Fine."

Dax didn't say anything else and moved to the opposite railing, to go stand by Patches and Scar. I stayed where I was and looked out at the water and the coast beyond. It was so beautiful. Even with an uncertain future and an eye swollen shut, I tilted my head back as the wind caught my hair, and couldn't stop the smile. I was really out of there.

"What's she so fucking happy about?" I heard one the pirates ask his friend.

"Didn't you see her hands before he put the glove back on? She's a Plaguer. She's nuts," his friend answered. "We're all going to be lucky if we're standing come tomorrow. I can't believe the captain agreed to this."

"Somebody should push her over."

"I'm not touching her."

"Me neither."

My smile didn't falter.

"We're going," Dax said to me some ten minutes later.

I nodded and watched as they rolled two of the metal bikes up and then lowered them down with ropes to a floating square made up of wood that also had Patches and Scar on it. The pirates rowed the raft to shore, dropped off its riders and then returned to the boat.

It was my turn and I was climbing down a rope ladder to an area tight with the last bike, a couple of pirates, including the big burly one who hit me, Dax and the last bike. I would've stayed closer to the center, even if it was near the burly pirate, if it wasn't for Dax steering me in a different corner. I'd never admit it but I was grateful for the arm Dax looped around my waist when I ended up by the edge of the raft, even if it did make me intensely aware of him. I couldn't wait until the pirates paddled us closer to the coast.

I wasn't prepared for Dax to jump off the raft with me in tow once we hit waist-deep water. Vacations with my parents flitted to mind again, memories of being in waters like this and a life that seemed like it had been too idyllic to have been real. It was the last time I'd been in a pool of water. The Cement Giant only had showers. Now that I could feel my feet touch the bottom and I knew I wouldn't drown, it was amazing. I wanted to dunk my entire body in it and splash around.

Dax moved ahead and the raft was towed in with ropes on two ends, and I moved along with everyone else, resisting the urge to submerge myself.

I slowed my pace as the burly pirate moved

in front of me. Seabirds caught my attention and I looked up only briefly when something caught my ankles and I was falling face first into the water.

I found my footing quick enough and came up invigorated. Dax was staring in my direction like he was pissed off. "What the hell? I tripped. Not a big deal," I said, getting stiff.

I pushed my now wet hair back from my face, feeling utterly refreshed even as the tension in the group seemed heightened. I was going to have to do some serious adjustments in my thinking, because these people in the Wilds were strange. That really said something considering I'd come from a place that housed all the crazies of Newco.

The raft was finally dragged up onto the shore and the last bike was rolled off when I saw Dax round on the pirate who'd punched me.

"You got water on my bike," Dax said to him as we hit the shore.

It was sort of a ridiculous statement, since they'd just been transported across a shitload of water, but the pirate seemed to take the question seriously, compounding my belief that people in the Wilds were just plain old weird.

"There's no water on your bike," the pirate replied.

He was bigger than Dax but looked soft where Dax was hard. There was another difference between them too that I couldn't quite figure out. Something in the way they stood, maybe? The way they talked? What was it that I sensed that was so different? This was really going to bug me.

"Don't tell me what I see," Dax said, and then hauled off and launched a fist straight into his face. The pirate fell like a ton of bricks.

Aaah, that must have been the thing I couldn't figure out. Dax could kick some serious ass and the pirate just pretended he could.

I turned to Scar, who seemed to stay within a five-feet perimeter of me now. "Dax really doesn't like water on his bike, huh?"

He grunted before he answered. "He doesn't like when people fuck with his stuff."

Dax helped the other pirate load his friend onto the raft and shove off back into the water toward the larger boat. That was one huge stretch of water I would have to get back over when I enacted my plan.

"There any other way across this?"

"No. Their gang runs this bay and most of the Atlantic in these parts."

"Runs the Atlantic?"

"Crossings. You don't get across any of the large waters around here unless you go through them. Only other way to do it is to go west first and add a ton of travel time." He turned away from me as Dax approached. "We heading out?"

"You two go ahead. Make camp at the place and we'll catch up within the hour."

Scar nodded and walked over to where Patches was. They got on their bikes and took off.

"Come on," Dax said, as he pushed the bike over to an alcove that was hidden from view. He stood the bike up and put out his hand. "Give me your sweatshirt," he said.

The dark fabric was hanging almost to my knees with the weight of the water as I took it off and handed it to him. He grabbed it and wrung it out vigorously before laying it across a fallen tree.

He turned back to me and froze for a second. I looked down to figure out what had thrown him and saw the now wet white of my dress hadn't left much to the imagination. I crossed my arms in front of my chest as he seemed to be making a concerted effort to act like he hadn't just seen all of my goods on display. The way his eyes had frozen on me and then turned away, as if he didn't want to see me, again confirmed what I'd feared. I was deformed in some way. That was why the guards never touched me. It wasn't because I was a Plaguer. They knew after being around me so long that I wasn't contagious. Dax hadn't seemed to fear catching anything from me either. So it was something else. I thought I looked like everyone else, but something was obviously wrong with me. Whatever; he didn't have to look at me if I was so ugly.

He reached a hand back and tugged the t-shirt he wore over his head and then held it out to me. I'd never seen a man without a shirt on in person and now I had one in close range.

I had a feeling most of them didn't look the way he did. There was a handful of scars scattered about his front and sides, but nothing that detracted from him. It might have even added to his appeal.

This was what I'd sensed earlier. He was a fighter. He was hardened and didn't take any shit and it showed. It was strange but I felt like he appeared to the world the way I was inside. Like we were the same, he was just inside out.

He shoved the shirt at me. "Put this on so you can take your dress off and lay it in the sun for a few minutes."

I took it from him and he turned his back without being asked.

I shimmied out of the wet dress and threw his shirt on. "So, why'd you break me out?"

"Because I need what you can do."

"Which is what?" I asked, thinking he'd messed up royally. I didn't have any known skills other than a larger-than-life thirst for freedom, and couldn't figure out how that would benefit anyone but me.

"I've been searching for a Plaguer for a while. I need to know what you see."

"You mean the stuff we make up?" I asked, wanting to hear him say he believed what I saw wasn't just stories. I'd spent so many years aware of how Plaguers were discredited that I found the idea of a stranger I'd just met believing me impossible.

"We both know that isn't the truth."

I moved past him to where the sweatshirt was laid out across the log and laid the white dress beside it, mimicking what he'd done. This was stuff I'd need to know, like how the sun could dry my clothes.

The simple action brought me a weird feeling of satisfaction. At the Cement Giant, we'd been given a set of clothes after we showered every day. I didn't own a white dress but had shared them with all the other girls my size in the compound. But that was my dress lying there. Mine. I still hated it and what it represented, but it was *mine*. I owned it.

"How does my thing help you?" Now the very thing that had landed me in the Cement Giant was the thing that had freed me.

"I don't know if it can but I'm looking for something and I've reached a dead end."

"What are you looking for?"

"You don't need to know that."

"Fine. I don't really care anyway, to be

honest." I shrugged. I had enough on my plate and this Dax guy could handle his own affairs. "All you want from me is to tell you what I pick up off people?"

"Yes."

What would Moobie do in this situation if he had some leverage? "And if I help you? What's in it for me? Will you help me in return? I've got to go back there and get my friends out."

"You've already been paid. I broke you out. After you help me, we go our own way. Never see each other again. That's what you get."

I put my hands on my hips. "I didn't need you to get me out."

He had the nerve to roll his eyes. "So you were there by choice?"

I straightened my shoulders and lifted my head. "I was waiting for my opening. Thing is, I didn't ask for your help. Why should I pay for it?"

"I think you've misunderstood. This is not a negotiation."

"And if I refuse? Then what?"

"There's ways, but much less pleasant."

I huffed out a half laugh. Did he really think that was going to work? "You did notice that I was strapped to a chair with electrical leads when you came, did you not? You should go ask them how much cooperation *they* got from me."

"You've got balls. I'll give you that. I know

about those places and I know their methods. Trust me when I tell you they're amateurs. The way I see it, you need me more than I need you right now. I cut you loose and you're dead in under a week, or worse."

"What's worse than dead? Is there a new ranking system in the Wilds I'm unaware of?"

"There is worse. You've got a strong will but you're weak as a kitten and you don't know the first thing about how stuff works out here. Unless you want to end up serving pirates like the ones back at the boat and getting raped by those men every night, I'd take my offer."

It might have been a scare tactic but I heard the truth in it. It was well known that only the hardest and toughest survived in the Wilds and the rest lived almost like slaves to the mighty. I was tough, no matter what I looked like, but I was weak in body, at least right now. It wasn't a bad offer, as long as there was an end in sight. "How long is this going to take?"

"Maybe a month."

I'd need a month anyway to start working out the details of my plan to bust my friends out. "Then we cut all ties? No strings attached?"

"Yes, and in return, the time you spend with me, I'll teach you how to survive the Wilds so that when you do leave, you might actually live another week or two."

"Thanks for your vote of confidence." I sat

down on a free corner of the log to think for a minute, the bark scratching at my thighs reminding me how undressed I was, not that he seemed to want to get a look. "It's not a dependable type of thing. I can't guarantee what I'll find out or if I'll get anything at all." I didn't want any reneging on his part, saying I didn't live up to his end and him wanting something else from me, or worse, prolonging the deal.

"I'll take that chance." He held out his hand to me and I looked at it. "First rule of the Wilds: you shake when you make a deal with someone."

That was one I'd known about, but no one had ever wanted to shake my hand before, especially not the right, the one that had the brand. I reached out my hand and he took it in a firm grip before releasing it. I smiled. I'd just made my first negotiation in the Wilds with a man that I was fairly certain was pretty badass.

"You shook on it. Don't cross me."

I narrowed my eyes and tried to look as intent as he did. "Don't give me a reason to cross you." Then I ruined the whole goddamn effect by smiling. It was hard not to, though. I'd always wanted to be able to say stuff like that, like Moobie would. I'd wanted to live, and after almost eighteen years, I was doing some serious, hardcore living. My smile got even larger.

"Why are you smiling?"

I narrowed my eyes again even as my smile wouldn't budge. "If I told you, I'd have to kill you." It was classic Moobie.

Dax shook his head.

He didn't get it, but Moobie would've been so proud.

Chapter Nine

"Here," Dax said, handing me my white dress and the darker sweatshirt. "They aren't dry but they're better."

We'd been sitting in the alcove for a half-hour or so if I had to guess. We hadn't talked but he'd shared his canteen of water with me and some bits of dried meat he'd called jerky, which had come from the pack on his bike.

"So your big plan is to go back to the compound after I'm done with you? Going to go rescue your friends?" he asked.

"You got it," I said, already knowing he was calling me all sorts of stupid in his head.

"Everyone has their own path and is responsible for themselves." He looked at me, and I knew what he was going to say even before it came out. Not because he was transparent or any easier to read, but I knew what the situation looked like to an outsider.

"You're going to get yourself killed," he said. It was exactly what I'd expected.

"No, I won't." He hadn't sounded overly concerned, but I still had to try one last time for the girls. I knew what failure would mean. "You could help."

He shook his head and said, "Not my responsibility, either," before he took a swig from his canteen.

"You've got your secret plans and I've got my—well, not-so-secret plans. The point is we both have plans. You do you and I'll go be the decent person." Leaving them there was something I'd never do. Not to mention it was so un-Moobie-like. You didn't leave a man behind.

"You'll go be the dead person, but it's your choice."

The way he'd said it, I could tell it wouldn't really matter to him. Maybe he felt he had to warn me for some reason. Maybe he had a code, like I did, but just not as strong or good. I guessed a weak code was better than none.

"Yes. That's right. It's my choice." Everything that happened from this point on was going to be my choice and I was going to start them off right. I'd seen lives go bad from too many wrong choices. Even little bad choices piled up after a while into a whole big mess. It was all the choices you made in your life that determined who you were, not some abstract notion you made up in your mind, with motivations and feelings filtering out the ugly.

Thinking of ugly, my white dress wasn't such a prize right now. Clothes in hand, again I didn't have to ask him to turn his back. He just did. I really wished I knew what was so wrong with me that he was so averse to seeing even a flash of skin. Not that I wanted to put myself on display, but I didn't want to feel like an ogre either. It had never bothered me, men's lack of interest. Maybe now that my first goal of freedom was achieved I had more room to think about these things?

I made quick work of changing and handed his shirt back to him.

He tugged it on. "Let's get going. We need to catch up to them before nightfall." He kicked out the metal bar that kept the bike upright and settled onto it.

"Why before nightfall?" I asked, super aware of every place our bodies touched as I climbed on behind him, remembering exactly what his flesh looked like beneath the places my hands now lay.

"I don't want them to be alone after dark."

"So it's true what they say about the beasts? They come out at night?"

"Yes," he said, and then the bike woke up, stopping any more questions.

We slowed to a stop just as dusk was upon us, in between strange hills all lined up in a row. It was the oddest forest I'd ever seen, but I hadn't seen many.

He pulled alongside one of the larger hills

and we got off the bike. He started walking it around the side of it but I stayed in one spot and turned, taking in my surroundings.

"Why's it look so weird here?" I asked. "What's with all the hills?"

He stopped walking and looked around the place as if maybe he'd forgotten how it appeared. "They aren't hills. They used to be homes. People lived in them. Most of the people in the community probably died. The few who survived probably went looking for others survivors and nature claimed this place back for itself."

"Why would they want to live in little mountains?"

He shook his head. "They weren't once. They were buildings that nature grew over." He tilted his head toward the back of the hill. "Come on."

I followed him to the other side and watched as he pushed back some vines that revealed an opening. He rolled his bike into the hill.

Scar and Patches were inside already. It looked more like a cave I'd seen in pictures, but I could see the remnants of walls where vines and leaves didn't cover what used to be a house. They were sitting around a fire and the smoke drifted up toward an open sky, the roof probably having caved in long ago and lying beneath the dirt I stood on.

Dax pointed toward Scar. "That's Tank." And then his finger jumped to Patches. "And that's Lucy."

I guessed we were far enough away from Newco that it was okay to exchange names. I nodded to them. Tank nodded back. Lucy ignored me.

"Your bikes filled up?" Dax asked.

"Yeah," Lucy replied, and then pointed to a red container sitting beside the opposite wall. "But we're running low."

Fuel. That was what the machines ran on, but I knew it was incredibly valuable in Newco. I thought it was almost priceless in the Wilds. I wondered if they stole it from within one of the countries, but maybe not. I couldn't really take anything for granted. Everything I knew about the Wilds was gossip and hearsay that trickled into the Cement Giant.

I found an empty spot and settled down. Dax pulled out some more jerky from his pack.

"Can we go hunt for dinner?" I asked. "If someone lends me a knife, I'll go do it." Actually I wanted to do it, but tried to downplay it for no good reason.

"Not at night," Tank said, looking at me skeptically, as if he didn't think I *could* catch dinner. "The beasts are territorial."

There wasn't much talk after that. I figured that had to be on account of me. What did they think was going to happen? I'd get scooped up from their camp and spread all their local gossip? These people must have something they could talk about. Or maybe not?

I grabbed a nearby stick and started drawing in the layer of dirt beside me. It was the shape I remembered of the Cement Giant from all I'd seen. I'd been piecing together what I knew of the inside and what I'd seen outside.

A pair of boots stopped a few inches away from taking out one of my walls, and I looked up to see Dax staring down at my sketch. He didn't say anything but he shook his head before he walked back to his spot.

"You do you," I said as he sat not far from me.

"I didn't say anything."

"No, but you think obnoxiously loud."

I didn't know what Tank or Lucy thought of our little snippet of conversation but they didn't say anything. They must have been having so much fun not talking at all. I mean, yeah, I didn't have any good stories because I'd lived in a jail. After I lived in the Wilds for a while I hoped I'd be a bit more interesting than these three.

The sun had been down for hours when Tank and Lucy both finally lay down and closed their eyes. Dax sat wide awake, a branch in his hand as he stoked the fire in front of us.

"Get some rest," he said to me. "Tomorrow is going to be a long day."

"What about the beasts in the forest?"

"I've got it covered."

I took the sweatshirt he'd given me and used it as a makeshift pillow on my bed of dirt, but it would be a long time before sleep would come. I heard every branch that broke and leaf that rustled. It seemed like I'd barely fallen asleep when I was being shaken awake. I was just about to let out a wallop of a scream when I heard Dax say, "It's me. Get up quickly. We're getting company."

"Who?" I asked as I rose. I looked upward, through the open roof, and saw the stars still bright in the sky. Tank and Lucy were grabbing their stuff together and kicking out the fire.

"Probably from Newco or the jail," Dax said.

"I thought you said we'd be safe in the Wilds? I thought they didn't come here?"

His eyes flickered over me. "They don't. Not normally."

I listened keenly but didn't hear a thing. I wasn't going back there. If he thought they were coming, that was enough to get my feet moving.

They rolled out their bikes in a row with me behind them. Just as I climbed on behind Dax, I heard the dogs and the bikes roared to life. Did Newco use dogs too or was it Ms. Edith sending them after me?

***

We didn't stop until late morning, and by then I understood why they had us shower every day at the compound. I had dirt everywhere, under my dress, logged in the tiny crevices left of what nails I had left. I'd probably swallowed more bugs on the ride than were stuck to my shirt, and I wasn't the only one looking worse for wear.

But when Dax started to slow the bike, a shower was the last thing I was concerned with. "Is it safe to stop?"

"We aren't stopping for long but I think we've put enough distance between them and us for a quick break." Lucy and Tank slowed down and stopped beside us.

"Take her down to the stream with you," Dax said to Lucy as she was getting off her bike then took off toward the trees.

Lucy stopped moving and shot me a dirty look once Dax was gone. "Will I need to carry you there, too?"

"I don't want shit from you—" I started to spit back, and then Tank was in between us, his back in my face as he spoke to Lucy.

"Dax said to go do it. Now stop arguing and do it."

I couldn't see her expression but she didn't say anything, just turned and headed off.

"I don't need someone to go with me. Just point me in the right direction," I said to Tank.

Tank just lifted his arm and pointed toward where Lucy was heading. I guess it made sense the direction would be where she'd went.

God, I hated this chick, but I followed her, wanting the fresh water more than I disliked her. We hadn't stopped long enough to drink since we'd left the camp, and I was anxious to wash the dead bug taste from my mouth.

Lucy moved through the woods and roots like she was strolling across a ballroom. Not that I knew what a person in a ballroom looked like, but Moobie had described it in his last book and it had made me envision something just like this. I was a bit slower picking and choosing where I stepped since I didn't have shoes.

It took five minutes for us to reach the stream and I watched as she stripped off her shirt. She was all lean muscle without the larger breasts I had hanging off my chest. Maybe that was why men didn't like me. My lumps were too big and the rest of me was way too skinny.

I tried to rinse my arms but was ashamed to take anything else off, feeling deformed in comparison.

She looked up suddenly from where she was washing and caught me staring. "What the fuck you looking at me for? What? You want a kiss?" she sneered.

"No, I just…"

"What?"

I turned away, flustered and then embarrassed. First I'd gawked and then I'd stammered. It was just she looked like she belonged out here. It was the first time I'd ever really been jealous, and it had been like a wrench thrown into the spokes of my brain.

"Figures a dirty Plaguer wouldn't wash," she said loud enough for me to hear.

The stammering had only been a minor glitch in my brain and she'd just pissed me off enough to push past it.

I turned and looked back at her, not flinching at all now. "You're right. I do like dirt. I like digging big holes in it to bury all the people I kill with the Bloody Death." I smiled at her like I was truly as insane as they said.

She shot me a dirty look. Her movements gained steam and she was throwing on her shirt and then heading back to the guys in no time. I had a nice little chuckle. That was much better.

I washed up in the stream as best as I could before I walked back by myself to the group. Tank and Lucy were there waiting, but Dax hadn't returned yet.

Lucy, who was only a few feet away from me, made a huffing noise loud enough to make it obvious she had some sort of issue and then turned to Tank. "You know we're lugging around a dead girl. We aren't going to make it home with her in one piece. She's an idiot and we know what happens to even smart Plaguers."

I wasn't as stupid as she thought. I'd heard, probably more times than she had, what they did to my kind. I knew about the killings and torture.

My feet were heading in her direction before my brain had made a decision on what it was going to do. "Go ahead, try and kill me," I said to her. The only thing stopping me from closing the final distance was Tank stepping in between us.

Tank held out a hand in both of our directions and said to Lucy, "Shut. Up. Dax didn't ask you to come. You volunteered and you knew what for."

It didn't matter if she said another word. I'd hit my limit. "I don't need this and I don't have any overwhelming desire to help a boy killer."

"What did you call me?" Lucy asked with much less of the bravado than what she'd had before.

I'd zeroed in on her soft spot but I hadn't let loose the killing blow. Yet. "Boy killer? What was he, ten? Twelve?" I asked, underestimating the age on purpose. They didn't understand, and I didn't either until that moment. I'd shut up for so long and taken so much shit, I wasn't sure I was capable of holding back anymore. It was like the restraints were off and the anger spilled out. "How did it feel?" I asked her. "Did you enjoy killing that little boy before he'd even hit the prime of his life?" I asked even though I knew she hadn't.

"See, Dax? She's fucking crazy like they say." Her voice cracked as she said it, and I turned around, realizing he'd come back. I'd just been about to feel bad for what I'd said to her when she had to go and call me crazy.

I turned and looked at Dax. He didn't say anything, but I saw the warning there. His stare was telling me to shut up or else. Then he was tugging me along with him until we were a good twenty feet away.

"Don't do that again," he said once we'd stopped.

I looked up at him undaunted. "She had it coming," I said, but with a lot less heat than a few minutes ago.

"She had something coming. Not that."

"What about all the shit she's been spewing at me?" I asked, getting angry again, but this time it had nothing to do with Lucy. It must be nice to have someone protecting you.

"Different level."

I backed up. "How do you know what hurts me and to what level? I didn't get out of that hellhole to be dictated to by anyone." I put my hands on my hips, broadcasting *who the hell do you think you are* at full blast in his direction. "You might be in charge with them but you aren't with me."

"You think so?" He shrugged. "Fine. Stay here." He looked up at the sky and then back at me. "You're not in great shape, so my guess is they'll catch up with you in about two hours. Have a nice life, whatever you've got left of it."

He turned and walked away from me.

Shit. He was totally right. I didn't even have shoes and Newco probably wasn't that far behind. This stuff didn't happen in the Moobie books. Moobie always had the upper hand.

I followed after him, cursing as I went but knowing I was screwed. "I'm coming," I said.

He stopped and turned to look at me, and I knew it wasn't going to be that easy. "Are you going to keep teasing Lucy?"

I looked over at Lucy where she was waiting by her bike looking...well, pretty emotionally fucked up. I guessed I could've held back a little, but who knew what a delicate flower she was going to be? I'd been called worse things... Maybe not worse but a lot more often, and I was fine.

"Fine."

"When we come in contact with other people, don't speak. You're a mute.

Understand? And don't take your gloves off again."

"Why am I mute?" I asked, looking down at the gloves I'd just put back on.

"Because you don't know the way of the Wilds. You start talking and you might give up the fact that you're an outsider."

I nodded but he still didn't move to get on the bike.

"Do you hear me? Keep your hands out of view and don't speak."

"Am I supposed to be deaf too? Because you don't have to keep repeating yourself." Hmmm, on a Moobie scale of ten, I wondered where that comeback rated? Probably a five. Certainly not my best.

"I am starting to wonder," he said, but finally went to get on the bike.

I wasn't stupid enough to wait for an invite.

Chapter Ten

We rode through the woods for a while before we hopped onto a path that seemed to be more well traveled than anything we'd taken thus far. Every now and then I'd see an old metal sign along the side. The last one we'd passed had the first three letters "VIR" still visible and made me think that this had once been part of those big roads they'd had in the Glory Years. As much as Dax said I wouldn't make it a week in the Wilds on my own, I definitely wouldn't be taking any road used as much as this one appeared to be.

It made more sense once we slowed and I looked over Dax's shoulder and caught sight of the largest bridge I'd ever seen. The thing was an engineering marvel. Seeing something like this made me wonder what the world looked like once upon a time.

As we got closer, I could see a gate blocking the lanes to the bridge, and no one was getting off their bikes to go open it.

"Why are we just sitting here?" I asked. The gate didn't look that sturdy. "Uh, hello? People still chasing us? Anyone remember that?"

"Shhh. You're supposed to be a mute," Dax said.

I was about to argue the point that I was

only a fake mute. If he thought I wasn't going to be talking on a regular basis he was as crazy as Moobie's sidekick, Doxie. Then I stopped because I doubted he'd know who Doxie was.

Before I got my brain back on the original argument, Dax's hands went to mine where they'd dropped to the tops of my legs. He grabbed them and put them back at his waist. He tugged his shirt up and over them, my fingers on the flesh of his stomach.

"What are you doing?" I said, about to pull my hands away. His grip on them stopped me and made it worse. All I could think was I hoped he couldn't tell that my palms were sweating through the gloves. Even if he could, it wasn't like it was touching him that did it. Maybe I was just nervous because I was on the run for my life? Huh? What about that, Dax?

I saw a guy stepping out of the trees that lined the road. His approach interrupted my silent self-defense and saved me from myself. The guy looked exactly how I'd always heard most of the people from the Wilds described. Leather pants hung low on a wiry frame, shirt ripped in several places and greasy hair slicked back into a thin ponytail at the base of his skull. He also looked like he could use a meal as much as I did.

Dax nodded while remaining seated, but this signal seemed to set Tank into motion. Tank got off his bike and grabbed a capped glass jar with liquid from his bike's pack. He walked over to the man, who was now positioned in front of the metal gate that blocked the bridge.

The guy took the jar and held it up, eyeing the half-full contents, and shook his head. "There's four of you now."

"Three bikes," Tank argued.

The guy shrugged. "We charge by the head."

"We aren't giving you any more," Dax said. "That fuel in your hand is it."

"Not enough." The bridge man's eyes scanned our group. "What else you got?" And then the man's eyes settled on me.

"Why he's looking at me?" I asked. "I don't have anything to give."

"Shut. Up," Dax said, and nudged me with an elbow. "Do you hear anything I say?"

The greasy bridge man started talking. "I think you do." What he'd just said and the way he was looking at me finally sank in. This guy had to be mighty hard up. No one ever wanted to sleep with me. I looked over at Lucy, the only other girl present, but I totally understood why he might not want to go there. She was beautiful in the same way a praying mantis was, and he'd probably be just as dead after the deed was done.

"Buddy, you and me? It ain't happening." And then I said to Dax, "Why does this guy think he owns the bridge? Why are we listening to this crap?"

"I say she fucks him and we get the hell out of here," Lucy added.

Dax turned toward her for the briefest of moments and her mouth shut. He had that look down. It didn't work on me, but that didn't mean he didn't have some skills. Nothing really worked on me.

I looked over at Lucy, amazed at how she'd shut up so quick, and felt a tinge of pity creeping in. I did really lay a mental trip on her earlier. Maybe she'd earned a reprieve for a few days. But I couldn't let it go without saying something. She needed to know I was being gracious on purpose. "I've decided to give you a little leeway. We'll see how that works out," I said, not wanting to commit to unlimited cordialness.

"Where's she from?" the greasy bridge man asked. "Seems different. I never fucked a foreigner."

I heard Dax sigh loudly. "What did I tell you?" he asked me.

"You had to know the mute thing wasn't going to work well. I'd say that's just as much on you as me."

"Where you from, girl?" the man asked, taking a couple of steps closer.

"None of your fucking business," Dax said,

and was getting off the bike. I reflexively put out my feet and grabbed the handlebars to keep it from tipping over. He walked past Tank and grabbed the fuel on his way. "Stay by her," I heard him say as he did.

Tank got back on his bike and rolled it a bit closer to me, while Lucy was shooting me the evil eye but not saying anything.

Dax stopped a foot from the guy and handed him the jar. The bridge man shook his head.

I grabbed the handlebars and tiptoe-rolled myself a hair closer to Tank. If I was going to survive in this place, I needed to start learning their ways.

"What's going on?" I asked Tank, since the mute thing was blown anyway.

"He wants more fuel," he said, his eyes never leaving where Dax stood and his hand on his gun strapped to his hip.

"That's, like, your money?" I asked.

"One form and the only kind the pirates will take."

I looked around. The bridge spanned a huge expanse of water, definitely a nice-sized bay that probably let out into the sea. But there was no boat. "This guy's a pirate?"

"Pirates control all the waterways. From what I know, they alternate duties. The guys working the bridge are always pissed off." He looked at me briefly to stress his next words.

"They *hate* land duty." He shrugged a *not my problem* and went back to watching Dax's back. "I've never seen this one before, but Dax will work it out."

Dax and the bridge man walked a bit farther away. I couldn't hear what was being said but the bridge man's stance softened, from something confrontational to very accommodating.

Then the bridge man was shoving the jar back at Dax, shaking his head with one hand up in what looked like a gesture of surrender. Dax didn't accept the jar and walked away from the man and back to the bike. I scooted backward as he grabbed the handlebars.

"What did you say?" I asked. I needed these kinds of details to add to my arsenal of information on how to live in the Wilds.

"Not now," he said, and seemed annoyed for someone who'd just come out the winning side of a negotiation.

The bridge man was opening the gate while hollering some gibberish toward the tree line.

"Why's he yelling at the trees?"

"He's not yelling at the trees. He's telling the gunmen who have their sights on us that it's okay to let us pass."

"I don't get it," I said as we waited for him to finish opening the gate. "Why do the pirates get to say who goes over the bridge? It's not

113

theirs."

"Because they're the ones that keep this thing standing. It is their bridge. It would've crumbled a long time ago if they didn't."

Tank leaned closer. "Did he agree to the other thing?"

Dax nodded. "Yeah. If they come this far, they won't let them pass."

"They'll never pick up our tracks after that," Tank said.

We started moving again as I realized he was talking about the group from Newco following us.

***

After crossing the bay, we went deep into the forests again. I hadn't seen anything but greenery for a few hours until we stopped about thirty feet shy of a large wooden building. It had the kind of detail in the woodwork and a certain character that made me think it had been standing here for a very long time. There was a large porch that ran along the front, with a few wooden chairs sitting unoccupied. A painted sign over the entrance read *Eat, Drink, Sleep.* There were a handful of horses lined up to a hitching post and a barn out back where I guessed a few more horses might be.

The place was amazing!

Dax got off the bike and I was doing a mad grab for handlebars again, wondering what he'd do if I just hopped off with him and let the bike drop next time.

He took a few steps toward the building and started his commander act again. "Tank, you stay out here with Dal. Lucy, you come with me. We'll get some supplies and be back." He took another step or so before stopping like he'd forgotten something, and nailed me with one of those *I mean business* stares. "You don't move, talk or do anything."

I rolled my eyes but he was already walking off again.

I watched their backs as they went inside, leaving me and Tank behind. I leaned forward, arms resting on the bike's handlebars as I viewed my very first experience with a true-life establishment in the Wilds. Even the knotty wood of its siding was cool.

"It's not that great," Tank said from beside me.

"Yeah, I'm sure it's not," I said, wishing I knew what I was doing that looked so pathetically longing. "I've just never seen one, is all."

"One what?"

I waved a hand toward the building. "You know, an *Eat, Drink, Sleep* place."

He nodded.

I leaned my chin on an arm. I wondered what it was like in there. Were there men drinking and flirting with women? People having bar brawls? Groups playing cards with pistols ready? The more I thought about it, the more it drove me plain crazy. There were all sorts of windows, but I wasn't going to go shove my nose against one no matter how much I wanted to get a peek in.

"Why don't you go look through a window and see how they're making out?" Tank said. "They're probably fine but you never know."

I scratched my head. "Yeah, if it'll help you out." What else could I do but press my nose against the window if it was for the better of the group?

He nodded. "But don't go in."

My tired muscles felt invigorated. I was finally going to see some of the real world. And not even the regular Newco world, but the lawless Wilds where only the toughest survived. I could barely control my enthusiasm. I was hopping and twitching all over the place as I crossed the distance at a jog and climbed up a box to get to the window.

I looked through a thick coat of grime; there were mostly men, and a rough group at that. The place was hazy as people smoked. I'd seen some of the guards do it at the compound and I remembered my father smoking before I'd gone away.

A long wooden bar ran the entire length of the back wall and there was a man standing on the other side of it. I saw Dax and Lucy speaking to him. The rest of the place was filled with tables and chairs and people were eating here and there. There were a couple of girls carrying trays, and they both had these large lumps pressed up toward their chin in a very uncomfortable looking position.

One of the girls served a table not far from the window and the guy yanked her down on his lap. He looped an arm around her waist and she started squirming and fighting him.

I started banging on the window. The guy holding the girl looked over and I wagged my finger, warning him he was doing something bad. Moobie always gave a warning. He thought it was only fair. I was inclined to agree.

The attacker wagged a finger back, but it was his middle one.

Luckily, Dax noticed me and I pointed at the offensive behavior. All he did was point for me to go back to the woods and mouth *get out of the window*. He tried to nail me with another *I mean business* stare.

Poor Dax. Didn't know how long it was going to take him to realize they didn't work on me.

But I did do part of what he asked. I stepped

out of the window. Then I went to the door. Someone had to go help that girl. I'd been bullied in the Cement Giant for years, and hell if I was going to be another person who stood by and watched another person get abused without helping. Some of the world's greatest atrocities could've been stopped if people hadn't just stood around watching.

I stepped into the place as I heard Tank screaming, "What the fuck you doing?" from the direction of the woods. I was in before he could stop me.

No one noticed me at first, but once they did, they kept staring. I knew even without the brand, I didn't look like I belonged. Maybe it was the white dress—I'd left the darker shirt by the bike—or my red hair. No one seemed to have hair like mine. I wasn't sure what, but something about me seemed to be sticking out to these people. It didn't matter. I was fine with being different and they could stare all they wanted.

I came up behind the man who still had a firm grip on the struggling girl. He hadn't noticed me. I grabbed a glass from the table beside me from some guy whose forehead was on his arm. Contents and all, I smashed it over the offender's head. He slouched over and his arms fell to his sides. I didn't feel any remorse. I'd given him fair warning he'd crossed the line.

His friend screamed in outrage and even the girl I'd just saved looked pissed. Now that she could get free she was all righteous indignation. "You idiot, you just cost me a job."

I looked about the place. They all saw me now, including Dax in the corner by the bar.

"I saved you," I told the waitress.

"You better pay me now!" she screamed.

My unconscious target's friend grabbed my arm in a death grip. "Oh, she's going to definitely pay for that."

I saw Dax heading over from the other side of the bar not bothering to hide his irritation. I straightened and made the most of my diminutive height and said to my accoster calmly, "I'd unhand me, sir, if you knew what was good for you."

His mouth just gaped open and I figured I needed to bring this down a bit for him to understand. "You want a piece of this? Because I'll give you a lot more than what you think. You like a little—"

"Don't do it," I heard Dax say just as the words "Bloody Death with your afternoon drink?" came out of my mouth.

The man's hand jerked away from me like I had worms oozing from my skin.

The room went deadly silent and I heard Dax say to someone, presumably Tank or Lucy, "Get the bikes ready." And then he wrapped an arm around my waist and was carrying me out of the bar just as the place started going crazy. People screamed "Plaguer" and were becoming altogether frantic.

I heard someone scream, "Block the door," as others yelled, "Kill her." But whatever their intentions, Dax cruised through the crowd as he held me in front of him like a shield of death and they scrambled out of our way, although I had fists ready and legs primed to kick.

Just as we were leaving, though, I saw a man stand up in the farthest, darkest corner of the place and I thought I caught a wisp of storm-gray haze around him. A Dark Walker? Here? It was so quick it could've been just some heavy smoke. It didn't make sense that one would be here. All the stories I'd heard whispered over the years had said Dark Walkers stuck to the countries. We were out the door too quickly for me to confirm if I'd actually seen one, and on the bikes a minute later.

I was forced to cling to Dax for fear of falling off the bike, and I had a feeling it wasn't from fear of people chasing us that he was going so fast. We were both riding high on adrenaline. Now that was going to be a good story.

He finally skidded the bike sideways, bringing us to a stop at a violent angle.

He hopped off the bike and I had to jump off myself or I would've gone down with it.

Tank and Lucy slowed a bit past us, clearly not looking to do the kamikaze slip and slide stop, hoping your legs made it through intact.

He stormed off a few feet and then turned on me. "What was that?" His finger pointed in the direction we'd come from.

He wasn't screaming but the little vein in his neck was popping out and he had a new stare going on. I didn't think he'd actually hurt me, but I'd go so far as to name this one *I'm going to kick your ass.* Didn't change anything. It wasn't like he'd kill me. He needed me.

"I thought the girl could use some help." I threw my hands up and tilted my head. Enough said, no?

"And you thought you should be the one to do something?" His voice had gone down a couple of decibels and I heard Lucy and Tank rev up their bikes.

"We'll just be a little up ahead," Lucy said quietly, and the two of them took off like they were the ones about to get reamed. Wusses.

"Yes. Someone had to. I thought I handled the situation pretty well."

He advanced on me but stopped just short of stepping on my toes, which was a good thing because they were much smaller than his boots.

"We had to run out of the place because you attacked a client that she *wanted.* That's well done?" We were almost nose to nose.

"I get what you're saying but hypothetically, if she had been in need"—I stopped for a dramatic pause and laid my hand on my chest—"I would've saved her." I couldn't wait to tell the girls this story.

"You're right. That would've been just brilliant, but she didn't need help." He walked away again as if he couldn't decide whether he wanted to beat me or run away from me. He ran both his hands through his short, dark hair. "You know, maybe you Plaguers are fucking crazy."

I shrugged. "It could be true." Maybe I was. Lucy and Tank had made a run for it while I didn't fear taking him on. Yeah, he had a lot of bark and I didn't doubt there was a serious bite to back it up, but so what? I had some teeth too. And the other thing? A bad day out here was still better than a good day back at the Cement Giant.

He let out a long sigh, the kind that told you just how exhausting he found me. "Why did you have to announce to everyone that you were a Plaguer?"

"To get the guy off me."

He shook his head. "I was walking over toward you. You knew I was going to handle him and don't say you didn't."

"It was in my arsenal and I used it. I'm sorry if that bothers you. Should I be meek and embarrassed of it?"

"You wanted to shove it in their faces."

I snorted, not bothering to respond.

"You know, you're a very hard person to like."

I put my hand to my chest and started fake crying. "Oh Dax, please, not that! Please say you like me."

He shook his head and walked to the bike that was lying on its side. He got on and I didn't wait too long to follow. He might not kill me, but I wasn't so sure if he wouldn't leave me hanging out there with a possible mob on their way just to screw with me.

The look I got when I climbed on confirmed my suspicion that he'd thought of it.

We caught up to Lucy and Tank only a few minutes later and we didn't stop again until it was nearly dark.

Tank set about making a fire, and it looked like we'd be camping out here for the night. I settled myself against a boulder while Lucy started digging through her pack.

"What do we have left?" Dax asked.

"We've got four jerkies left. One each."

"One and a third each," Tank said.

"One each," Lucy said, surprising the hell out of me.

"Why does she get to eat?" Tank asked. "She just cost us our dinner and now we're going to have to drive through the night because she tipped off everyone in the area that there's a Plaguer around."

"She eats," Lucy said. "I might've done the same thing." She shot me a look that was far from *hey, let's be friends* but close to *maybe I don't totally hate you.*

"Those aren't the rules. She cost us a meal," Tank said. "You cost the group a meal, you go hungry. That's the way it's always been."

I thought Dax was going to let them fight it out but then he spoke up. "I don't want to feed her right now either but she's a walking skeleton, and I need her alive. If there was one jerky, she'd get it before any of us." He reached over and grabbed two dried meat sticks from Lucy and tried to hand me one.

"I'm fine. I don't need it," I said, looking at Tank.

Dax grabbed my hand and shoved the jerky into my palm. "I took you out of that compound for a reason. I will force-feed you that jerky before I let you starve yourself."

"Fine. I'll eat it. Whatever. You don't need to get so bent out of shape about it." I was hungry as hell so it wasn't actually a concession, but he didn't know that. I mean hell, I knew I needed the calories and the Cement Giant wasn't going to blow itself to smithereens.

I took a couple of bites as Dax got up and walked out of the camp.

I gnawed on the stuff as I leaned against my rock. "What flavor is this? It's really good stuff."

Lucy and Tank looked at me kind of oddly. Hey, if I was going to eat it I didn't see a lot of reason to pretend it sucked. These people were weird.

Chapter 11

We arrived at Dax's home the next day. I knew it was his because when we pulled up to the man guarding this gate nobody had to dig around for glass jars filled with fuel. The man just opened it once he saw us. His eyes fixed on me as we passed, and I had a feeling there weren't too many strangers welcomed here.

A large farmhouse sat in the middle of a huge field and dominated the area that looked like it was gated all around, except for where it backed up to a stone cliff. There were other buildings spread out as well that appeared to have been built more recently, all smaller than the main house. Some looked like small ranches while others looked like one-bedroom cottages. There were a couple barn structures and scattered sheds, and there was a windmill too. Off in the distance I could see animals roaming the area outside and other gated, partitioned-off areas, which looked greener than the rest. A couple of specks in the far distance looked like people riding horseback along the perimeter.

We pulled up to a porch that ran the length of the main house and two people came out. One was an older lady with a head of white hair who had to be about seventy.

I'd heard people in the Wilds died young but

I'd also been told they had no fuel. I'd decided very little of my information was reliable. Half was Newco propaganda and the other dreamt up internally, probably by Ms. Edith. At the current rate of propaganda I'd been fed, for all I knew, my head full of information could have been ninety-five percent bullshit. I was willing to give it a five percent accuracy rate, because even bullshit usually had a thread of truth running through it.

There was another guy there who looked close to my age with a mop of shaggy, dark hair. He was tall and broad but lean, like he hadn't had time to fill out all the growing he'd recently done. It was the first boy I'd been around that was close to my age since I'd gone to the compound.

He waved a silent greeting and I instantly liked him. I didn't even have to get close enough to see the dark memories. Some people were like that, so good their insides sort of just glowed through their eyes. In this case, large hazel ones with thick black lashes that looked so wholesome they made me think of peach pies like the ones Moobie would describe.

"I see it went well," the older woman on the porch said as her gaze landed on me.

"Dahlia, this is Fudge and that's Bookie." Dax stepped up on the porch beside her, wrapped an arm around the woman's shoulders and kissed her cheek. "We're starving. What do you have brewing?"

"Don't act like you don't smell my meatloaf cooking," she said with a smile. "It'll be ready in a few hours. There's some fresh fruit and dried meat to pick on until then."

Dax glanced at me and then back to Fudge. "Can you handle this?"

"I'll take care of the details. Go take care of things."

"Thanks," he said, and patted her on the shoulder as he left.

"I'm Fudge," the woman said, and waved me forward as Bookie walked down the stairs to help Lucy and Tank with their stuff.

I looked up at the woman and hesitated, not wanting to know what bad thing I'd find. When I'd gone into *Eat, Drink, Sleep*, there had been too many people close to me at once. If I didn't center in on one person, they all sort of blocked each other out. It was kind of like too many people trying to get through one door until no one could. One on one, it was a lot harder to avoid what was lurking underneath.

"Come on, now," she said, and I pushed myself to move closer but I had a really bad feeling about this one.

When I got near people, sometimes it was the worst things they did that would come to me. Other times like these, it was the worst thing done to them, the deepest scar they had that they couldn't outrun, delivered up to me on a silver platter, garnished with scents and feels. If I was lucky, it was a little fuzzy around the edges, and other times it was like I was right there going through it with them.

Fudge had been a young girl when it happened. She was sitting in the middle of the woods while people were draining her parents of their blood in front of her, slowly and methodically. I could feel the hands on her, holding her tiny frame in place.

After there wasn't a drop of blood left, they skinned them and threw their hides on a pile with the rest of the ones they'd gathered. I'd heard about these people, even in the countries. They sacrificed humans in belief that it would save them from Bloody Death outbreaks.

They finished with her parents and turned to her, but a blur of activity stopped them, wisps of hair as two creatures tore through the area. I couldn't see anything clearly but I heard the growls. The creatures moved so quickly it was hard to figure out what had happened until there was nothing but dead bodies, torn apart and lying before her. So these were the mighty beasts of the Wilds I'd heard about. It was said that the strongest ruled in the Wilds. Fudge's tormentors had just dropped a rung on the food chain.

I stumbled but caught myself with a hand on the top step before I did a face plant. It was one of the most terrifying things I'd ever seen, and I wanted to know how she'd escaped the beasts with her life but I wouldn't ask. That might have been one of the most frustrating things ever. I hated the damn cliffhangers but I wasn't stupid enough to try and get the sequel.

By time I was straightened back up, she had a look that said it all.

"So it's true?" I could hear the wonder in her voice.

I nodded. "I'm sorry," I said. The two words fell short for my having intruded on such an experience, but I wasn't used to getting caught and didn't have a better line ready. I wasn't sure what I was apologizing for exactly, that she'd been through that or for my encroaching on her hurtful memory. It just seemed the appropriate thing to do.

Margo had said it a couple of times when talking to other people in the compound after hearing their sad stories—and there was *always* a sad story. Margo had been a late bloomer, as we called them, and come to the compound after ten. I didn't understand why she was saying sorry when she heard their stories, since none of it was her doing, but it had made them feel better. Since she'd had the best social skills, I'd followed her lead.

"Not your fault. You don't get to choose, do you?"

"No. Sometimes if there's a lot of people around, they'll cancel each other out, but I don't really have any control of it." I'd wished I could stop it sometimes. It was hard to explain to others what it was like to have your first memory of most of the people you meet be something so terrible. If I let it, it could make the world seem like a very horrible place, but that wasn't the world I chose to see.

"We've all got our burdens." She turned and headed into the house.

I followed her as the simplest things were setting my senses off into delirium, like the sound of our feet crossing the wood of the porch. I walked into the house with her and desires I'd tamped down over the years were trying to flood up to the surface all at once. In all my years in the Cement Giant, when I imagined what a home should look like, this was it. A massive fireplace sat against the wall, competing for attention with the spindled staircase. A table not that far away looked like it would accommodate a huge family for a homemade dinner. Nothing was bright and shiny but everything was clean and warm, like the things had been used for years with love and adoration.

She turned toward the wooden stairs and

began climbing them. I followed as I tried to not touch everything within reach, like the flowers that sat on a well-worn table on the landing, or reach down and touch what appeared to be a braided rug that ran the length of the hallway.

She stepped into a bedroom at the end of a long hall and waved me in. "You're going to stay in here."

The four walls and a door were the only similarity between this place and where I'd slept at the compound. Instead of a harsh gray cover it had a soft white blanket that my fingers itched to touch.

"I'll bring you a snack and get you something to wear. Didn't know who was coming or how big you'd be so didn't have anything prepared."

"I'm staying here?" I asked, probably sounding like the mental patient most thought I was.

"Yes. I'll be right back," she said. I had a feeling it was as much to get distance from me, and the hurtful things I'd made her remember, than to do anything else.

She left and I didn't know what to do. Afraid to touch all the wonderful things in here, like the fluffy pillows or the frilled curtains hanging above the picture window. I was still standing in the middle of the room when she came back ten minutes later with a pile of things in her hands.

"You can make yourself comfortable," she said.

I nodded even though I didn't move. I wasn't sure what that meant. No one had ever told me to "get comfortable" before.

"Here's a few shirts and pants." She looked me over. "They might be large on you but that couldn't be helped." She looked down at my feet. "I found you a pair of boots but they might be a bit big as well."

"I'm sure they're fine," I said as I watched her place the brown leather shoes by the wall.

"Come with me."

We walked back down the hall into what I recognized was a bathroom. "I thought there weren't working bathrooms in the Wilds?" Even in the country, only the rich could afford these kinds of amenities.

"We don't heat the water except in the winter, but it's functional. There's a water reserve attached to the house that catches rain. Just be warned, we've had some good rainfalls recently, but come drought time, you take more than a five-minute shower and you'll be catching some serious flack around here. We run the generators from sundown to ten, but if you want to stay up later than that you'll have to use candles."

"You've got fuel?" I asked.

She smiled. "Don't get the wrong impression. This isn't how things are in most of the Wilds, but Dax…" Her words trailed off until she caught herself again. "Dax is a resourceful one. We live pretty good here."

"How many people live here?"

"In the house? Only a handful, but our community has probably a hundred or so. There about twenty or so within this immediate area but there's more beyond the gates."

She moved to a cabinet and pulled out a tannish-brown bar of soap and a large cloth. "This is yours. We only make soap once every month, so don't leave it in a puddle of water. Make it last." She walked over to the door. "Now that Dax is back, we'll be having a feast tomorrow, so rest up."

"What's the feast for?" I asked as she was shutting the door.

"Dax's return. Everyone will come."

"How long has he been gone?"

"Few weeks now. I'm guessing you're from the country of Newco?"

I nodded.

"Figured. Your country was the last on the list. He's been trying to track down a Plaguer for a while."

I didn't know that much of the world beyond Newco, and even that was limited. I did know there were a handful of other countries, though.

Did they all have compounds where they stashed Plaguers away? "And he couldn't find one?"

"Not if he ended up in Newco."

Were there any more Plaguers left? Was I one of the last ones?

"Don't worry. Things will work out," she said with a smile.

I nodded and she shut the door but I didn't believe it for a second. Things didn't just work out. That was only what you told little children.

***

There was a sandwich sitting on the table beside the bed when I got back to the room. I was starving, but what if there was something to what they had said in the compound? What if eating a lot would make me sick again? But it would make me healthier, so wouldn't that do the opposite of getting me sick? But what if the virus was still in me and it made that stronger too? I'd take a couple bites only. That should be safe.

Two bites had turned into inhaling the sandwich.

I'd chewed my last bite while standing and looking at the bed. She did tell me this was my room. She had to assume I'd use it.

I stretched out on it and wondered how they

made their mattresses. The ones at the Cement Giant had been a thin layer of feathers, but this one felt like I was lying on a cloud.

It was dark when I awoke. I'd only meant to lie down for a minute, but that intention went to the same place as only having a couple of bites of food.

My drowsy brain thought I was still back in my cell until I smelled the smoke and looked up to see a small girl of maybe five or six hovering over me. She had riotous red hair just like mine sticking out every which way, and was holding a bundle of what looked like weeds that were smoking. She smiled widely at me.

I drew a big fat blank on the memories, and I was grateful. Kid memories were the worst, just unfiltered pain with a nice serving of shock because most of them didn't see it coming. Nothing had scarred her too badly...yet.

"I'm Tiffy," she said.

"Hi, Tiffy." I looked at the smoking weeds as she moved her bundle back and forth a couple times as if she couldn't decide what was the best spot for them, over my chest or closer to my head with a couple gratuitous ashes for flavor. My brain searched for some explanation that made this normal but came up with nothing.

"What are you doing?" I asked.

"Checking your magic." She was very intent on her job.

"What do you mean?"

"Look," Tiffy said, pointing to the smoke.

"At what?" I asked, not getting the point of this.

She dragged a finger through the stream. "It's bluish."

"It looks normal to me."

"No, no. You're mistaken. Look closely. I know you can do this." She patted my hand with her free one in an encouraging way.

"Okay," I said, wanting to placate her because she believed it so firmly.

She waved her hand over me again. "See? The sage's smoke is blue."

I looked closely, my eyes focusing. Still looked gray to me. If I was splitting hairs, maybe a bluish hue, but that could've just been the dark lighting in the room.

She moved the bundle away from me. "See? Now it's gray." She moved the bundle back again. "And now it's blue again."

If it changed, the difference was so slight it might have been a placebo effect of her suggestion.

She must have realized I'd had my doubts, because she said, "It takes a while to get the hang of it. I've got more experience but you'll

137

learn."

"Do you do this to everyone?" I asked, letting her finish out her experiment.

"No. My friends asked me to do it for you."

"What friends?" This didn't strike me as a Dax or Fudge thing, unless I'd made a serious miscalculation.

"I can't talk about them."

The door that was left ajar opened and Fudge appeared. "Tiffy, what are you doing in here? You shouldn't have bothered Dahlia. She needs to rest."

I sat up on the bed now that the burning bundle wasn't hovering over me. "No. It's okay. I should be getting up anyway. What time is it?"

"It's the middle of the night and you've been traveling for days. You need more sleep. Tiffy, go back to my room."

Tiffy leaned in close. "I'll let you know what they say," she whispered, and then skipped off after a last smile in my direction, only stopping as Fudge took her bundle of sage on the way out.

The soft feel of the room suddenly made sense. "Am I in her room?"

"Yes, but don't fuss about it. She never sleeps in here anyway. She hates to sleep alone." After she heard the door shut down the hall she continued. "Lost her family to the Bloody Death when she was a baby."

138

Her brain must have been too young to form the memories, and I was glad for it.

I stood up, thinking of what they'd said at the compound, how even too much sleep might bring back the Bloody Death.

"What are you doing?" Fudge asked as I moved about the room.

"I'm not tired anymore."

"That's nonsense. You've slept for only a few hours and you've been traveling for days on almost no sleep. Get back in bed."

Fudge was standing there pointing at the bed. Even as scrawny as I was, I knew I could take her down, and yet I found myself getting back into bed like she had some old woman magic.

Fudge left the room while I pondered who Tiffy's "they" might be.

Chapter 12

I walked down the stairs to the sound of bustling activity early the next morning. At the compound everyone would be up by six, and it didn't seem to be much different here. There were lots of people here, and I couldn't help myself from wondering if they all knew I was a Plaguer.

People were coming in and out of the dining area, where it looked like a buffet had been set up on that large table I'd admired yesterday. The heaping pile of food on display smelled like it would be as good as it looked. I caught a couple of glances as I paused at the bottom of the stairs but no one said anything to me.

Fudge walked out of the kitchen and spotted me instantly, like she had some sort of radar that told her my whereabouts. "I put breakfast out at six thirty sharp every day," Fudge said. "You miss it and you fend for yourself."

"Sounds good to me." I didn't need any more prodding. I waited for a break in the line to slip in and grabbed a plate from the stack. I'd never been able to choose what I ate before and I wasn't sure what to go for first. I reached over and grabbed eggs. Those I recognized from the compound, but I didn't know what anything else was. Eating the sandwich hadn't struck me down dead, so I threw caution out the window and started piling up some of everything. There were spongy yellow-looking foods and little grayish tubes, flat strips of striped food and round slices of pink.

A few people looked at my plate as it was growing vertically and then looked at me, pants bagging at the hips and skinny arms poking out of the sleeves.

"What? You've never seen someone eat before?" I said after the third look from some portly guy in overalls.

There were forks and knives piled in a cup at the end of the spread. Grabbing a pair, I took my plate and went outside to a bench on the back porch and started to chow down. Even the eggs here tasted better than what I'd eaten at the compound. Plus I could eat as much as I wanted.

By time I was done, I realized that not eating wasn't the only way to knock someone out. I felt like a beached whale. I wasn't quite sure what that was, except I'd read it in a Moobie book where it was used to describe something bloated that didn't want to move. Sounded about right.

I didn't give the food too much time to sit, though. I had to go find Dax and see if it was time to "work." If not, I had my own agenda to get started on. Being here in this place made me think nonstop about my friends being where they were.

I went back into the house and poked around and then stopped by Fudge. "Do you know where Dax is?" I asked.

"He won't be back until later on today."

"Is there anything you need me to do?" I asked, hoping she'd say no.

She shook her head. "I think everything's pretty well in hand at the moment."

I looked around the kitchen until I located what I was hoping for—a couple of sharp knives sitting on one of the counters. "Could I borrow one of these? I've always wanted to try whittling and since there's nothing else I'm needed for…"

She shrugged. "Okay, just make sure to bring it back."

"Will do."

I took the knife and left the kitchen. I tried to keep it angled out of view as I walked out of the house and toward the gate to the property. It was the only way out, since the rest of the area was fenced in or surrounded by rocky cliffs.

There was a different man than yesterday guarding the entrance, an intimidating machine gun in his hands. I'd seen them on occasion at the compound. That was what I really needed, but since it was a long shot, the knife would have to suffice for now.

"State your business," he said as I came closer.

"Is that necessary? The business stating

stuff?"

I took a couple of steps closer and he backed up a bit, his eyes shooting to my right hand with the brand, not my left that was holding the knife. I was wearing the gloves but he obviously knew what lay beneath, which meant everyone here probably knew.

"For you it is," he sneered.

What an idiot. Did he really think he was going to make me feel bad? I'd been shunned since I was four. Did he think the fact that he didn't give me a warm hug on greeting was going to make a difference to me?

I rested my weight on one foot as I scratched my chin. "Do you know what Plaguers can do?"

He made a show of spinning his gun. "See shit about people? Bunch of hogwash, you ask me."

It was almost unfair how outmatched he was, and he was going to make this almost enjoyable for me. "I wonder if your sister would agree with that."

The color in his cheeks drained completely and then came back with a vengeance a few seconds later. "Don't be saying shit about my sister."

I wondered if the joy of getting the upper hand on jackasses would ever fail to bring me such happiness. "I didn't plan on talking to anyone this morning. Just looking to take a walk in the forest. Of course, plans can change and I could get stuck with nothing else to do."

He yanked back the latch that held the gate closed and flung it open. "Go. I hope you don't come back. I hope the beasts eat you."

I smiled brightly as I passed him. "Thanks so much. Hope you have a great afternoon, too." What a lightweight. He wouldn't have lasted a week in the Giant. I was starting to think these people of the Wilds wholly overestimated themselves. They broke awfully easy.

The trees swallowed me up and I breathed deep of the forest air and listened to the birds chirping and hoped I'd never get so jaded that I would take this paradise for granted. I moved farther into the woods and I didn't stop until the main house and gate were out of sight. The forest felt old here, like it had been growing way before a plague wiped through the world.

I was getting pretty deep into it but I wasn't worried about the mystery beasts so many feared. Want to talk made-up bullshit? The beasts sounded like tall tales to me. Even as I thought of the animals in Fudge's memory, they might have been a pack of wolves. That was the thing about other people's memories. They weren't exactly objective.

I spotted a dead tree with a trunk that still stood eight or nine feet high. It was time to practice. When I got back to the Giant, I'd need to be able to handle myself. That was part one of my plan, become a honed killer. Part two? Gather enough explosives to blow the place to bits. As daunting as training myself to be a killer seemed, I knew the massive amount of explosives I was going to need would be the worst of it.

I'd take it one step at a time, starting here. I held the knife in my hand, imagining I was traipsing through an enemy's country on assignment and the dead tree was an assassin come to finish me off.

I turned sideways, making myself a smaller target, and tried to balance the knife on my finger. I'd never checked a knife out before. I wasn't sure what the point of trying to balance it on a finger was, but Moobie would've done it. That was about all I had to work with right now. If Moobie did it, I did it.

I looked up, preparing to take aim at the tree.

"You, sir, have taken on the wrong person. It is time to meet your death," I said in a fake aristocratic accent toward the center of the tree, as if I could see the villain's face.

"What are you doing out here?" Dax asked from behind me.

How did I not hear him coming up on me? My spine stiffened, preparing to weather the storm of humiliation. "Just goofing around," I replied, not looking at him.

"Oh, because I thought you were preparing to mete out death to that already dead tree." He wasn't laughing, but I could hear he was barely holding it back.

He stepped around to the side. "Please, I don't want to stop you from finishing off this tree," he said, acting quite serious.

"Thank you." I tilted my chin up and held my tattered dignity together as best I could.

I was hoping he was going to leave, but instead he leaned against a nearby tree and looked like he was settling in to watch the show. There was nothing to do but take my best shot. Really, how much more embarrassing could it get?

I gripped the knife lightly, just as Moobie would've done, and flung it at the tree. The handle end bounced off the bark about a foot off the ground.

Nope. I was wrong. It could get more embarrassing.

Dax straightened, walked over, grabbed the knife and then moved back about ten feet farther away from the tree.

"Come here," he said.

I walked over to him, figuring he wanted me out of the line of fire as he threw the knife himself. I mean seriously? Did he have to gloat over being better?

I stopped a few feet to his side and he

handed the knife to me. "Try it from here."

"I couldn't do it from up there." I knew there had to be something wrong with him. He was hot but he was brain dead.

"Try it anyway." His tone alone said he was prepared to make an issue of it.

"Fine." I took the knife and this time I didn't even manage to hit the bark.

"Go get the knife and try from back there," he said, pointing another two feet away.

"I'm not doing this. It's ridiculous." I'd come back out by myself again and practice alone. It wasn't like he was giving me pointers. I was failing and he kept making the target harder.

"Do it."

"I don't want to play this game anymore." I crossed my arms over my chest. Why was he being such a dick? I couldn't do it.

"Do it anyway."

Why was he digging in about this? He stared at me and I didn't flinch but my wheels were spinning. This place was perfect. I didn't have to worry about somewhere to eat or sleep while I could devote most of my energies to putting together my plans.

If that meant throwing the knife at the tree, I was going to have to do it. I broke eye contact first and went to get the knife, swallowing my pride like I'd hoped I'd never have to do after I got out of the Giant.

I took my position, not really thinking about my stance or anything else at that moment. I reached over my head and let the knife fly, expecting to not even come close to the tree this time.

I was stunned. I'd nailed the tree dead center. How the hell had that happened?

I looked over at Dax. He was quiet and not surprised like I was. It took all my control to not hop and dance around.

"Dax, did you see?" I asked, even though he was looking right at it.

"You got the plague when you were four, and you're eighteen," he said, musing to himself with none of the enthusiasm I was feeling.

"What does that have to do with anything?"

He looked to me now. "You ever wonder why they nearly starved you in that place? Gave you just enough to let you survive at the lowest level of existence?"

I stiffened but didn't turn away. He sure knew how to take the fun out of a moment, and how did he *know* so much? "I survived just fine," I said, not having to fight the urge to jump around now. My happy dance was completely deflated.

"I'm stating facts. You can't be emotional."

"I'm not," I said, knowing I sounded defensive but couldn't help it.

"Yes, you are. If you want to survive, you need to be an independent variable. You are the cause, not the effect."

"What are you talking about?"

"I'm talking about teaching you to survive. You can't feel so much."

"I wanted out so that I could live, not die."

"If you want to live, part of you has to die."

I kept my mouth shut, not saying a word, but he was wrong. I hadn't gotten out of that place to become a machine. He could think whatever he wanted. He wasn't changing me.

He walked over to the tree and yanked out the knife before returning to me.

He put the knife in my hand. "Don't do this in front of anyone."

"Why not?" I asked, doubting I could do it again anyway.

"Because it makes you look more different than you already do."

"You already told them I was a Plaguer." I knew how to spot the looks, even if the gate guy hadn't said anything.

"The glove trick wasn't going to work here on a daily basis. I needed to stay in front of the subject." He started walking out of the clearing. "Come on. You shouldn't stay out here alone."

"Why?"

"Because of the beasts. We haven't seen one around for a while but that doesn't mean it's safe. Plus, you might want to get cleaned up a bit before everyone shows."

"What's wrong with me?" I asked. I'd showered yesterday. I wasn't that dirty.

"Don't you want to, like, I mean…" He waved a hand in the direction of my head.

"What?"

"I don't know, do what girls do? Maybe brush your hair or something?"

My hand went to the nappy mess of red. I'd never wanted to attract positive attention, not that I was sure I even could, but him pointing to my hair had me trying to smooth it down. "I don't see the point," I said, contradicting my actions as I followed him back to the house.

"Suit yourself, but when we go to work, it would help if you could look a little more low key. Your coloring, the bright eyes, you don't blend well. Having that"—he gestured at my hair again—"sticking out all crazy doesn't help matters."

"Ow." I slapped a hand to the back of my head.

"What?"

"What kind of weird bugs you guys have out in these parts? I think one of them just ripped a hair from my head."

"That might be an improvement," he said as he walked toward the house.

He didn't get to see the face I made at his

150

back.

Chapter 13

With all the things Fudge must have been juggling today, goddamn if she still didn't manage to track me down an hour later with a brush in hand. I saw her coming out of the corner of my eye and stopped in mid-turn because yeah, I was slick like that.

I darted off in the opposite direction as if I hadn't seen her, and maybe by some stretch she didn't know I had. I moved across the field that led to absolutely nowhere but I couldn't outrun the old lady as she yelled across the distance, "Don't you run from me, missy," while she waved the brush in her hand.

I didn't know what it was about Fudge, but I stopped in my tracks. Anyone else and I would've been flipping them the bird, and I resented every frozen moment of it.

"Hi, Fudge."

"You're coming back in the house with me right now. God only knows how long it'll take to straighten out this mess," she said, and was trying to drag the brush through my hair even as she spoke.

It was still the tangled mess it had been earlier this morning when Dax had criticized it. The first thing I'd done after we'd gotten back was go into my borrowed room and look for a brush but then I'd stopped. How pathetic was I to let some guy's opinion count for so much? This was my hair and he could take it or leave it. I wasn't looking to impress anyone.

"Did Dax send you after me?"

"No, why? By that comment I'm guessing he said something? You think he's the only one that noticed this mess?"

I tried to pull my head of hair away but she wouldn't let go of the brush already lodged into it. The only thing I accomplished was moving us both a couple feet to the left. "There's nothing wrong with trying to look pretty," Fudge informed me.

"I don't care what people think of me." I tried another evasive dodge of the brush.

"Of course you do." Fudge was much more agile than she looked.

"Fine. I'll do it myself," I huffed, trying to get the brush from her while avoiding the onlookers.

"It's too knotted. You need help."

"Really, I don't."

Fudge utterly ignored me. I'd been beaten more times than I could count in my life and never gave an inch, but the urge to whine was strong as she took that brush to my hair. Of course I didn't whine, because that would be, well, frankly, just too embarrassing. But so was letting this lady brush my hair. What was becoming of me?

I should tell her to get the hell off me but her hands were all bent with arthritis and she'd run after me like… Actually, I wasn't exactly sure what she ran after me like, since I'd only had people running after me to kick my ass, but it was good, whatever it was.

I'd always thought that if someone ever broke my will to theirs, they were going to be one mean son of a bitch and they'd have beaten me until I couldn't stand. It appeared that I'd seriously overestimated myself.

"Can we at least go inside?" I asked, and even my tone made it hard to keep my head up.

"Of course, dear."

At least she was merciful in her victory. I was laid low by grandma. This was pathetic.

The sounds of the feast floated up through the window of my bedroom and so did the smells. It was weird how my nose recognized good food that my taste buds had never experienced.

The party had been going on for a little while already as I moved in front of the full-length mirror in the room. It was the first time I'd ever seen all the parts of me at once, besides in a window's nighttime reflection.

My hair looked okay I guess, but the pants bagged on me and I realized that I wasn't just skinnier than Lucy, I looked downright scrawny compared to her, like a stick figure with bulges coming out here and there. The unfitted dresses of the compound had been more flattering than what I was currently wearing because at least they streamlined the differences.

I turned from my image. It didn't matter. I knew that I hadn't been left alone by the guards because I'd been a raving beauty. Looks didn't matter that much anyway. They weren't what counted, and when I walked into this party, it wasn't my hair or outfit they'd be looking at anyway. I tugged the gloves on my hands, hating how damp my palms felt.

I headed down the stairs, following the laughter and music to the back of the house. There had to be close to a hundred people there, all having a good time, smiling and laughing. The area was lit by several fires. This was just as I'd imagined a party would look like in my mind. They all had glasses in hand and some of them were eating. I couldn't get over the smells. I'd never experienced such smells before.

There was a man singing with a guitar in his hands off to the side, and Bookie was pounding a drum. He missed a beat to lift up his hand and give me a wave from across the distance. I did the same as I took a step forward.

Slowly, an awareness seemed to spread through the crowd. The looks started. They already knew I was a Plaguer and I wouldn't pretend I was anything else. It was one thing to do it when we were on the run, but I was supposedly here to help Dax. They didn't like what I was, then that was their problem.

I walked around the area, chin frozen in an up position. Fudge was directing some men over by the food and I made my way over. Even if every single one of them resented my presence there, I didn't care. I'd be eating good tonight.

Fudge was making up a plate and then handed it to me as I approached. "You need to get some skin on those bones," she said.

I took it with a smile and then carried it over to a dark corner on the back porch where no one else was sitting to get a good view of everyone laughing and dancing.

I looked down at the plate, knowing I'd been pressing my luck lately. What if the people at the compound were right about the Bloody Death coming back if I kept eating? The source of the information wasn't great. Could I really believe anything the same people who tortured me said? Dax had made it sound like they'd wanted to keep me weak. But who could I really believe? People who had kept me alive for years or some guy I'd just met with shady motivations he wasn't disclosing?

There were heaps of meats piled up beside this white fluffy stuff I knew was mashed potatoes and a pile of corn. There was some sort of very yellow bread that I'd never seen the likes of, and it had a glossy surface in spite of its rougher sides.

"It's not poison," Dax said, walking up to me. "Are you going to eat it or just stare at it?"

One more good meal wouldn't be likely to kill me, would it? It would really suck to have finally made it out of the compound and then die less than a week later. But I was out and I wanted to live. I didn't get this far to get stuck still living by compound rules. What if Dax was right? They'd been trying to make me weak?

I took a spoonful of potatoes as Dax watched. He knew there was something I wasn't saying, his expression almost screaming to either eat up or fess up. If I told him about how food might make the Bloody Death come back, he might take my plate, and I wasn't risking it. I loaded down a fork with meat, potatoes and corn all in one pass.

The first bite hit my tongue in an explosion of joy. Fudge's food might be worth death. I actually moaned over how good it was. I started shoveling bites into my mouth before I'd swallowed the last.

He sat on the porch railing while I attacked the food on my plate. "We're going to start soon. Going out and canvassing areas."

I nodded, my mouth too full to speak.

"I'll leave you to your..." He waved a hand to encompass my feeding fest.

I nodded, realizing a little belatedly that the rate at which I was shoving food in my mouth might not be very flattering.

I still had a few bites left on my plate that I was gearing up the strength to eat when Tank walked over and sat a jar down on the arm of my bench.

"What's this?" I asked, picking up the jar and sniffing it. This didn't smell anywhere near as good as the food.

I must have made a face, because Tank laughed before he said, "Booze to wash the food down."

"Booze?"

"Yes. Alcohol. Whiskey, to be precise."

Ah, alcohol. I'd always wanted to try some of that. It would probably be okay. I mean, the food hadn't killed me...yet, and I was all about living on the edge these days. I took a large gulp and then my eyes watered with the burning feeling and my insides felt like they were being cooked. I coughed, wondering why people liked this stuff. The taste was rough but then I noticed the warmth settling in my stomach, which was delicious.

"I wouldn't drink it quite so quick, okay?"

"Yeah, sure, got it. Thanks." I held up the glass and took another tentative sip as he left.

I pulled my legs up underneath me, sipping my whiskey as someone sang a song I'd never heard and people danced in between the fires that lit the area. This was heaven. I'd figure out a way to bust my friends out of the compound and we would build a life just like this. We'd all have this soon.

A lovely feeling was starting to build in me and I looked down at the glass that was close to empty. I liked this booze stuff. I tipped the glass back and emptied it. Where were they hiding this wonderful stuff? I was going to drink this every day for the rest of my life.

I made my way to the table by the food that had jugs set out that looked like the same stuff and refilled my glass, right up to the brim.

By time I'd finished that glass, I was moving not so steadily on my feet to the heart of the crowd dancing. They all made room for me as I mimicked the steps I'd watched them make, minus a stumble or two here and there, but I thought I was doing pretty well.

I spun around and the crowd got wider. "Dance with me," I said to the people, but couple by couple, they were all stopping. "Why aren't you all dancing?" I asked before my brain kicked into gear, a little slower than normal. They didn't want to dance with me? My feet started slowing until I was standing alone.

Then an arm wrapped around my waist and swung me around. A hand took mine and I realized it was Dax and we were moving around the area.

"Dance," Dax said loudly.

"I'm trying to," I said.

"Dance," he repeated even louder.

"I'm trying!" I shouted, doing the best I could, but he was moving a lot quicker than my feet wanted to go.

I looked around and others had gone back to dancing as well. Maybe they'd just taken a break? I had a feeling I was missing something, but my brain was too fuzzy to worry about it and too damn happy. I really liked whiskey.

We twirled around the area, my hand on his shoulder, and I couldn't help but notice how handsome Dax looked and how nice he smelled.

His face looked a little softer than normal when he looked down at mine and I blurted out, "You're pretty. Not in like a girly way but a guy way."

He smiled but looked away. "And you're a lot tougher than I thought you'd be."

I frowned. I'd wanted him to tell me I was pretty, too.

The song ended too soon and instead of steering me to the porch and leaving me there, or better yet, dancing some more, he was guiding me inside.

"Where we going? I want to *dance*!" I did a wide flourish of my arm and banged my knuckles against the door we were passing.

"I think some sleep might be a better idea for now."

"But I want to dance and drink and live."

"I think that's enough living for now."

His arm around my waist kept me moving up the stairs and down the hall to my room. I fell upon the bed, curled onto my side, boots and all, and realized that this sleep idea wasn't such a bad call.

The door closed as he left the room and a breeze came in through the open window. That was another new thing. The windows opened here.

I kicked off my boots without getting up and crawled under the covers with all my clothes still on. As I lay there on my back, I could hear the party dying down. They didn't like me. I'd expected that, even if I'd secretly hoped for a different outcome. I'd never been popular, not even at the Giant.

I wasn't good with people and I knew that but it didn't matter. They were using me and I was using them. Like was an unnecessary emotion. It certainly wasn't going to keep me awake at night.

It was nice here but a month was plenty

enough time. I'd get strong. I'd figure out a way to get my friends out of the compound and then I'd build a house of my own.

I woke a couple of hours later to the most intense thirst and found a glass of water sitting at my bedside. Had to love Fudge. At least I thought it was Fudge. I couldn't imagine Dax bringing me water.

While I was chugging it down, I thought I heard Dax's voice below the window. I placed the glass on the nightstand quietly as I crawled out of bed. The fuzziness was still with me but I was at least mobile. I knew I was eavesdropping, but a girl had to do whatever she had to do in times of survival.

"Do you think they'll come here?" Fudge asked. "You said they already followed you across the Great Bay. That's unheard of."

"You remember the last time one of the governments tried to come into the Wilds," Dax said, like it was something she couldn't have forgotten. "They won't come in large forces. They lost too many people but they're going to come. I'll deal with it when they do."

"Will it even work?" Fudge asked.

"I don't know. But I've run out of leads."

"Do you think she knows she's one of the

last ones left?"

"I think she has an idea. It's good she's tough. She's going to need to be." I heard some movement and scraping of chairs. "I'll see you in the morning."

"Night."

Chapter 14

When I woke the next morning, my head felt like it was trying to revolt from my body and holding violent protests to accomplish its goal. Oh no, maybe eating too much did bring back the Bloody Death, because I felt like I'd died and been reheated. I better not do that again. It had tasted so damn good, though.

What if there was no redo? What if I was contagious already? What if I was already spreading it to everyone? I had to get out of here.

I didn't bother changing clothes. I grabbed the discarded boots from last night and only stopped long enough to pause at the door, listening. It sounded relatively quiet, so a lot of people were probably sleeping in.

I tiptoed down the hall, ran down the stairs and was out the front door before the people at the buffet noticed me. It was a good thing I wasn't hungry, because I couldn't risk close contact with the breakfast crowd, even lighter as it was today. The sun seemed brighter than normal as I made it to the front lawn.

"Where are you going?"

Shit. Of all the people of course it would be Dax, and damn he sounded louder than normal. My head was already about to split open from the Plague as it was. I'd hoped to slip out and not have to tell a soul that I was sick.

I turned to find him leaning on the corner porch post, suspicion in his eyes. I'd learned one thing about Dax. You either read nothing on his face or what he felt like showing you. This look was a warning.

"Nowhere. Was just taking in the morning air."

He pushed off the post and walked a few steps in my direction. "You wouldn't be thinking of running out on our bargain?"

"No, of course not."

He nodded but his face still looked suspicious.

"How are you feeling today?"

Not only was my head pounding but I felt like my heart was also looking to exit my body. If I told him what I feared, that maybe I was getting sick, he might kill me. It was amazing that someone from the Wilds would be so open-minded toward a Plaguer in the first place. How far would he go? If I was sick, would he let me walk or kill me here where I stood like generations of his people before him?

"I'm feeling great."

"Really? I'm surprised after all that whiskey you drank."

"What do you mean?" It was the booze that made me sick? Not the food? Please say it was so.

"As much as you drank, men twice your size would still be laid out or vomiting their guts up."

I wasn't sick and I could still eat? I wasn't dying? I wanted to jump into the air, or would once my stomach settled down some and the world got steadier.

I still felt close to death but I couldn't let that stop me. The people at the compound had stolen enough years of good food from me.

"Breakfast buffet still out?" I said, moving closer to the house and peeking through the door, knowing I'd gotten up later than normal.

"Yeah," he said, and for the first time ever, it looked like he was actually really going to laugh. He didn't, but he got really close.

I left him on the porch while I struggled toward the buffet line. Nothing smelled the same today, but I was eating whether my body wanted it or not.

With a heaping plate of food, I made my way out to the back porch to eat in peace. Then Lucy showed with a heaping plate of food of her own and made a loud disgruntled noise when she saw me, making it clear this was her spot and she was annoyed. I felt like saying this wasn't my first morning in this spot either but didn't bother. I had a job enough getting all this food down. I couldn't add talking to the chores.

She sat on the other bench and then stared at me while I tried to pretend she wasn't there.

"I'll share my breakfast spot but I will not be chitchatting with a Plaguer every morning," she finally spat out.

"Uh, yeah, sure," I said, wondering why she thought I would have any desire to have chitchat, as she called it, with her. I hated small talk. I wasn't good at it, and if I was going to make an attempt, it would not be wasted on her.

I looked out at the land, imagining I was alone, as I took in the beauty and told myself that I would not throw up.

"You stupid girls all want to talk about your hair or what dress you want to make and what stupid colors to dye the fabric. And if it's not that stupid shit, it's who's a good provider and who just wants a quick lay."

I looked back to Lucy where she was now shuddering in distaste, and just nodded. I didn't feel the need to mention that my hair looked like a rat's nest again and that I was in the same clothes I'd worn to the feast last night. I didn't care enough to bother.

"And we aren't going to become best buddies and start jarring jams together."

Oh geez, when would this chatter stop? "Noted," I said in between mouthfuls, hoping an acknowledgment might help.

She stabbed at some of the food on her plate.

"And I know Dax is attractive, but seriously? You just *met* him. You think you'd wait at least a week or so before falling into bed with him, even if he did come along to your rescue."

I had to pound my own chest with my fist to dislodge the sausage stuck in it so that I could speak. "What?" I asked even as a piece of meat was still trying to cling to a tonsil. "I did not sleep with Dax. Who said I slept with him?"

She looked over and cocked her head to the side. "You didn't? Sure looked that way to me."

"No, I didn't."

She leaned back and made some hmm noises. "Okay, I see what's going on here."

I coughed free the last bit of meat, enough to squeak out, "Mind sharing?"

"After he took your drunk ass to bed last night, he didn't come back downstairs until about twenty minutes later and looking quite more disheveled than before he'd taken you in the house."

"So?"

She rolled her eyes. "Clearly you don't get it, but I, more worldly than you, got the distinct impression he'd just gotten laid, especially after all the cow eyes you were giving him letting everyone know you were ready and willing."

He was good looking but I hadn't thrown myself at him or anything…had I? My mind shuffled through blurry memories and the words *you're pretty* came to mind. Then I remembered how soft his hair was. Had I curled my fingers into it when he'd danced with me? Oh shit, I had.

I didn't say anything while I waited for the first wave of mortification to pass, hoping it would get better soon.

"You could see how a person would come to a certain impression. No one else was in the house," she said like I was dumber than the patch of dirt five feet away.

"But why would he do that?" I asked. I sifted through more memories. He hadn't touched me at all. Not a hint of anything sexual, but then he walked back out and made everyone think he had?

Lucy exhaled the longest drawn-out sigh I'd ever heard before she said, "So no one else would touch you."

"I don't get it."

Her look made me think I'd dropped in her estimation, but I couldn't think of anything dumber than dirt.

"Looks like I'm going to have to school you on this as well. It's all about ass kicking when you get right down to it. There's two types of women in the Wilds. Ones like me, that kick ass, and ones like you, who get their asses kicked. You're either on one side of the line or the other. Although you might have shown some

169

aptitude in willing to kick ass, you are still on the shit side of the line and look primed to get a boot to the butt at any second.

"Dax, on the other hand, is such an ass kicker, no one screws with him, like ever, because they know they'll get their ass kicked. He's almost got his own line. It's such a sure thing that he can kick everyone's ass that him claiming you as his keeps your ass from getting kicked by association. No one will mess with you now." She made a little flair gesture with her fork and then said, "You're welcome."

There was only one problem with her spiel. "But isn't this place his? Couldn't he just say something like 'don't kick her ass'?"

"I'm not saying it wasn't overkill, but it's not like he's here twenty-four-seven, either. Things still happen. He was probably being safe."

"But he didn't try…" I shut up, realizing I was disclosing more than I wanted but it was too late.

"Of course he didn't. He's a gentleman. He would've wanted to wait until you were sober." She looked at me, eyes round and eyebrows raised, with a *do you finally get it yet* kind of look.

I leaned back. It was just like the guards at the compound. But I hadn't asked for his protection, so I certainly didn't see the need to pay for it in that manner. Not that he was a bad-looking guy or anything, but it wasn't how I saw my first time happening.

Or was it? I could do worse, way worse. After last night I could hardly deny finding him attractive. Apparently everyone in the immediate area knew it now. I was human after all, and he did have this thing about him. He'd probably thought I had initiated it too. The girls at the compound had done much less to get their guard boyfriends.

And I was in survival mode.

And he was hot.

And I was also eighteen, fully grown. I'd told myself after I got out of the compound I would live life to its fullest potential. Shouldn't that include sex? Maybe I should sleep with him? I mean, Moobie had all sorts of sexual conquests, and if I were being completely up front, I was curious what the deal was about.

The backdoor swung open and Dax was standing in between Lucy and me on the porch. "You ready?"

"For what?" I asked, almost stuttering. Did he want to do it now? I'd just accustomed myself to the idea of doing it but I needed a little time to prepare.

He was facing me, and Lucy was behind him and nodding an *I told you so* face.

"We've got work to do."

"Oh, sure."

"Here," he said, handing me a pile of clothes.

"What are these?"

"Something to make you blend a bit where we're going. Meet me in front in fifteen." He walked back in the house.

Chapter 15

Bookie was the first person to see me in my new getup when I came down the stairs. He looked me over in the non-creepiest of ways before announcing his verdict: "Cool outfit."

"Thanks." He was probably being nice, but my hands ran over my new clothes anyway. These fit, almost like someone had altered them especially for me, and when I'd looked in the mirror, I looked a little like Lucy now. I had a sleeveless shirt and leather patches on my pants. I'd pulled my hair back so the red coloring wasn't quite so obvious. I might even blend, like I was a Wilds native.

Bookie leaned on the balustrade with a book under his free arm. "Dax is out front, waiting. Said you'd be back for dinner."

"Another buffet?" What would there be to eat tonight? Dinners were even better food then breakfast, and I was finding that the highlight of my day was mealtime.

"No, that's only in the mornings and special stuff, like Dax coming home. Everyone does their own thing at night. It'll just be us, you know, the people who live in the main house."

I had no idea who actually lived in the main house but I nodded anyway. "Okay, I'll see you later," I said, heading out to the front door, knowing without anyone having to tell me that Dax wasn't going to be big on waiting.

Dax was sitting on his bike just where I expected him. He looked me over as well but wasn't as forthcoming with an opinion like Bookie. I'd heard that men were supposed to compliment a woman when they wanted to sleep with them. Even the guards at the compound had told the girls they were sleeping with how pretty they were.

Dax must have thought I was somewhat attractive if he wanted to sleep with me. Then again, it wasn't like I was going to tell him he was pretty again, not while I was sober. Maybe we wouldn't have that kind of relationship. On the other hand, he had said I was "tougher than he'd expected." Maybe that was the "you're so pretty" in the Wilds?

"Get on," he said, jarring me from my musings.

"So where are we off to?" I asked as I climbed on the back of the bike, much more aware than ever before of where my hands touched him, wondering if maybe we would do *it* tonight?

"A traveler's hole."

"What's that?"

"People who do business with the different countries go up and down certain routes. There's one that runs from Myers all the way up to

Newco and it has stopovers every so often."

"Have you ever been to Myers?" I asked. Once upon a time, the country of Myers had been the state of Florida, back when the world had been full of people and promise.

"I've been to all of them," he said, leaving me wondering if it had been in his search for Plaguers.

I'd hoped he hadn't had to look that hard. It added another preoccupation to the list of things spinning in my head at any given moment, which was already juggling: break the girls out, avoid the Dark Walkers and the newest addition, have sex with Dax.

The bike roared and that was the end of conversation, which I was kind of grateful for. If I was one of the last Plaguers, I didn't want to know. I didn't even want to contemplate it.

We drove for a couple of hours south before he stopped the bike outside a brick building, about half the size of *Eat, Drink, Sleep*. This one only read *Bob's* over the door. I couldn't help but wonder if we'd be meeting this illustrious Bob inside, who was so important his name encompassed all other needs.

Dax got off the bike and said, "We need to talk about—"

I held up my palms to stop him—so much for what he knew about Plaguers. "Before you say anything, I can't choose what I see and I can't always get a read, either. There is no prepping and there is no control." After I schooled him, I tugged at my gloves, admiring how they added a certain something to my new tougher look. I just needed a gun holstered to my hip or a knife strapped to my thigh and I'd *really* look the part.

"I don't want their histories. That's not what I'm after."

I dragged my eyes up from my fascination with how cool I looked in my new clothes to his face. I shook my head and then froze. "Then what do you want?" I asked, hoping he didn't mean the only thing left I could do, mark people as Dark Walkers. The look he was throwing at me was as promising as storm clouds over a picnic.

He was staring at me like a man who knew what he wanted and this had nothing to do with my conversation with Lucy and sex. I wished it had. The decision on whether to have sex with him or not was a lot easier than giving in to what I thought he was going to ask of me.

He lifted his eyebrows as if chastising me for trying to fake ignorance. "I needed a Plaguer for a reason. I could've dug up people's backgrounds on my own. I'm looking for Dark Walkers."

I hadn't heard that term outside my own head since I'd entered the Giant. There were only two things that truly scared me on this Earth. Number one wasn't an immediate problem, but number two on my list was about to get trampled all over. I wasn't messing around with Dark Walkers until I was ready to bust the girls out. Drawing their ire prematurely was a really bad plan of action. Tipping people off about their identities? That was guaranteed to piss them off and get every one of those things after me.

I'd been locked away long enough with my thoughts to come to one firm belief. The Dark Walkers were somehow responsible for the condition of the Plaguers. I didn't know how many of them existed but I knew that if I started outing them, they'd come for me en masse, deep in the Wilds or not. Breaking my friends out of the compound would become impossible. I'd lose all the advantage of a surprise attack. Instead of biding my time and planning when to hit, I'd become the hunted again.

It could not happen.

I started shaking my head vehemently and then got a hold of myself. I couldn't act defensive. "You heard wrong. There are no such things as Dark Walkers. You put too much faith into rumors."

"Don't deny it. It's beneath you to run scared."

He looked at me like he was disappointed. I

tried to shrug it off but it bugged the shit out of me.

He had to hit my soft spot with the scared comment, didn't he? No matter, I wouldn't go down that easy. "Not scared. There's nothing to tell."

"We have a deal."

I shook my head and stepped away from him. "I promised to tell you about the flashes, the scars people have."

"No. You didn't."

I thought back to that first conversation and he was right. I'd *assumed* what he'd wanted was histories. He'd never specified. "You have no idea what you're talking about." I backed up a couple more steps.

"That first meeting at the compound, Ms. Edith was one, wasn't she? I could tell how you acted."

"Or maybe she was just a bitch?"

"Bullshit."

Denying wasn't going to work. Time to switch tactics. "Dax, I don't know if what I see is even real."

"We both know it is."

It was nice to have someone finally believe me, but this wasn't the time to get all conspiracy buddies, thick as thieves, on each other just because he might be as crazy as I was.

"If you wanted one so bad and you knew

Ms. Edith was one, why didn't you go after her? Why bother with me at all?"

"Wasn't conducive to my plans."

"But you think there might be one in this place that will work better for your plans?"

"I got you out. You would've died there. You made a deal, now honor it."

"I've told you a gazillion times now, I was going to get out. I wasn't going to die in that place. You didn't 'save' me." And he thought I had a problem listening to what he said. "If this is the big reason you *helped* me escape then tell me why? What do you want with them?"

"That's my business." He took a step forward and the shutter on his expressions dropped all the way down and it said this was happening one way or another. "Don't tell me you aren't going to do this."

I wasn't going to get out of this, at least not on the up and up. Hands on my hips, I asked, "What are you going to do if I point a Dark Walker out?"

"It won't be your problem."

"According to you," I said. I shook my head and made some grumbling noises like I was really going through with it. "Fine. Let's get this over with."

He shot me a look.

My hands dropped along with my will to argue the point anymore. "Enough with the looks. I get it already."

He did the most unexpected thing then. He laughed and I felt my legs go weak, because when Dax laughed something very strange stirred within me and I had no idea what the hell the feeling was but it made me want to laugh with him.

Luckily he stopped before I made a fool of myself gawking at him and he headed toward Bob's front door. He paused on the stoop. "No fighting today."

"You act like I enjoy fighting."

"You don't?" His eyebrows shot up. "Few words of advice, just because your hands are free doesn't mean you should use them to punch everyone in the face."

I opened my mouth and then paused as his words really sank in. Maybe I did like to fight on some level, enjoyed the surge of feeling it brought to me. When I'd been at the compound, fights had been the only time I'd felt like I was among the living. "Still, not why I did it last time."

"I know why you did it."

"Why?" I said, doubting him.

"Because you can't stand to see someone weaker getting pushed around."

I shrugged. So he was a good guesser. I'd clearly been in a weaker position in my past. Guessing that my inclinations lay toward helping the underdog wasn't that much of a leap.

"It's an admirable trait, but you need to learn you can't always help others, especially when *you are* the weaker one. Sometimes it's smarter to sit back and wait."

I dug deep into my well-honed theatrics, wanting to accent each word. "And sometimes, you wait so long there's nothing left to fight for." I threw my hands up. "The war's lost while you're still sitting around waiting to get in the game."

Instead of him being impressed with my wisdom, his eyes rolled. "Fine. But no wars today."

"No matter what?" No way I could agree to that. "What if it's something really bad? War-worthy bad?"

"No matter what imaginary plight of the hooker you might think you see, talk to me before you do anything stupid."

"I never do anything stupid," I said. "Saving the hooker was not stupid. It was noble."

"If she'd needed saving, maybe. She didn't, so it was a little stupid." He held up his thumb and pointer finger to emphasize.

I pulled open the door to the great and powerful Bob's and walked into the dark interior, debating whether I would sleep with him after all. He sure didn't know how to woo a girl.

The place was dark and smelled stale, with the odors of people that lacked the resources of fresh clothing and proper hygiene. I was actually grateful for the smoke filling the room from a group puffing away in the center, who looked like they were doing some tobacco trading.

I scanned the place, not from any desire to do due diligence but because I needed to act the part. Wasn't as if I could walk the room shuttering my eyes and play it off while chanting, *No, no, no, I see nothing*.

My gaze passed right over a Dark Walker in the first thirty seconds. Figured there'd have to be one sitting in the corner, all ready to be plucked out of obscurity.

He looked just like someone from the Wilds, blended perfectly, but he was definitely a Dark Walker. Why would a Dark Walker look like a native to the Wilds? Only one reason. They were not only deeply involved in the country but they'd infiltrated the Wilds too. How many more were there? Were they watching over every aspect of the human race?

We stepped over to the bar as I made a show of looking at the entire place and trying to ignore the one who should've been my target.

Dax placed a coin down on the rough wood. It was Newco money and I guessed most of the people here did enough business with the country to make it a viable currency. "Two ales," Dax said to the scruffy guy behind the bar whose beard was about a year overdue for a trim.

I wanted to ask why it wasn't fuel, but that would show my ignorance to the barkeep who was still in hearing distance. The bartender placed two foaming mugs down a minute later, one right in front of me garnished with a dead fly floating on top.

The barkeep moved away and I looked for an excuse to not drink.

"Where does all the fuel come from?" I asked. He had to have a steady supply for the bikes. "I thought fuel was scarce in the Wilds?"

"It is. I've got a rig," he said. Dax grabbed the ale with the fly that was in front of me, flicked the offending bug out and then took a swig. He pushed the other mug my way, obviously expecting me to drink it. "You want to survive, learn to blend." His eyes shot to the ale.

"A rig?" I asked, more concerned with the mug I was to drink from. All those years in the compound, I never thought I'd miss anything about the place, but clean mugs were making it a close call. My drink, the cleaner of the two, still had a layer of greasy film that coated my fingers as they wrapped around it. I had to make a conscious choice not to throw up as I tilted the fluid back. Surprisingly, it had a nice taste. Not good enough to completely overwhelm my gag reflex but I managed to keep it down.

I placed mine back on the bar and tried to not look at the filth surrounding me so that I could gather up the fortitude to repeat the process, figuring if I had to drink it, I probably had to drink all of it.

"An oil rig. I drill my own. Well?" he asked, and I knew he wasn't asking if I liked the refreshments. He wanted to know if there was a Dark Walker here.

"No," I said.

"Don't let me find out you're lying."

"Why would I?" That was believable, since there was no real rational reason to lie that he knew of. But instinct born of long exposure and a deeply ingrained survival instinct told me that the Dark Walkers were not the ones I wanted to cross until I was good and prepared. There was something much larger at work here and I wouldn't put my life, and that of my friends, at risk for some obscure plan he wasn't bothering to share.

I geared up to take another swig of filth, while Dax tilted his back until there couldn't be anything left. He reached for mine and finished that as well before he nodded for the door.

I guessed that not finishing an ale was a huge no-no, but the guy you're with drinking

184

your share didn't seem to ruffle any feathers. Good to know.

Following him out, I contemplated what else had just gone down. He'd drunk from the very same mug I had. In the Giant, the girls had said something about swapping spit. And he'd finished my ale like we were a couple or something. He *did* really want me.

Chapter 16

Tiffy was setting the table for seven people
when I walked into the dining area that night.
Other than her and a glimpse of Fudge in the
kitchen, no one else had shown up yet, but the
table was already laid out with food, including a
big bird-looking thing in the center.

"You sit right here," Tiffy said, pointing to a
chair to the right of the head of the table. She
seemed quite pleased when I did as she told me.

When Fudge walked in the room with
another bowl, I backed my chair up to see if she
needed help carrying things until Tiffy stopped
me.

"No, you stay there."

"Tiffy, are you being bossy?" Fudge asked
as she came in on the tail end of our interaction.

"No, Fudge. I'm helping her."

"Do you need help?" I asked, but Fudge
shook her head and then she shot Tiffy an *I
know what you're up to* kind of warning look.
This didn't seem to so much as tug at the smile
on Tiffy's face. I wished Fudge would fill me in
on what she thought Tiffy was up to.

Tiffy sat down across from me and Dax
came in shortly after. He looked briefly at the
sitting arrangement but didn't make a comment
as he sat down. Tiffy's grin seemed on the verge

of becoming permanent.

Tank walked in with Bookie behind him, both grabbing a seat.

Lucy came in after and then stopped short a few feet from me. "You're in my spot," she said.

Before I could respond, Fudge spoke. "We don't have spots, Lucy."

"Okay, she's in the spot I've been sitting at consistently every night, if that's more accurate."

"I'll move. I don't care where I sit." I pushed my chair back. Of all the things I thought were worth fighting over, this was not one of them. Plus, I didn't want any delay to the eating portion of the evening.

"No," Tiffy spat out.

"Lucy," Dax said at the same time.

Lucy let out a disgruntled moan but sat at the only seat left open at the table.

Tiffy smiled at me, looking quite pleased with herself. Dax didn't seem to care as long as everyone shut up.

"I found a great book today for my collection when I was going over by the ruins," Bookie said, trying to smooth out the ripple as Tank was ripping into the big baked bird. Lucy was scooping out heaps of fluffy potatoes. Tiffy kept giving me a look like I was in on some secret but she'd forgotten to tell me what it was.

"You have a collection of books?" I asked,

remembering the one I'd seen him holding earlier. I'd thought only the rich had collections. That was how it had been in Newco anyway.

"Bookie is a bit of a bookworm," Fudge said, smiling at him.

"What's it about?" I asked, excited that there was a collection of books so close by that I might be able to get my hands on.

"The one I found was about cities, printed during Glory Years. The shit they had was amazing. It's so crazy to even think about. Do you know that there were so many people that they had to have these big buildings just for the sick? They were so big they could house our community five times over! And they had roads in these big cities that got so busy it could take you an hour to get a mile even though they all drove in cars then."

"It'll come back again one day," Fudge said.

"Not if this plague doesn't stop creeping back up every twenty years. Jesus, even killing the Plaguers didn't fix—"

"Bookie," Dax said.

"Sorry, I didn't mean that—"

"Not a big deal," I said, not wanting the added attention that subject brought to me. I might be human but I was still different than anyone here.

"Hardy, he says that a lot of people were really miserable back then," Bookie continued.

"Who's Hardy?" I asked.

"He's a philosopher," Bookie explained.

"He's a drunk," Dax added.

"Okay, he might be a bit of a drunk but he's very interesting. He's got a theory about why a lot of people were depressed during the Glory Years. He thinks the way the world had become, so many people were doing things so opposite from our hunter-gatherer ways it messed with their inner inclinations. He says at heart, we're all still hunters or gatherers."

"I hate that hunter-gatherer shit," Lucy chimed in. "Just because I don't have a dick the men on this world think I should be out gathering berries."

Bookie shook his head. "Girls can be hunters. Me, I know I'm more of a gatherer. Dal, what do you think you are?"

For some reason, the whole table stopped what it was doing to look at me and hear my answer. I was a hunter. I knew it down to my very core—even when I was throwing the knife and it clattered to the ground, it had still felt so right. But I also knew what I looked like, so instead of being honest, I said, "Gatherer, probably," and was immediately mad at myself. I'd told them what I thought they'd expected because I wanted them to like me. I'd wanted to fit in. "No, I take that back. I'm a hunter."

A couple of shrugs and a random nod and

they were back to chewing. It hit me then that they didn't really care. It was like at the compound. They were too busy surviving themselves.

I glanced to my left, where Dax was. He wasn't looking at me but he was smiling.

Bookie started talking about some other geography book he'd found and Dax went to answer a knock at the door.

No one seemed alarmed by a person just coming to the door, but unexpected company still registered in my brain as a problem. I gripped the knife I was using to cut my meat a little too tightly as I watched a stout man in his fifties walk in and stop right inside the front door. He was the guitar player from the feast and looked a lot less jovial than when he'd been singing. I saw the stranger's eyes shoot to the table and pause on me.

He was talking in a low voice with Dax, who seemed to grow tense as the guitar player spoke. Dax nodded and was shutting the door behind him before he walked back to the table.

Fudge was the first person to speak up when he came back. "Everything okay?"

"Fine," he said, shutting the subject down. If something was wrong, Dax wasn't sharing.

The subject was forgotten as Lucy took up Dax's stance and started arguing how Hardy was a drunk for the rest of dinner.

It was an hour before the time Fudge had warned me the generator for the house would be turned off, or nine p.m. for everyone else in the area. I was curled up on the window seat in the bedroom, staring off at the forest. As far as rooms went, it was perfect. I already missed this room and I didn't even know for sure when I was leaving. I wished I could have a place like this of my own, no strings attached, but wishing didn't change anything. I'd learned that a long time ago. You had to do things for yourself in this world and I would. I'd build an even better home and room.

Footsteps alerted me to someone climbing the stairs and my pulse picked up. Was it Dax on his way to my room? They sounded like they were retreating in the opposite direction and I went to peek around the door I'd left slightly ajar. I saw Lucy's back as she went inside her room.

I went back to my seat without closing the door. After getting over the novelty of being able to shut it when I wanted, I'd started to enjoy that I could also leave it open.

Bookie had gone to his room an hour ago, and Fudge had gone to hers with Tiffy. I'd found out at dinner that Tank had the basement when Lucy had called him the Basement Troll. It left one door unaccounted for.

I didn't think he'd come up yet but there was a suspicious light underneath. He had to be in there but why hadn't he come to me? Maybe I was supposed to go to him.

Or what if he wasn't interested? What if Lucy had been completely wrong and he wanted nothing to do with me other than finding Dark Walkers? But at dinner, Dax had backed Lucy off to keep me seated by his side.

The girls at the compound had always said there wasn't a single guard that would turn down a sexual invitation. I should go to him. Yes, I was doing this. I wasn't chickening out. How many nights had I told myself that if I got out of that place, I'd live every second to its maximum capacity? Sleeping alone was a world away from max capacity. Moobie slept with people all the time. This was a part of life outside and I should know about it.

I took a deep breath and prepared for my evening. I ran my hands through my hair and then had to smooth it back down after I realized I might already have the tousled look. I tugged the shift nightdress Fudge had given me down on one shoulder. I was still skinny but I looked a little healthier than when I'd first gotten here.

I walked out of my room and straight to his door. Knocking might draw the attention of everyone else, so instead I leaned close and whispered, "Dax?"

"Yeah?" I heard from the other side.

"I've come to see you," I whispered back.

There was a long pause but I heard shuffling inside. Maybe that was the delay? He'd been getting his room ready for me.

I heard more noise as I waited outside the door, but when it finally opened it was a woman that appeared. I'd seen her at the feast and also in the gardens, pretty brown hair, quite a bit older than me but nowhere near Fudge's age. She had a warm feeling about her and nothing horrible floating in her past, which was a nice perk.

"Hi, Dahlia. We haven't met yet but I'm Becca. I was just leaving, so you go on in." I took a step back as she exited, smiling and patting me on the shoulder as she did.

I wasn't sure I liked my future boyfriend having women in his bedroom, but she seemed so nice I decided I'd let it slide with her.

I walked into the room where Dax was walking out of an adjoining bathroom with only a pair of pants on.

"What's wrong? You needed to talk to me?" His eyes flickered over me and I thought he liked what he saw, but then he became more interested in looking at a clock he had on a table beside his bed.

"Why was she in your room?" I blurted out after I'd decided to not be one of those jealous girlfriends.

He looked up at me and I could see the surprise. "We were working on something."

I nodded. Garden stuff, maybe? I'd thought I'd heard her name in connection with plants.

He ran a hand over his short, dark hair. "What did you need to talk to me about?"

I knew I was naïve to this sort of thing, but something about this situation wasn't feeling right. Shouldn't he be trying something or moving closer to me at this point? I wasn't going to chicken out either, though, as I kept remembering how the girls said the guards never turned sex down. None of the guards looked like Dax but I'd taken it to be a generalization about men.

I surveyed the room and the bed that seemed to be partially unmade. There was also a couch that sat under a double-wide window.

Couch or bed? Moobie would be all balls. Bed it was.

I sat down, flipped my hair about and then leaned back on my elbows with the best come-hither smile I could conjure up.

"What are you doing?" he asked, watching me.

Maybe my come-hither look was wrong? Switch positions. I turned on my side and rested my head on my palm and then used my other hand to raise my shift up my leg slightly.

"Dal—"

"I know what you did. How you claimed me and offered me your protection." I flipped my hair back and then decided to just go for broke.

I dropped back onto the bed, my arms spread at my sides and eyes closed. "I'm here to let you use me for your manly needs." When I'd read that in the sex book Margo had gotten, it hadn't sounded so weird. Maybe it was the saying it out loud part that made it not sound as sophisticated. Still, it got the point across, so not so bad.

As I waited for him to ravish me, I thought about how after tonight, I'd be a woman. His woman. I'd know what love to a man was all about.

Nothing happened. It could be he wasn't understanding what I was offering but I was certain I'd made it pretty clear.

I opened my eyes but didn't have the nerve to check the room to see where he was or what he was doing. I settled on, "Dax?"

"I think you might have misunderstood." And then there was silence again.

I closed my eyes and didn't want to open them again, like maybe ever with the way I was feeling. Wow, this might have been the worst idea I'd ever, *ever* had, because that did not sound like he wanted to sleep with me. Okay, I needed to get out of there and pronto. But that meant I'd have to open my eyes.

Unless maybe I could do it without looking? No, that might even top coming here as my stupidest idea. I was going to kill Lucy. He hadn't looked disheveled because of me that night, he'd been doing it with someone else, probably the woman I'd just chased out of here. Why had I listened to her?

"What you're feeling, it's just a crush. It doesn't mean anything."

Now I really needed to get up. He thought I was still waiting for him. Oh geez, this was getting worse and worse.

I sat up like the bed was burning, and not from the hot love I'd thought we'd be making on it. One look at his face and I felt about two inches tall. Pity was written all over him. Of all the times he decided to show me how he felt and he couldn't keep that stuff shuttered?

He might be rejecting me but I didn't need his pity. Without even thinking, I stood a little straighter and kicked into defensive mode. "I am not a child. I'm eighteen, two years past legal adulthood in most countries. I'm a little old for crushes." Shit, that hadn't come out like I planned. Now it sounded like I was begging him.

I tried to find the quickest way out of the room, because I knew my skin was on fire, while simultaneously trying to avoid looking at him. I never got like this. Years of being called a dirty Plaguer rolled off my back and now I was laid low by a rejection from this man.

His hand gripped my wrist as I moved forward. "Dal—"

"It doesn't matter. You're right. It didn't mean anything. I just thought, you know… Actually, I wasn't even thinking." I yanked my wrist free. "Really, I'm fine."

"It can't happen. Not with us, not in this world. You don't understand."

He looked like he regretted it but it didn't matter. He was like everyone else and I was a Plaguer. "I might not have experienced what goes on between a man and a woman and I might have misjudged this situation. Sometimes I might not use the right words or know every intricacy about the Wilds, but don't tell me I don't know how the world works. I learned that very well a long time ago. I know plenty."

We stood, not even a foot away from each other, and I saw some sort of emotion flicker across his face. The woman in me, and she was in there whether he acknowledged it or not, liked to think maybe he was regretting a hasty rejection. Or maybe it was uncertainty, that he'd misjudged me and the depth of who I was. Of that I was sure. I'd spent years in a man-made hell but those devils had forged me into someone special, whether he saw it or not, whether he wanted me or not. If he couldn't see past the Plaguer label, I didn't need him.

I lifted my chin and walked out of his room.

"Dal, it's not—"

"Don't worry about me. I'll be fine. I always am."

Chapter 17

I was humiliated. Why had I thought he'd wanted me? In all those years at the compound, not once had a single guard tried anything with me. They hadn't ever even flirted, and it wasn't just because I was a Plaguer. Most had known me long enough to know I wasn't contagious.

It was after dusk but rules or not, I needed out of the house. The beasts roamed at night, they said. Bunch of made-up bullshit in my opinion. If these so-called beasts were so rampant, how come I'd never seen one or heard one in all the distance we'd covered? Miles and miles we'd traveled and not a single hint? I'd lived by other people's rules for way too long to abide by a new set.

I popped in my room but only for a second to change, and then left it again. I made one stop in the kitchen to find the knife I liked and tucked that into the waistband of my pants. Then I grabbed a couple pieces of jerky and shoved them in my back pocket, just because you never knew when the urge to snack might hit.

I approached the guard on duty and lucked out that it was sister-lover. He didn't bother arguing with me. He simply opened the gate.

"I hope they eat you," he said as I was walking by him.

I didn't bother to call him a wuss but I couldn't let it go completely. "Care to join me? No?" I shrugged. "Suit yourself. Make sure you lock up nice and tight so the boogeyman can't get you." I turned back around and marched straight into the forest. Beasts or not, I wasn't willing to give up my freedom again that easily.

The sounds of the crickets were loud and the coolness of the air filtered through the trees and leaves.

My assassin was standing right where I'd left him, dead bark and all. Ever since the other day I'd wanted to see if I could hit the target again.

I stood about eight feet from the tree and damn if the knife didn't widely miss its mark and then bounce to the ground. I tried it a few times before stepping back far enough that I could barely see the tree anymore through the darkness.

I could tell by the sound it had stuck this time. It was like I could make the expert shots but not the easy ones. I walked up to the tree and found the knife lodged just where I'd expected it. It was almost like if I tried, it would miss. If I let it just flow from my hand without a care, like I did when I'd assume I'd miss, I struck right where I wanted.

I yanked the knife out of the bark and took a step away before turning back and doing a little handiwork. A couple of eyes and a mouth and my assassin was looking much more respectable.

I tossed the knife a another twenty or thirty times before I worked enough of the humiliation from my system that thought I'd be able to sleep when I hit the bed.

I went up to retrieve my knife but stopped short of it. I was starving again. It was as if once I'd opened the floodgates to eating I couldn't stop. I reached in my back pocket for the jerky I'd snagged from the kitchen. Leaning a shoulder on my assassin, I listened to the crickets as I chewed on the beef and tried to forget how I'd flopped down on Dax's bed and told him to take me.

I didn't hear anything coming up from behind until there was a low-pitched growl not even a foot behind me. Whatever it was, it was large and tall and that sound came from right behind my head. My entire being froze, even my hair if that was possible.

The knife was stuck in the bark behind me, right in the eye I'd carved out. I didn't have a weapon. Stupid. I should've brought another knife or not left this one stuck in the bark out of reach. I'd left myself vulnerable and now look at me. Maybe I *was* a goddamn gatherer, because any good hunter would've had a knife in their hand.

While I was deciding my best course of action, it came closer. It hadn't attacked yet. Maybe kicking it in the balls—hopefully it was a male—wasn't the best idea. Maybe I should just wait it out and play dead, albeit standing up, which if it had any kind of higher intelligence might be a non-dead giveaway.

My heart felt like it was going to burst and I had a hard time keeping my breathing under control, another thing that screamed *I'm alive*. I could feel it sniffing at my hair. Its fur grazed the back of my bare arms.

This was the beast, the one I didn't believe existed. But what was it?

Its nose or mouth, I wasn't sure which, made its way down and was breathing on my neck now. It was definitely big and I was fairly certain whatever the beast was, its teeth were going to be huge to match the rest of it. It could kill me in a second.

I wasn't going to go down like this. Fighting it without even a knife was suicidal. I had to make a run for it. Decision made, I took a deep breath and got ready to make a mad dash until a wet tongue darted out and ran along the back of my skin. And then it did it again.

Was the thing licking me? The big tough beast everyone ran from? Or was it tasting me? Trying to see if I'd make a good dinner? I didn't know if I should run or turn around and give it a scratch behind the ears. Maybe movement wasn't such a good idea. What if it jarred the creature into action and it remembered that it ate people, not licked them?

The decision was taken out of my hands as I heard it move behind me. It was growling again. Oh shit, did it like how my skin tasted? The massive amount of body heat it threw was diminishing and I heard the sound of movement.

I whipped around, trying to get a glance of it before it was completely out of sight. All that was left of it was a flash of grayish fur disappearing into the trees. A *big* flash of gray though. Like, real big.

I grabbed the knife from my assassin's eye. "Until tomorrow, my admirable foe." I did a little bow but stopped short to add some final words in the tree's direction: "Just a heads-up. We'll probably be back to daylight hours from here on out."

My pace back to the house was a bit faster than my pace coming here had been, whether I wanted to fess to it or not.

I felt like my whole body let out a groan as I got closer to the gate. Sister-lover was gone, replaced by Dax. Yay, just who I was looking to see. I almost turned back to the forest. Dax or beast? It was a tough call but I moved forward. I didn't think Dax would eat me if he was in a bad mood, seeing as he already had plenty of food.

He opened the gate well in advance of my approach.

"It's three in the morning," he said as I walked through.

"I was thinking closer to two, but okay, I won't fight you over the hour." I walked past him toward the house.

He was right on my tail and I really would've preferred a bit more space after tonight's earlier encounter.

"You were told not to leave the grounds at night." He gripped my shoulder, jolting me to a halt and then spinning me around.

I looked at the offending hand on my shoulder. "You aren't my keeper."

As much as I couldn't get a read on him so often, I seemed to be getting under his skin almost effortlessly right now.

"You need a keeper. Anybody with any fucking sense wouldn't have gone out there alone."

"Did you break me out just to put me in a new jail? I said I'd do what you needed. I didn't agree to follow your every command."

We were standing nose to nose on the front lawn and if it weren't for an errant sneeze, neither of us might have realized that we had an audience. I looked back to the house and saw a sudden movement in not one but several of the windows.

"Brilliant," I said to him before I started walking back to the house.

"This conversation is not over."

"Yep, it is," I said as I kept walking to the house, knowing just how badly I was infuriating him. No, I was relishing in how pissed off he was.

I took a step on the porch and paused. I was almost in the house and I knew instinctively that I'd pushed Dax to his limit.

He was letting me go though, and instead of walking in the house, I stopped and turned back to look at him.

He was standing on the grass still and I could actually see the tiny little thread holding his temper in check, and part of me wanted to clip that last little bit. I realized I hated how much control he had. I wanted to know the real man, not the cardboard cutout that he showed the world, feeding little tidbits here and there when he felt like it.

"Dahlia, come inside. It's late."

Shit, where the hell had Fudge shown up from? That old lady was the nemesis of my free will. There she was, all ready to ruin my fun. Thwarted again.

"Dahlia," she repeated.

I mumbled under my breath all sorts of bad words and then turned toward her. What was this power this old woman wielded over me?

"I'm coming."

Chapter 18

I woke up at the first light of day feeling as if I'd never gone to sleep. It was hard to determine what had kept me awake—images of throwing myself at Dax, almost becoming dinner for a beast or the aftermath on the lawn. I'd sensed a crack in Dax's cement wall last night, and for no reason I could fathom, I'd wanted to take a sledgehammer to it, split it open and leave it crumbled on the ground around him.

The opportunity had passed; the cement wall was probably intact again. I wasn't sure when or if I'd get another opportunity. I didn't know what had set him off so bad to begin with.

I got out of bed and dressed to go downstairs, pushing it all from my mind. There were too many other things to worry about, namely three friends still locked away in hell who I needed to break out.

Breakfast wasn't ready when I got there but Fudge had it in the works. Standing in front of the oven, she gave me a look that warned of what was to come even before she spoke. I wasn't overly concerned. Nothing was too horrible when there was Fudge's breakfast on the horizon.

She started waving the spatula in her hand

around in between using it for the eggs in the pan. "I should make you cook your own breakfast. He's in a mighty bad mood. Up and out of here before dawn. And don't plead innocent on me either. I saw you about to dig your heels in last night when you two woke the whole house up."

"Sorry. I didn't realize we were so loud." It was true. I wasn't sure what had happened, but I'd forgotten everyone and everything when I was standing on the front lawn with Dax. He did that to me somehow, made everything else sort of fade to the distance when he was around, and it seemed to be getting worse.

Fudge's disapproving expression slowly broke into something a bit closer to neutral. "It's all right."

"Okay, well, I've got some stuff to do so I'll get out of your hair." That *stuff* was hanging in my room until more people were around. Once the place was crawling with hungry stomachs, I'd sneak back down and eat in peace.

"Not so quick," she said, stopping me before I could make it out of the kitchen.

I'd had a bad feeling there would be more. I hopped up and took a seat on the counter but not before I snagged a piece of bacon. I'd been informed recently that was what those tasty brown striped meats were called. If I was going to have to listen to how I shouldn't go out at night, I was going to be fed for my troubles.

"You and Dax are a lot alike," Fudge said as she shoveled eggs into a large bowl.

This didn't sound like the lecture I'd expected about running around late at night. She was heading into uncharted waters and I wasn't a good swimmer. This might not be worth bacon, or not one piece, anyway. It might be worth a plate, though. "We're not even a little alike."

"Stubborn with a hell of a temper when it lets loose," she said, as if she hadn't heard my denial.

"He doesn't have emotions. He's a glacier except he doesn't melt seasonally, just the same cold frontier day after day. The only time he bothers with facial expressions is when he's not in the mood to talk and prefers to make you *guess* what he wants." I crammed another piece of bacon in my mouth.

"If that's what you think, then why were you poking at him?" she asked as she pretended to be more interested in eggs.

"I had the situation under control."

"I'm warning you now, he's not someone to press. Watch your step, Dal. I know Dax. You might think you've got a handle on him but you're biting off more than you can chew. Don't be nibbling unless you're sure you really want a taste."

I had no idea what she was talking about, but I had other issues to worry about instead of nibbling or some such nonsense. "Fudge, the only thing I want to eat is your cooking."

She tsked but then told me to take a plate and go. She didn't have to tell me twice. I wasn't looking to go back in the waters she was splashing around in today.

I made my way to my spot on the back porch and was sitting quite comfortably when Lucy strolled out with her plate and took her spot, the bench on the other side of the porch. Her spot was a little too close for comfort to my spot, especially after last night. One of us was going to need to get a new spot. If she'd be quiet, though, I'd let her keep her spot until I finished my food.

When she didn't speak for a few minutes, I was lulled into a false optimism.

Then she started eyeing me up over a bite of sausage before she started in. "So yeah, I might have called that one wrong. I can't believe I didn't know he was doing Becca."

My bacon lost a little of its flavor, but before I had to stoop to ask how she knew this, she began talking again.

"You do realize how close my room is to Dax's room, right?" She didn't bother waiting for a response. "First, I heard noises and I figured, fuck, there goes my good night's sleep.

I think to myself he must be in there banging Dal, and pretty good from the sounds of it. I'll admit to you now since it wasn't you in there, I might have been *trying* to listen. I mean, there's only so much to do after lights out." She stopped speaking just long enough to get a couple of bites in before she started back up. "Then I heard you calling his name from the hall, which made no sense since I thought you were already inside. Of course I'm confused, and then I heard Becca in the hallway. Then you went in and weren't in there more than a few minutes before I heard the door again. It was all quite a fiasco if you ask me."

I hadn't asked, but that didn't seem to matter much as I tried to ignore her.

A couple of more bites and she was raring to go again. "I just can't believe I called that one so wrong. He must have had sex with her the night of the feast after he brought you inside. I could've sworn the way he was looking at you that he wanted to bang you. And how hadn't I heard them before? They must have been doing it at her place." She pointed to a smaller cabin on the property. "Her and her sister live there. My point of all this is, I really called that one wrong."

I looked at her and finally understood she was trying to apologize in the most convoluted and roundabout manner I'd ever experienced.

She was stuffing her mouth full of food again but I knew she was waiting for me to say something. It took a minute before I saw the one good thing that could come from this. "Lucy, you know that shit I said to you when we were traveling?"

"Yeah."

I knew she'd remember. I'd done a bit of a head job on her. "We're even."

"I can see that."

I stood, hoping to not have to hear about how wrong she'd been about Dax and Becca anymore. I was ready to move on anyway. There were bigger fish out in the world to fry and I knew just the person who might be able to help. "You know where Bookie is?" I asked.

"Why? He's not going to be a very good protector if you're thinking of moving in that direction."

She just wouldn't leave it alone. "I don't want a protector."

"I'd rethink that. You could use one."

There was zero malice in those words. Lucy truly thought she was helping me. I couldn't even get mad.

"Do you know where Bookie is?"

"I think he's in the barn," she said. I was already walking away as she kept speaking. "But don't say I didn't warn you when the shit hits the fan and he gets knocked out by one of the paddles."

The barn door was open and I could see the top of Bookie's head a few stalls down beside a horse.

"Bookie?" I called as I walked toward where he was.

"Hey, Dal," he said, sounding genuinely happy that I was there.

He was running his hands over the brown mare's pregnant belly when I got to her stall. "What are you doing?" I asked.

"I help out Carter. He's our resident doctor. Two legs or four, he's got you covered. She's due soon so I'm just checking on her." Bookie moved from her belly to run a hand down the horse's muzzle. The mare turned into him, bumping her nose into his hand when he petting her. "I'm glad you're here. I wanted to talk to you about last night. I hope you didn't get the wrong impression at dinner. I didn't mean that I thought the Plaguers should be killed."

"Not a bit," I said. I knew what haters looked and sounded like and I'd never put Bookie in that category. There was something really easy about being around him and it was probably his antithesis of hate. "I had a question for you. Where do you get all your books?"

"All over. I've been collecting for a while. Just found a huge stash recently that I've been going through. It's got a ton of books but it's a little dangerous." His head seemed to perk up a little as he warned me.

"Dangerous how?" I asked. If it wasn't swarming with Dark Walkers I was there, like, yesterday.

He tilted his head as he mentally assessed the dangers. "Old city, crumbling building, sinkholes, the usual problems."

Crumbling buildings were all I had to worry about? "Could you take me there?"

"I could lend you some books instead. What are you looking for?" he asked as he moved out of the stall where I was standing by the opening.

I hadn't realized how awkward it might be to explain to someone I needed to blow shit up. "I just want to browse."

His eyebrows rose, making it obvious that sounded a bit suspicious when he'd just offered the use of his own library. He didn't say anything about it, though. "Dax might get pissed if I take you to a ruins. I know you're helping him with stuff."

Dax was becoming a damn thorn in my side. "So you won't take me?"

He shook his head quickly. "No, of course I'll take you. I'm in full support of your stance on the lawn last night and a strong believer in personal autonomy." He glanced back through the open barn doors. "We just need to figure out when he isn't going to be around, is all."

"Bookie, I think we are going to be good friends."

Chapter 19

I hadn't seen Dax at all yesterday but by time Bookie had been done with his work, it had been too late to go to his book place. This morning, I was awoken to a knock and Dax saying to be ready by nine on the other side of my door. He didn't wait for a response before I heard him walking away.

So there I was, sitting on the back porch, a glass of iced tea in my hand waiting for Dax, as ordered, when Tiffy came and sat down beside me.

"Hi, Tiffy."

"Hi, Dahlia," she said with the cutest little smile I'd ever seen. This was what children should look like, healthy and smiling, not how I'd seen them at the compound.

She looked around, her curls bouncing as she did, and then leaned closer. "I heard you met Hairy?"

"Harry? Who's he?"

"No. Not Harry. Hairy. That's what I call him, the beast."

This kid had some serious intel. No one knew what happened out in the forest with the beast. I certainly hadn't fessed to it after what happened with Dax afterward. "Why do you say that?"

"My friends told me."

Were her friends spying on me? "Who are these friends?" I kept my voice light as I asked.

"Can't say. Hairy's nice. We play together sometimes but only when I can sneak out. I'm not supposed to play with him, any of beasts, but I think that's mean. They get lonely out there. And they don't mean to hurt anyone, even Hairy. He just does what makes him happy."

I was really starting to think this kid shouldn't be left alone at all. Whatever had happened to her, even forgotten or buried so deep I couldn't see it, seemed to have stolen a few chunks of reality. After everything I'd been through myself, I felt like a total hypocrite thinking she was crazy, but using the beasts as playmates didn't have another label in my book.

"Tiffy, I don't think you should do that. The beasts are dangerous."

"Not to us," she said, and took my hand.

Don't feed into her delusions. Don't ask; just tell her to stop. "Why not?"

Her little eyes rolled to the sky. "Because we are magic, silly."

"That's right. I remember you saying something about that."

"My friends are waiting to meet you, so let me know when you're free. They get impatient."

She kept talking about friends and I thought back over the last couple of days. Not once had I seen another kid.

"Are they around?"

"They don't live here."

"Oh, okay." I was starting to think these friends were of the invisible variety. But how had invisible friends known about the beast in the forest? Unless it was a lucky guess?

The backdoor opened and Dax looked at the little girl. "Tiffy, you aren't telling stories, right?" he asked.

She rolled her eyes again. "Dax, I'd never do that," she said with the most authoritative little voice I'd ever heard.

God, I liked this kid.

"Just make sure it's okay."

It was an odd conversation to be sure, but I let it go. I had enough oddness in my own life to question anyone else's. Compared to what I had going on, they were regular ole Janes and Joes.

"We're leaving now," he said to me. Not asked, told. He was making a point and I didn't particularly care for it.

"Yeah." I smiled at the little girl. "Bye, Tiffy. I'll see you tomorrow, okay?"

"You're coming back, right?"

"Yes. I'm coming back." I looked at Dax for confirmation of time. "Tonight?"

"Late tonight or early morning."

Her little head nodded and then she pulled me closer to her so she could whisper in my ear.

"We'll talk later."

"I've got the bike up front," Dax said, and I followed him as he walked around the house. Awkward and tense was an understatement, but I was having a hard time pinning down who was the main culprit. Was I projecting my uncomfortable feelings or just picking up on his general mood? Or was it a little of both, ricocheting back and forth until we were repelling each other like the same poles of a magnet?

He halted beside the bike but stopped short of getting on it. "She really likes you. You're good with kids."

"Thanks," I said, waiting for the *but*, and there definitely was one.

"She's got attachment issues. Since you aren't going to be around for the long haul, it's best if you keep your distance."

My head dropped. I knew he was right and I felt bad for not realizing it myself. I nodded, not needing to say anything. I got it. Boy, did I get it.

He got onto the bike and I climbed on behind him, swearing I'd keep my distance from him and her.

That turned out to be the most talk we did all day. We rode about an hour and a half away, to another "hole," as they were called.

We didn't talk on the way in.

We got ales, I spotted not one but two Dark Walkers, but I shook my head and denied their presence and we drove back.

Dax was gone by dinner.

Chapter 20

I awoke to a knock the next morning, but instead of this one being followed by orders direct from Dax, it was Bookie whispering, asking if he could come in.

I jumped out of bed and ushered him in. He closed the door behind him and then said in hushed tones, "Word is Dax has to go out to the rig for something that should keep him most of the day. How quick can you be ready?"

"Five minutes," I said as I was already gathering my hair into a ponytail.

He moved to the door as I grabbed my traveling outfit.

"Show your face at breakfast. I'll drop a couple of comments how I'm going to give you a tour of the area so as not to arouse suspicion with anyone while we're gone. At my signal, meet me behind the barn."

"Got it."

He left to go downstairs and spread the lie and I was downstairs five minutes later, like promised.

I choked down a plate of eggs while waiting for Bookie's signal, which turned out to be nothing more than him nodding toward the vicinity of the barn. He had a bike waiting and ready to go. Neither of us wasted any time chatting. I hopped on the back and we were off less than a few minutes later.

We slowed down an hour later and I knew without anyone telling me that this used to be a city. The partial frameworks of buildings still stood tall in places, and other than the Cement Giant, I wasn't sure if I'd experienced anything so creepy. It was like I could feel the ghosts of the world that once was.

I climbed off the back and Bookie pushed the bike along, talking to me as he did. "It's better to walk this part. You can see sinkholes coming easier than if we were riding. Problem with these old cities is, if what's left of the buildings doesn't crumble down on you, the ground might fall out from underneath. All the metal that held things up is deteriorating to nothing. Then there's the other diggers."

"What are diggers?" I asked, looking at the buildings we passed. Some still had a window or two intact that you could see the sun reflect off underneath a heavy veil of vines.

"Diggers are people who come out looking through wreckage for things. You could call me a digger even though I'm mostly after books. Diggers are usually harmless but you've always got a couple bad apples, ones who try and stake a claim to a certain ruin as theirs."

"But after so many years, what's left?" When I caught a glimpse into some of the places, they didn't look much different on the inside than the outside.

"How much do you know about the Bloody Death?" he asked then quickly added, "Other than the obvious, having had it."

"Showed up out of nowhere and decimated the human race."

"You know how quickly it spread?"

"Like a bat out of hell."

"Once it hit and people realized what was happening, they were dead or hiding. Lots of stuff left behind, even now. There's still niches, here and there, that survived the elements. Like that." He pointed down what once was a street to a building ahead. "That's the book place. A library, they called it."

"I've heard of those." The "library" looked like half of it had been swallowed into the ground. It didn't look any better as we got closer.

He grabbed something out of one of the bike's side bags that looked like a little mini lantern and handed it to me. He laid the bike on its side and started covering it with vines.

He lit the lantern I was holding and then took it back. "Follow me and watch your step."

I followed him into the dark chaos. It was

like crawling down into a cave, a really musty one. I couldn't see too far beyond us with the one light, but I was actually climbing over books as we walked farther in.

"So what did you want to look for?" he asked, stopping. "I've figured out some of the sections."

"Instructional-type stuff. Like how to build things."

"How to build what? Maybe I already know how to do whatever it is you want this book to tell you to do," he said.

"Probably not."

He shrugged. "Try me."

"Do you know how to build bombs?"

His face scrunched for a minute like he was trying to find the knowledge in his head, as if he'd read so much he had to scan his internal database. He finally said, "Drawing a blank. Why do you want bombs, though?"

"Because I left people back where I came from and I have to get them," I said as I squatted down and started looking through the pile on the ground: *History of George Washington*, *World War II*. "I think were in the wrong section."

He nodded and we walked, partially climbed, over to a different pile about ten feet away. He was looking through some books on the ground as he said, "I've heard about those places, the kind you came from. Was it bad

224

being there?"

"Yeah, they pretty much suck." I picked up *Sweet Southern Desserts* with a picture of the nicest-looking pie I'd ever seen. No bombs but this looked like a keeper.

"Why do you want to risk going back?"

Now that I was out of that place, I wanted to wipe the memory of living there clean from my mind, but I couldn't. After I got them out, though, I was going to get a big jug of that whiskey stuff, and me and the girls would have a grand night where we could get out all our grievances. Then we'd torch the memories like they'd never happened. Or at least I hoped. I knew how sticky memories could get, but I had a lot of faith in that whiskey.

"I can't leave them behind. But I'm going to need these bombs. It's the only way I'll be able to do it on my own. I'm going to blow the place up." I flipped open *French Cuisine*. "I think we need to try a different pile or we're going to have to hunt some food down."

"I'm going to go help you."

"Help me what?" There were some awesome-looking desserts in this book, too.

"I'm going to go back with you and help you get your friends out."

"You are?" I'd thought it impossible a second ago, but *French Cuisine* was forgotten.

He nodded and smiled at me.

"But you don't even know them. Why would you risk yourself?" I asked. "You could die. I might die." Death wasn't an outcome I hoped for but I wasn't delusional. It was a real possibility, and I was avoiding tallying up the odds because I knew that they'd be stacked against me.

"I know that and I know you and I know what is right. I've read the history, and this isn't how the world should be. People used to help each other. It'll never get back to something like that unless *we* make it like that."

I fell back on my ass in the middle of food books. Bookie didn't look anything like a fighter—the exact opposite, actually—and yet here he was willing to go to the compound with me because it was something he thought was worth fighting for. Or maybe he looked exactly like a fighter because he had more heart crammed into his lean frame then anyone I'd ever met besides myself.

I forgot about the fact that I was a Plaguer and jumped up, throwing my arms around him. Before I thought of what I'd done, he was already hugging me back.

It only took a second or two before the awkwardness kicked in and we were breaking apart. I wasn't sure who stepped back first.

He was quick to break the unease of the moment. He was good that that way. "I don't know if you should be this happy. I'm not sure how much math they taught you at that place you came from, but although two is twice as much as one, in our equation, two still equals fucked."

I laughed harder than I should've, and he joined me as only two people in over their heads together could. We might have been idealistic in our reasons, but we were realistic in the outcome.

"I've got some other good news,"

"Besides having company going out in a ball of flames?" I asked, still making a joke of it because if I didn't, the idea of him dying with the rest of us was too much.

"I already know where we can get what we need."

"Explosives?"

"Yes. And they're not far from here. Come on." He was grabbing my hand and tugging me after him.

Instead of going somewhere else in the city, we got back on the bike and didn't stop until we were in the middle of an empty field.

"There's nothing here," I said, getting off the bike.

"Yes, there is." He kicked out the stand and

walked four feet from the bike and then knelt down. He was on the ground and digging through the dirt, tugging on something, when all of a sudden a square chunk of grass and dirt rose up.

"What is that?"

"It's a silo. A shelter someone made to weather the storm."

He climbed down and motioned me to follow him. He disappeared completely. I walked over and saw the room below he was standing in and climbed down the ladder behind him.

The place wasn't that big but it was certainly well stocked.

There was a set of metal bunk beds along the wall and a table against the other.

"Somebody made this to prepare for the end of the world but it doesn't even look like they used it," Bookie said.

"Talk about missing the boat." What a waste. All that time and planning and they still bit the dust. They must have waited too long, and like so many others were dead before they got out of Dodge. I kind of wished I could go back and talk to whoever built this and say, *Buddy, world's ending. What are you waiting for?*

Bookie walked to the far-off wall where a metal cabinet was and opened the latch. "This is what I brought you here for."

I'd read about explosives in books but I'd never seen them in person. "These all explode?"

"Yep. Well, I think so anyway. Whoever made this probably figured if they ended up having to use the place, they'd need to booby-trap it. I'm guessing they're landmines and grenades, but we'll have to do a bit more research. I don't have extensive knowledge of explosives."

"I think we start moving the stash closer to home—I mean the house. It's going to take us a bunch of trips just to get the stuff there. Then we figure out how we're going to get it to the place I came from to blow it up." Seeing the mound of grenades piled up, the reality of what I was getting him into, hit hard. "This is going to be a tough job," I said, looking at him and wondering if he really knew what he was gearing up for.

"I'm ready. Are you up for it, Doxie?" he asked.

Doxie? That was Moobie's sidekick! "You read Moobie?" I didn't think copies made it out into the Wilds.

"Who doesn't?"

"We've got to clear one thing up. I'm Moobie."

"I'm the one with the supplies. I'm Moobie."

"It's my plan," I said, confident that he'd

come around to my way of thinking in time. "But okay, you can be Moobie, for now." I might get the kid killed. I guessed I could let him think he was in charge for a little while.

***

"I knew we took too long," Bookie said, using the back of his hand to hit my arm before he pointed toward the house.

Even in the dark, I could see Dax's silhouette standing on the porch, feet shoulder-width apart and arms crossed in front of his chest as he watched our approach. One of the perimeter guards had probably tipped him off that we were coming.

When we'd left the silo, hitching that wagon we'd found to the back of the bike seemed like such a great idea. We'd already gotten four times the amount of explosives we would've been able to carry back and stashed them in the forest. It had also taken four times as long to get back. It wasn't like we could abandon our load halfway when we figured out how much slower we were moving.

My back was already stiffening at the sight of Dax. "He doesn't have any right to say where I go. I'm not his prisoner."

Bookie made a groaning noise before he said, more to himself than me, "Oh God, this is going to be ugly. I thought I'd at least live until we bombed the compound." He was joking, but I could hear the nervousness underneath the humor.

I walked determinedly toward the looming Dax. His eyes flickered over me, then moved to Bookie. I stepped closer to Bookie in response, drawing Dax's eyes back to me. He seemed to be getting more pissed by the second.

"I know you took a bike. Where did you take her?" Dax asked, looking back at Bookie.

"I—"

"I asked Bookie to show me around," I said, cutting Bookie off and bringing Dax's anger back to me. This was my heat and I wasn't going to let Bookie burn for me. He was already doing enough.

It redirected easily. "I didn't break you out so that you could get killed touring the Wilds. You don't leave here without me." He looked back at Bookie. "And you—"

I stepped completely in front of Bookie this time.

"I agreed to work with you. Not to listen to your almighty commands."

"Dal, what the hell—" Bookie started saying from behind me until I cut him off again.

"I'll do whatever I want," I said to Dax, making sure I was the sole target of his anger. If I got him angry enough at me, he'd most likely

231

forget about Bookie.

"We'll see about that." Dax turned on his heel and walked in the house.

"Dude, he's *pissed*," Bookie said.

I shrugged. "I didn't think that went so bad."

Chapter 21

I turned off the shower and yanked the curtain back to find Tiffy standing there, waiting for me. Luckily, I'd gotten used to her unexpected visits enough that a scream didn't well up.

"How long have you been here?" I grabbed my drying cloth from where it hung nearby, as I became immediately self-conscious over her appraisement.

"Do you realize you have unusually large mammary glands for someone so lean?" she asked, her eyes on the vicinity of my chest.

Even though the cloth was now covering said glands, she was still staring. "Yes, I'm very aware of how lumpy I am. Did you need something?" I asked, hoping there was a purpose to this visit and it wasn't going to become the norm to find her outside the shower, maybe with an entire bush burning next time.

"Dax wants you. I volunteered to locate you. He's waiting in the back."

It was almost dusk. Were we going somewhere or was this the reckoning for last night's digressions? I'd been wondering how long it would take to pay for what he considered crossing his lines. Dax hadn't struck me as the type to not get payment eventually. It wasn't something I'd been told. It was something you just knew without asking.

"Okay, thanks." I maneuvered my way around her, grabbing my things as I headed back to my room. Tiffy's bathroom shower visit was slightly less creepy than the "hovering over me while I slept" visits, but just barely. I really did like the kid but she was an odd one.

I threw on the work clothes, in case we were going somewhere, and headed down to the back of the house. Dax was waiting on the back porch like he was there to collect payment.

"What's going on?" I knotted my wet hair into a bun as I walked over to where he stood.

His eyes appraised me but his expression was blank; his emotions tucked back behind the cement wall once again. But I might have been getting better at reading him, because I could feel the anger boiling within.

It would've been easier if he ranted and raved. He was giving me nothing to rage against, nothing to retaliate over. The only thing I could do was wait for the hammer to drop, and it might drop pretty heavily but I'd take the blow willingly. I'd directed Dax's anger toward me, since I wouldn't have Bookie paying the price for helping me.

"Come on," he said. He didn't wait for an answer and started across the yard, expecting me to follow.

"Where are we going?" I asked as I realized we were heading toward one of the larger buildings and not where he'd usually have a bike waiting in the front. It was definitely payment time.

"You think you're ready to handle yourself in the Wilds?" he asked.

Hell if I knew, but I certainly wasn't going to confess that I might *not* be, not after his reaction last night.

"Yes, I do." I didn't consider any of this his business anyway. He'd busted me out and now he acted like he owned me. I didn't have time for that nonsense.

I needed to be out there. There were explosives to stockpile and plans to work out. That was the thing Dax didn't understand. It didn't matter if I *was* ready for any of this. I had to be ready and I'd handle whatever came.

"Prove it and I won't say a thing about you leaving this place without me."

Shit. I'd walked right into that one.

"What proof would you like?" Whatever proof he required, I'd manage. If I failed, it didn't much matter anyway. I'd still do what I had to. I had people waiting for me and every day that went by they probably lost a little more hope that I'd be coming back. The idea of anything else being taken from them made my stomach hurt. They didn't have much left to lose.

He stopped in front of the building that looked like a smaller version of the barn and paused before he opened the door. "Knock me off my feet a single time and—as long as I don't need you—you're free to come and go whenever you want."

I eyed him up and down. Even in the loose-fitting pants and t-shirt he had on, he looked like he could take me on in duplicate and not break a sweat. My gaze stopped at the gloating look on his face. Oh, so now he was ready to be a human being with feelings? "You're almost twice the size of me."

He lifted his shoulders and dropped them. "You don't get to pick your opponents in the Wilds."

How could I argue that point? He was right. But he wasn't saying I had to be able to beat him, just take him down once.

I could do this. I had to do this. If not for freedom's sake then to get that damn look off his face. He was better when he was blank. I didn't know why I ever wanted expressions from him. His sucked.

He pushed the door open wider, as if beckoning me to my own funeral within. "You ready?"

My shoulders straightened as I tried to milk another inch of height out of my spine. "For anything you've got," I said, and walked into the building looking cockier than I felt.

I stopped and looked around. There were mats laid out on the ground and some stuffed bags hanging from beams, which looked like they were just asking for a set of knuckles to pound into them.

He walked farther in before he stopped about ten feet away from me. He shook his head and force-fed me another obvious expression. This one was along the lines of *you are so young and stupid*. As if that weren't clear enough, he had to verbally expand on it. "Don't you understand? You aren't a character in some Moobie book. When you die, there's no fucking sequel or close call. This code you have is idiotic. The only thing you should worry about is staying alive. But you don't get it because you've never had anyone teaching you anything. You grew up and the closest thing to a role model you had were these stupid books, but it's time to wake up."

Out of that whole tirade, the first thing that hit me was how did he know about my fascination with Moobie? Had Bookie told him? Nah, I didn't think so. Then I remembered he'd read my file. I'd caught more than a couple of beatings over having hidden Moobie books. That mystery solved, I could move on to the other matter.

"I'm not delusional. Moobie's not real, I get that." But it did hurt a little somewhere in my chest to fess up to it. Bastard. "But if I'm supposed to listen to people tell me that I'm too weak and I can't do this and I can't do that, that I should let my friends rot away in that hellhole, I'd rather have a fictional mentor, because the real ones are failing pathetically." Then Tiffy and Fudge popped into my head. "And if we're going to lay it all out, I think you're full of it. I don't think you'd leave your people there either, so cut the preaching."

He shook his head, shooting another look that I couldn't read, although I knew I didn't like it.

"What's that supposed to mean?" I asked, clearly indicating his new look.

He shot me another new look—a *you really didn't understand that*—and then elaborated. "I'm me. You're you. Big difference there. You're not ready."

I put a hand to my hip and my chin inched up. "Maybe I don't need as many years of practice as you did."

He let out a loud breath, or more likely an annoyed sigh. "You go. You die."

"I could've died when I got the Bloody Death. I could die tomorrow from a cold. I'm not going to become a different person just to squeeze out a few more days. I'm going to step up because they need me."

"This is exactly what I mean. You talk like you're a fucking character. You won't go in there and walk out a hero and you won't die a martyr. You'll just cease to exist."

"It doesn't matter. If I don't try, I won't be able to live with the person left anyway."

I watched him, his cement crumbling a little around the corners of his psyche again. "You act like I'm crazy, but you do get it. I can see it."

He was standing there one second, and then a flash of movement before an arm was across my chest. Flat on my back a second later, I was sucking in air like I'd never breathe again, and wondered what the hell had just happened. No warning. No *hey, you ready for this?*

"What was that?" I asked a minute later after my lungs stopped being flapjacks in my chest.

He walked over, feet beside my shoulder, looking down. "That's all you've got? I figured you'd fight back. Not drop like a stone." He made a clucking sound with his tongue. "You can't save anyone. You can't even take care of yourself yet."

Anger got me to my feet before I'd even fully reinflated. Even though I'd just landed flat on my back, this still felt nothing like when one of the guards had taken a shot at me. Dax had taken me down but that was it. He hadn't landed a kick to my ribs once he'd put me there.

I did a little hop back and forth and then moved my head from side to side, trying to crack my neck in vain. I meant business and I'd get the best of him one way or another.

"Try it again, now that I know what's coming," I said.

He circled me. "You think your enemies are going to tell you when they're going to attack? You think the people out there are going to not kick your ass because you tell them it isn't fair?"

I turned with him, keeping him in sight. "Just stop your blathering and come at me already."

He lunged and I dodged just in time, then my legs came out from underneath me and I landed on my ass.

He circled around. "Don't let your target out of your sight. You need a few minutes?" he asked, but in a way that made it clear he'd be calling me a sissy if I did.

This wasn't like the compound, where if you tried to fight back you'd have every guard in the place jumping into the fray. This was one-on-one combat where I hadn't lost before I'd even thrown a punch, and I was discovering very quickly that I enjoyed it, so much that even being outmatched wasn't detracting from it. I felt completely alive, like I was high on the elixir of life. It also made me wonder what sex would be like. Would it compare to this?

"Nope. Do you?" I asked, getting to my feet again.

He threw back his head and laughed. I knew we'd picked up some spectators. I saw the light of the door increase as a couple people came in to see what was going on. Yet when he was standing across from me, it seemed like we were the only ones there.

I watched him move and I knew just when he was coming for me. I ducked quickly to the side and then low as I tried to round on him from behind and sweep his legs out.

I failed, but I came close. I was starting to realize that not only did I like this sparring business, but I might be a natural at it.

He laughed like he thought it was funny I'd almost taken his legs out. "You almost got me." He was smiling as he said it, like he would've been even happier if I'd succeeded.

His smile did bad things to me, like short-circuiting my brain and making other parts of me flutter. I paid for it too when he dropped me again, because it also threw off my concentration.

Lying flat on the ground, for the first time I really doubted my sanity. I couldn't understand why I was finding this whole thing so damn entertaining. I was going to be one big bruise tomorrow and I still wanted to keep going.

Dax reached his hand down. I took it and he gave me a lift to my feet. It was the first time he'd done it since we'd started tonight, and there was something more there than just a hand up. It was as if he was encouraging me to keep playing with him, that he was enjoying this as much as me, as if we had found common ground between us.

"Come on," he said. "You're getting close."

It was ridiculous to me why, but the encouragement from him had me taking chances I wouldn't have. I moved in to try and take him by surprise, and instead of him going down, he had me pinned against him, one arm trapped between us and the other in his grip behind my back.

"Say it," he said, his face inches from mine.

I shook my head.

"You know you're beat. Say it. Concede."

"No."

"Why?"

"I'll concede defeat when I'm dead."

"You won't be able to do shit then, let alone concede."

"I guess it'll never happen, then."

His lips were soft but his stare was intense, like I could see the fire that raged underneath the cold exterior.

We were in a standoff. He loosened the grip on my arm but didn't let me go. Something flickered in his gaze and his eyes moved to my lips, and this overwhelming desire for him to kiss me surged up.

I tried to stomp it away but I couldn't help the feeling from welling up in me. I was happy for the flush the activity had brought to my skin, as I hoped I wasn't as transparent as I felt right then. It didn't seem to matter that he'd turned me down; I still wanted him. But he had turned me down because he was taken and I couldn't forget that.

"Maybe you should take a break," I heard Becca say in the distance. I hadn't noticed Becca make her way into the barn, but it reminded me again that we weren't alone. I looked at the small crowd now gathered, all watching us.

It was as if he'd just remembered as well. He stopped asking for a concession and dropped my arm, taking a few steps back quickly.

"That's enough for tonight," he said, and made his way out of the barn.

Show over, the barn emptied out quickly behind him, including Becca. I dropped to the mat below as I tried to figure out what had really just happened between the two of us.

Chapter 22

Becca laughed. "You've got to keep adding flour," she said as I was trying to free my fingers from dough. She'd arrived before dinner and the next thing I knew, the two of us were elbow deep in flour, making some special biscuit recipe handed down in her family.

Becca's laugh was warm and open, and sounded like she'd had plenty of practice. It made me feel even worse about throwing myself at Dax. Then I started thinking crazy thoughts, like maybe she knew how Dax was starting to affect me.

I had to it get out, woman to woman. It had to be said or I'd never get past this uncomfortable feeling. "Becca, remember how I showed up at Dax's room?"

"Sure."

"I didn't—"

Dax had the unfortunate timing of walking in the backdoor at that precise moment. Well, wasn't that just the special sauce to make this moment perfect?

He moved into the kitchen and was pouring himself a drink, barely more than five feet away from where we were making the biscuits at the table.

"Um, I didn't know that… I didn't mean

to… I wouldn't have…" I started tripping over words. It was tough to explain you wouldn't have thrown yourself at a man when that exact man was close enough to hear, and more than likely listening.

Her eyes shot to his back and then to me. "I know. It's all right," she said, smiling.

I could see why he liked her. She was all smiley, bright and clean. The worst memory she had was of someone dying from natural causes in her arms. If I were a guy, I'd be all over her. Why would Dax want someone like me when he had her?

"Like this." She pushed the dough this way and that, covering up the conversation we had been having as Dax made his way across the room.

When he passed by us, I saw her eyes go to him but he seemed oblivious. I might be inexperienced in romance but I knew love when I saw it. It was all there written on her face, and she had a particularly open one. It was a strange pairing, the two of them on different ends of the spectrum, but maybe that was why it worked. Dax needed someone like her to counteract how closed off he was.

While she was preoccupied with Dax, I glanced back out the window to where Bookie was fiddling with one of the bikes in the last of the day's light. I hoped he was getting it fixed. If that bike were broken, we were done for. We were going to sneak out today for a run, but the damn thing hadn't started and it was the only one available. There weren't that many bikes to begin with.

"I noticed you and Bookie are getting along really well," Becca said.

I hadn't realized how obvious I was being, but luckily she'd misunderstood the interest. "Yeah, he's nice."

"I think he likes you."

"You think?" I asked. Although I didn't want to bring the subject up, guys weren't into me. Hadn't I just proven that again with Dax? "He seems like he's nice to everyone."

"I think he's sweet on you," she said.

I looked out at Bookie again just as he was looking up. He gave me a thumbs-up through the window and went back to work. A girl could do a lot worse than him. But the situation would be different with Bookie than what it might have been with Dax. With Bookie, it wouldn't be two people using each other. It would be sweet and real and hard to walk away from in a month's time.

Dax, on the other hand, wouldn't get attached. There would be no hard feelings when I left. It was better that he was with someone like Becca, who would feel enough for the two of them. I didn't have that kind of emotion available to give away, not right now.

I looked back up through the window, wanting to check on Bookie's progress. He shot me a nod and a smile. We were back in business. He gathered up his tools and was rolling the bike toward the shed when Dax stepped in front of my view.

"Bec," he said, and then nodded toward the door.

"Keep going, Dal. I'll be right back," she said, and patted my hand still working the dough.

He walked out the backdoor and she followed him. I heard the footsteps on the porch but they didn't go that far.

I knew they were talking about me. It was just one of those gut instincts that never steered me wrong. Margo had told me once it was rude to eavesdrop. Margo, who I loved to death, was still stuck in hell. Margo didn't have a bossy man named Dax trying to make her ID monsters for his own purposes. Screw polite. This was wartime.

I angled my ear toward the door but couldn't make out anything. I was mighty thirsty, and that pitcher of tea was sitting right out on the counter by the door. No one could say anything about a girl getting a drink.

I grabbed a glass and made it over to the pitcher, ready to pour the minute someone came in. From my new location I could barely make out their voices, but I couldn't go outside and pretend to not be listening so it would have to be good enough.

"Stop encouraging her and Bookie," Dax said.

"What's wrong with her having a relationship with Bookie?" Becca asked. "They're the same age and it's not like there's a ton of people for them to meet."

"It's not a good idea."

"Why?"

"Don't press me about my business."

"This isn't your business. This is two people's lives."

"I'm not discussing this with you." His voice was cold, even with her. Well that wasn't very nice. I'd thought being his girlfriend would shed a little of the arctic chill.

"I know why you won't talk about it. You told me you didn't care, but I can see it—"

"I'm not talking about this."

"Don't you walk away from me," she said, but I could hear her voice breaking and was glad I couldn't see her.

"This has nothing to do with you."

"I used to pretend that you cared for me—as much as you were capable of caring for anyone. I could believe that before."

"I never lied to you. I told you what this

was."

"That's the thing, you did. You said you couldn't care for anyone, that you weren't built that way. But I see the way you look at her. I saw you in the barn."

"I look at her like she's an asset. That's it."

"You're lying to both of us."

I didn't know what happened next, but they went quiet and I backed away from the door quickly. I dug my fingers into some dough, pretending I'd heard nothing when I spotted Dax through the window walking away from the house.

Becca walked in, and as she crossed the room, I could see the tears start rolling down her face. I hadn't cried since I was a child and couldn't imagine the pain that would make her do so. All thoughts of pretending I hadn't heard a thing washed away with those tears.

"There's nothing going on between the two of us," I said as she grabbed her bag to leave. Where was she going?

Bag in hand, she turned to me. "There is. You just don't understand it yet."

I tried to grab her arm, anything to stop her. "No, Becca, I would never do that to you. He's just using me."

"I'm not blaming you. But I can't be with him, not now."

"But nothing is going on," I said, trying to

stop her as she seemed determined to leave. "He's just using me," I repeated at her back as she walked out the door.

Then I was standing in the house alone with nothing but the dough. How had that gone so wrong? I was the one getting used and I was still getting stuck making the dough for tonight? Maybe I should storm out too, but then there'd be no dinner rolls and I did like to dip them into the gravy. And hell, being used just didn't seem like a big enough deal to leave.

Becca, on the other hand, seemed a bit more particular about her relationships. Goddamn, Dax really botched this one up good.

***

Dinner that night was almost worse than a session with Ms. Edith. Okay, maybe that was being a bit dramatic, but it wasn't a lot of fun either. I sat in my seat next to Dax, which forced me to keep my head to the left or I'd have to look at him, and I didn't want anything to do with him right now.

Whatever had gone down between Becca and him had turned out to be much larger than I had witnessed. I'd gotten word from Bookie fifteen minutes before dinner that she was leaving to go live outside the grounds. In fact, she was so eager to move in with some distant relatives that she was skipping dinner to pack. She'd fed him some bullshit that one of them was sick, because she must have found out by smoke signals or something. I certainly wasn't believing it, and no one with half a brain would either.

Something more must have gone on with her and Dax. Didn't he get it? There weren't that many good people left in the world. Did he have to run her off? Who knew what would happen to her now, out there? He thought I couldn't handle myself to the point that I wasn't supposed to leave the premises, but he didn't say a damn word about Becca?

Bookie sat across the table looking at me strangely because, well, Bookie was sensitive like that and knew I was upset. Fudge was quiet and so was Tiffy.

Lucy bounced in and sat in her *new* seat. "Where's Becca? Thought she was coming to dinner?"

"No," Dax said in a way that didn't invite questions.

I didn't think that tactic would work on Lucy, but she sat down in a surprisingly quiet manner.

When Tank, the last to arrive for dinner, showed up and asked where Becca was, Lucy answered, "Not coming," and gave Tank the *shut up about it* eye.

We all started eating in silence and I realized that in the hurried conversation over Becca, I hadn't confirmed whether Bookie had fixed the bike.

"I saw you working out there. Is the bike broken?" I asked Bookie, as if I had no idea of its state and that it wasn't crucial to our plans.

He cleared his throat. "Yeah. I think I'll have it back up and running in another day or so, though," he said.

We were both now avoiding looking in Dax's direction, but man, I could feel his eyes burning into me. Bookie started coughing. I didn't know if it was Dax making him nervous or the bite of biscuit he'd just taken, because on top of everything else, I'd somehow ruined the rolls. Even Fudge's intervention couldn't save them, and there wasn't enough gravy in the world that would fix them now. They broke apart like a dry brick and then continued to crumble.

Dax stood from the table and stopped behind my chair. "We're going on a run tomorrow. Be ready at six a.m."

"Fine."

Chapter 23

I came down the stairs that morning, dressed in my work clothes and ready to see no evil. There would be no Dark Walkers today, just like there hadn't been the last couple times, even though there were. Becca would be fine, no matter where she ended up, even if she wasn't. I had one target, and I couldn't lose sight of it because of distractions, no matter how worthy. I was letting too many emotions get in the way. I had to be cold, like Dax, at least for a while if I was going to get my friends out.

I walked out the front door with my tunnel vision set to straight ahead. If it wasn't something that sat at the end of my tunnel, I wasn't going to see it.

"Where's your gloves?" Dax asked as he got on the bike and I was about to get on behind him.

I looked down at my hands and realized the gloves were still in my pocket. For the first time in more than a decade, I'd forgotten about the brand, something that had defined me for so long. I tugged the gloves out of my pocket and climbed onto the bike.

We skidded to a stop a few hours later in the thick of the forest and in front of a structure that was barely more than a shack. He chained the bike to a tree but then did something he'd never done before. He looked into one of the small windows first before we entered. I didn't ask why. It wasn't at the end of my tunnel.

Whatever he was looking for didn't seem to disrupt our plans, and we went into the building, which consisted of a single dark room with only a couple of small windows for light. There wasn't a bar, but a man walked around with a couple different bottles to the individual tables.

My eyes adjusted to the light, and I took a good look around. The place was packed with Dark Walkers. It was like a monster convention or some shit. My brain was screaming to beeline it to the door, but I forced myself to follow Dax over to a table in the corner.

The waiter came by with a couple of glasses and Dax pointed to the smaller bottle he carried. He served us and was gone.

Acting normal in there might have been the hardest thing I'd ever done. I maintained composure while I sipped my drink, glad for the burn of whiskey to help steady my nerves.

We'd only been there a few minutes when Dax looked at me, asking his silent question. I did a single shake of my head. He kept staring. He'd never asked me twice before. I shook my head again.

He threw back his drink and I forced myself to finish my own. We left. Dax didn't say anything, but I feared he was starting to catch on to me. It wasn't until we were halfway to home, and he stopped in the middle of nowhere, that I was near positive the jig was up.

He got off before I did, and I was left doing a mad grab for the handlebars while my foot searched out the kickstand before I got off too.

He walked a couple of steps away but then circled back to me. "You've been lying."

He wasn't asking. I knew he couldn't prove it, but unfortunately, I wasn't sure Dax's personal justice system required proof. Now what? Lie until I died, or try reasoning? I knew this moment might come. I should've planned ahead, because the stare-down thing he was doing right now was jumbling my thoughts.

He took another step toward me, closing the already narrow space. "Do. Not. Lie. Again."

Well, that didn't help the brain jumble, but it did give me a more definitive idea of what not to say. "Why do you want them so much?" The stare-down continued along with silence. I didn't think I was going to be able to pull off *deny till you die*, so I tried a different angle. "You might not like it but I'm saving you. Whatever they have that you want, let it go. You don't realize what you're getting involved in."

"Yes. I do." There was no wiggle room in that answer.

He couldn't know. No one could. Not unless

they had seen them like I had, felt the cold that came off them, smelled the sickly sweet scent of their skin. I took a few steps away from him, and mentally away from the things I hated to think about.

"Hearing the stories isn't seeing and knowing." I shook my head. "You don't understand what you're asking me to do. You tell me how I'm acting like a character, that I'm clueless, that I don't know what life is about. I know too much. I understand what might come from this." He was the one that didn't get it. He hadn't been stuck with them for years and felt the evil that flowed from them, so thick it could suffocate you.

He also didn't understand how badly he could be screwing up my own plans. I didn't know what he wanted from the Dark Walkers, but if I started identifying them, I didn't doubt every one of them would come crawling out of their dark corners looking for the person who was to blame. There would be no sneak attacks and well-thought-out plans to free my friends. I'd be on the run.

I couldn't tell him that. If I did, I knew exactly who would be scrambling and left holding the bag. He didn't care about my friends or what would happen if I couldn't get to them.

He walked closer, following me to where I'd stepped away from the bike. "You want to lead your life on your terms but deign to tell me what I should do? You made a deal. Honor it." He took a step away as if he wanted space but then thought better of it. "You need to decide. You're either with me or you're not. If you're not, you'll be treated accordingly," he said, not yelling or screaming, but it was almost worse for the lack of it. This was cold Dax at his finest, or worst, depending on which side of the line you fell. If you were on his side, that ice-cold person in front of you was like a glacier buffering you from the fire. If you were on the wrong side, you were dead in the tundra.

"You better decide soon before I make my own determination," he said. "If you were smart, when I said jump, you'd be doing backflips. I got you—a Plaguer—out of that place. No one even wants to get near you people and I gave you refuge."

I knew he was mad, and he had the right to be. The only thing between us was a business arrangement and I'd reneged on the agreement. I'd been lying to him, but not because I wanted to. I had to.

And I'd been called a Plaguer in that way before, so often it was almost like saying *hey, girl*. I wouldn't trade being a Plaguer in for being normal, ever. At least I knew what walked this Earth. With age, I'd realized knowledge was power. I knew keeping your eyes shut could lead you right off a cliff.

So why was it so hurtful when he used the term, and in that way? Why were my eyes burning like I was going to cry? I didn't cry. I wasn't like other people. I was tougher than them.

I didn't say anything, just gave him my back as I tried to come to terms with the emotions roiling within. What was wrong with me?

"Dal?" He spoke my name in a tone heaped high with accusation, as if thinking I was ignoring him.

I opened my mouth to shoot back a nasty reply but came up blank. I couldn't think of a single retaliation.

I heard his footsteps near me and I started walking away.

"I need the bushes," I said before he could question me further.

He didn't say anything and the footsteps behind me stopped.

I found a group of bushes far enough away from him to get some privacy and squatted behind them, but not to go to the bathroom. I reached up and wiped away a tear that managed to escape. Fucking asshole made me cry and I couldn't even figure out why. So he'd called me a Plaguer in a way that implied that we might not be so popular. So what? It wasn't like it hadn't happened a thousand times before. I was going to act like a big sissy now?

It was ridiculous to get this upset. I moved over to a creek running about ten feet away, took my gloves off and splashed my face with water. I had to pull it together. It didn't matter if he was mad and I couldn't care what anyone thought of me. I pulled myself together and walked back toward him.

He cleared his throat and there was this strange awkwardness between us, as if he knew something was off.

He looked at me, his eyes narrowed like he was concentrating on figuring out a puzzle piece. "What's wrong with you?" he asked.

"Nothing," I said, with not a little bit of chutzpah thrown in for good measure. "Can you tell me what they have that is so important?" I asked, even knowing that there was nothing that would trump my friends' lives.

He didn't bother answering.

"I guess full disclosure only runs one way?" I said.

"You made an agreement with me and then lied. What disclosure?"

Chapter 24

We weren't speaking when we got on the bike, and I considered myself lucky that all Dax was doing right now was ignoring me. Then the bike wouldn't start. No matter how hard he jumped on the thing, it wouldn't roar. It didn't tank his mood—it couldn't. It was already nearing bottom.

"Get off," he said. "We're walking."

I'd already been climbing off, as if I hadn't figured that out.

He grabbed the handlebars and started off. I followed, wondering how long it would take to get back on foot, and then how long it would seem when those four words might be the extent of our conversation.

We walked until it was dark. It was probably only about four hours, but four hours times the not-speaking rate of a gazillion and it felt closer to a lifetime. Add in the bugs that felt like they were actually pulling hair from my scalp and it might have been closer to an eternity. Considering we'd be walking again in the morning, by the time we got back tomorrow, it was going to feel like we were near frozen in time.

"What are you doing?" I asked as he kicked stuff out of a small area.

"We'll sleep here."

I looked about the area and weighed his mood against my concerns, then decided my question was important enough to take on his bad mood. Plus, I had to cut him some slack in that area. I had lied to him. He just didn't understand he was giving me no choice. "What about the beasts?"

He stopped kicking shit to shoot me one of the most annoying looks I'd ever gotten. Eyebrows raised, and just short of rolling his eyes, he asked, "You're worried about them now?" I wasn't crazy about this new expressive Dax that kept popping up.

"Not if I was awake. I can't protect myself if I'm sleeping."

"They aren't a problem."

"Why?"

"That would be filed under full disclosure." And another obnoxious look, something close to *ha, see how you like it.*

I didn't like it one bit. *Damn your black heart, Expressive Dax.*

"Come on," he said, motioning for me to lie in a spot cleared next to where he was lying down.

"You want me to sleep there?" I asked as I watched him settle in and get comfortable.

"Yes. Don't act like my presence offends you. I'm not planning on attacking you. It's strictly for your safety." He certainly wasn't acting interested.

If I didn't lie down next to him now I looked like a fool who was self-conscious. "Fine," I said, walking over and settling down beside him but careful not to touch him anywhere. "But just so you know, I officially revoked my earlier offer."

"You revoked it?" he asked, adding an insulting half laugh to the end of it.

"Yes. It was only offered as payment and when I thought you might be a nicer person."

"Good to know." Instead of being insulted, he sounded amused. My couple inches of buffer space disappeared as he turned on his side.

I didn't like him anymore. I really didn't. It would be just like not seeing the Dark Walkers and Becca being okay. I had a mission. Nothing else could matter. Not liking Dax one day or not liking him the next, it didn't fit into my tunnel.

I woke up with his arm wrapped around my waist and his stubble grazing my cheek.

"Don't panic. Be still."

I hadn't been panicked until he'd said that. I hadn't even been awake, but now I was and at full alert. Also panicked. There was something very close to me, so close I could feel the heat off its body, its breath fanning my face.

I should've lain there and feigned sleep. That would've been the smart thing to do. Instead my lids flickered open and froze. I was staring straight into the beast's red eyes. They almost glowed they were so bright. It was covered in a wiry gray hair as it rested its weight on one dangerously clawed hand in front of me.

I bent my leg, raising my knee slightly higher so I could get my hand around the knife I'd borrowed from the kitchen and tucked into my boot. Last time I'd slept out here without it in my palm. From this day on, I'd be hugging that knife to my chest like it was the softest teddy bear, and I was four years old.

Its lips curled away from its teeth, which had to be five inches long, and it emitted a low growl. The beast knew exactly what I was doing.

"I wouldn't do that," Dax said, utterly calm considering that thing had teeth that could rip into the both of us, not to mention the claws.

I froze and it stopped growling although its lip was still raised, as if it wanted to make sure I didn't forget that it had a very large set of fangs and could bite me if I tried anything. It came even closer, its nose almost touching mine, and my pulse went wild. It moved its head lower and I felt its wet nose skim the flesh of my neck— the oh-so-thin layer right over my carotid artery, to be exact.

My breathing completely stopped as I waited for the beast to finish its inspection.

Dax, still lying behind me, didn't so much as tense. And yes, that made him an ass in my current opinion. Only an ass wouldn't care about getting mauled and dying as some beast's midnight snack.

It finally lifted its head. There was a blur as it stood to a towering height and then it was gone before I could even get a good look at its upright form.

I sucked down more air than my lungs could fit, trying to make up for their momentary lack of breathing.

"Holy crapola." I got up, sleep not an option anymore, and turned on him. "And what is wrong with you? Aren't you afraid of dying? I thought those things killed?"

"The answer to that would fall under the full disclosure clause." He yawned and folded his arms behind his head.

"You really aren't going to tell me why the beast didn't try to eat us?" I was on the verge of screaming. While I kept an eye out for another one, he was closing his eyes.

"Full disclosure." Even half awake and with only a partial moon to display it, his *You're the one that started this, not my fault if I'm better at it* face was about to make me lose it.

"I think that's some bullshit you're just using to keep your secrets."

"You would know something about that, now wouldn't you." He turned on his side and went back to sleep.

Chapter 25

We'd been walking along for a few hours on a not-so-traveled road when five men appeared in the distance. They looked a little rough around the edges, even for the Wilds. If they actually spoke, it still might be an improvement from current company.

"Where are your gloves?" Dax asked, looking at my hands as we saw them approaching us.

Oh shit. I couldn't believe I'd done it again. An image of them sitting by the creek, where I'd splashed my face with water yesterday, sprang to mind. This was bad. "I left them back by the creek."

"You. Left. Them. By. The. Creek?" he asked in a tone of disbelief.

"Yes. I. Did." I mimicked his tone.

"You think this is funny?" he asked.

"No, but there's nothing I can do about it now. It was a mistake." I wasn't going to tell him that I'd only forgotten them because he'd gotten me upset by calling me a Plaguer. A joke had seemed the best course of action. Looking at him now, maybe it hadn't been? He certainly didn't deserve an apology.

"Stay behind me and don't take your hands out of your pockets, even if they want to shake them."

"Why would they want to shake my hand?"

"Handshakes in the Wilds have two purposes. To make sure you don't have a gun in your hand and to call you out if there's a suspicion you're a Plaguer."

My hands went deep in my pockets. Enough said.

"And don't talk."

I moved closer to his side and said, low enough that there was no way the group could hear me, "I think it looks more suspicious when I say nothing."

"I don't care. I'm afraid of the shit that will come out of your mouth and I don't feel like killing any more people than I've already had to. I've got a cap on how much blood I like on my hands and I'm currently over quota this year, so please, do me a favor and just shut the fuck up for a little bit?"

"Fine. But why do you think they'll even bother with us?"

"Because we're outnumbered and we have something they want."

I looked at us. "The bike?"

"No. You. Did you see how they were carrying multiple guns on their hips?"

I nodded.

"There's a price on your head and only bounty hunters carry like that in these parts."

"A price?"

"From Newco."

"Do you have a price?"

"No. Just you. They're telling people that you are a live carrier of the plague."

"But that's a lie and they know it," I said. "I was around people for years and not a single one of them caught anything."

"They aren't doing it because they believe it. They're doing it to drive you out. They also said it was dangerous to approach you and that they should send message and they'll come and extract you themselves. But bounty hunters won't do that. Too afraid they'll get cut out of the money, plague or not."

The unexpected guest flashed in my mind. Dax had said it was nothing. "That's what that guy came to tell you at dinner the other night. Were you going to tell me?"

"At some point," he said, and I wanted to choke the blasé tone right out of his throat. I got it. I'd held back from him and now he was going to make sure I knew the consequences.

"If they attack, throw to kill."

"Kill?"

"Yes. Kill."

Conversation halted as the five stopped about eight feet in front of us. Any hope of passing peacefully was shot to hell as they spread out, intentionally blocking the road.

One of the guys stepped forward, placing him slightly ahead of the others. They were all looking down to where my hands were tucked in my pants.

They already knew. It wasn't like I was hard to ID. Young redheads walking about these parts were probably few. I'd only met one other redhead in my life, and that wasn't until recently, with Tiffy.

"How do you want to do this?" the guy in the lead asked Dax, not me. Maybe I should've been insulted he hadn't asked me, considering I was the target, but I had bigger worries.

"You don't want to do this," Dax said, like we were the ones with the upper hand. At that moment, a couple of things came into question about Dax: his sanity and his ability to count.

"I'm sure I do," the leader scoffed. I couldn't really hold it against him. I was near to scoffing.

"I guess it's going to be the hard way, then."

I didn't need an interpreter to know it was time to grab my knife. I'd killed a Dark Walker and a pretend assassin. I'd never killed a human before and I wasn't sure I had a taste for it. Didn't seem like I was going to have a choice, since that's all that was on the menu today. I'd die fighting before I let anyone take me back to Newco.

Their guns were drawn and bullets starting

whizzing past me. I heard movement to my left but I kept my eyes trained on the one guy coming for me. I didn't want to see Dax lying on the ground dead. I didn't know what would happen to me if I did. I couldn't look because if I saw it, it was real. It couldn't be real. Not if I wanted to keep my shit together.

I grabbed the knife from my boot but was afraid to throw it, not sure if I was going to be deadly accurate or lose my one weapon in the effort.

I heard shuffling to my side again and couldn't imagine what they were doing to Dax's poor body, but I was running out of time. I had to get away from here before all their attention was back on me. I wasn't going to win in close combat. The guy coming at me wasn't as big as Dax but he looked a lot stronger than me. His eyes shot to my left; he probably wanted to join in on the fight before it ended, since from the sounds, the beating was almost over. It was enough to send me over the top. I threw the knife at him and it found its home effortlessly in the center of the guy's chest.

The guy fell instantly. I needed to make a run for it, like this very second, but I couldn't stop myself from one last glimpse. I needed to know Dax was dead and not being tortured somehow.

There were four bodies dead on the ground

and Dax standing there, watching me.

"You're alive." I tried to hide the relief that welled in me. For the second time in days, I felt my eyes burning. It was in that second that I knew how much I was starting to rely upon him to watch my back, like we were partners or something. I'd expected him to get us out of this, and I'd felt panic over him dying. He was Dax; he couldn't die, and he hadn't.

But for that short moment, I'd thought he had and it had rocked my world. I was the one who was strong for everyone else. I wasn't supposed to be leaning. I was the *support*.

He looked at my victim lying dead on the ground. "You weren't horrible but you waited too long," Dax said, as he walked over and retrieved my knife from the corpse, stopping only to clean the blood off on the guy's clothing. "You need practice. You can't hesitate, especially once you're on your own. You're in the Wilds now, Dal. It's kill or be killed out here. When you fight, it's to the death and you don't start shit you aren't willing to finish. If you're soft, you're dead."

He walked back to me and handed me the knife and then went to look over the other bodies as he asked, "What's wrong? Reality not as charming as it seemed in your books?"

Yes, killing the guy was upsetting, enough that I didn't want to look at the body, but that wasn't why I was speechless. It was him. He was pissing me off. First I think he's dead. Then I don't get a chance to reset my internal compass back to north and get everything straight before he's complaining about how I'd taken too long to kill the guy.

"Not everyone is tough all the time." I didn't know why, but I resented him right now. It annoyed me that he always thought he was right, and it bugged me even worse that most of the time he actually was. But I had him on this point, and I knew it. "Not everyone is a machine like you." Some people even care when they think people die and might need a second, but I wasn't going to tell him that person was me in this moment.

He stood up from where he'd been squatting next to a body, ice-cold Dax back in place. "You have to be. You're going to be on your own. You don't have the luxury of emotions."

I wanted to be tough, not depend on anyone. But he was still annoying me. "I'm not going to be alone. I'll have my friends with me. We'll depend on each other." Or they'd mostly depend on me, but so what.

"I hope that works out for you," he said in a tone of voice that drove me crazy, like he knew all the secrets to the universe, and I was just a dumb, sheltered idiot.

"What about Becca? She went out on her

own, and she wasn't a machine."

"She wanted to leave. I'm not a jailor—most of the time. She got where she was going. What happens after that isn't on me." He walked over to the bike, done with the bodies. "People are who they are. You can't make someone fundamentally different."

He grabbed the handlebars and started walking while I remembered the last argument I'd heard him have with Becca and wondered who he was really talking about, him or her.

I had a long time to wonder, since it took us about four more hours to walk home. By time I saw the gates, all I wanted was some of Fudge's food and to curl up in bed and put the past two days behind me.

That wasn't how it was going to happen, though. It was stupid of me, but for some reason, when we got back, I thought there wouldn't be any ramifications.

Dax's first words to the guy when he opened up the gate were, "You let her leave this place without my say-so and it's your ass. Tell the rest of the crew." He didn't wait for a reply from the gate guy or myself, simply continued to the house.

"What is that about?" I asked, half yelling and forcing my exhausted body to catch back up to him after I'd stalled in shock.

"You need me to translate?" he asked, not

bothering to stop in his stride.

"That's bullshit."

"No. That's your new reality until you give me a Dark Walker."

I stopped chasing him and yelled, "What about 'I'm not a jailor?'"

"I'm not, 'most of the time.'" He walked around to the back of the house, leaving me standing alone in the middle of the front lawn.

Chapter 26

No one would let me out the next day, not alone, not with Bookie. I was officially on lockdown, and I didn't have time for this bullshit. Dax wasn't even around to go hunt Dark Walkers, so what was the point? I was wasting valuable hours for no reason. Bookie and I still needed to try and find books in the library so we could come up with detailed plans of how many explosives we'd need to blow through cement. Neither of us knew what kind we had or exactly how strong, how many to set off and where. The questions seemed endless. But instead of doing any of those worthy things, I was sitting in my room, basically grounded like a child.

When I did get out again, there was a whole new issue. Bounty hunters. I had a price on my head. In one strange and overly dramatic way, it was kind of cool. It was just like some of my characters. I wondered if I had a poster, too.

In a real-life sort of way, it sucked the big one. I toyed with a lock of too-bright hair. It was like a beacon.

Maybe there *were* some things I could do while I was stuck here.

I went downstairs and saw Fudge in the kitchen.

"I need to borrow a couple of things if you don't mind."

She narrowed her eyes. "Borrow or keep?"

I knew she was thinking of the knife, which I returned every evening and re-borrowed every morning.

"Borrow-ish?"

She rolled her eyes. "What do you need?" she asked as she continued to mix some dark brown concoction, which may or may not have been fudge. I'd recently found out her real name was Mary. She got the nickname Fudge because she liked to make it once a month. I'd never had it myself, so I was hoping that's what she was about.

I rattled off my list and she directed me to the various cabinets to find the items. Luckily, there was coffee in abundance. She had a nice stash of rags and she warned me not to drink too much when I took the small bottle of whiskey for good measure. Living in the well-stocked main house had some perks.

"What are you up to?" Her mixing arm stopped mid-motion as she took in my small collection.

"Nothing much." I smiled and hightailed it out of there.

"What did you do to your hair? It's darker."

Dax's voice startled me a few hours later. His timing was the pits. I hadn't heard the door open, and he didn't knock.

"Thought it might be a good idea." I hadn't managed to get my hair to the brown I'd hoped, but at least it was more auburn now than bright red. There were limits even to the miracle of coffee.

"It was," he said as I could hear him take a couple more steps into the room. "Are you dripping blood?"

I kept my back to him, holding the rag to the still bleeding hand. I looked down to see a small puddle had formed in between my feet. "It does look that way."

I turned around, keeping the rag pressed to my skin, figuring the cat was out of the bag. "A brand leaves no doubt. A scar leaves them guessing. I should've done it before now."

"Let me see it."

"It's fine." I didn't need someone to care for me. I'd cared for myself well enough for a long time. Besides, it was better now, other than the blood and some pain and the almost disgusting flap of skin I'd sliced off… Blah, blah, blah; it wasn't worth making a big thing over it.

He shrugged. "Fine, handle it yourself." He walked over to the window seat and made himself comfortable, watching me with a *go ahead, you said you had this under control* look on his face.

"What is it with you and the faces lately?" I shot at him, annoyed that he was insisting on sitting here and watching me. "I either get no emotion or the most obnoxious expressions known to man."

The bastard laughed at me.

"No, you and your gloating *I know it all* expressions are not funny."

He laughed harder. Damn if the sound of it didn't shoot right inside me and start churning stuff around, even as annoyed as I was with him. Now not only would he not leave my room, I was going to be his evening's entertainment.

I grabbed one of the longer strips of rags and tried to wind it around my hand but I couldn't get it tight enough to do any good, even when I tried to stick one end underneath my chin.

"You don't have that many outfits. I'd think you wouldn't want to bleed on the ones you do have," he said from his comfortable perch.

I looked down and saw a speck of blood that had already stained the dark pants. Bloodstains wouldn't be the worst thing in the world, but I would've preferred they were my enemies', not my own.

"Fine. If you're not going to leave, you might as well help. I guess."

He got up, walked over to where I was and

took the rag from me. He pulled off the rag and held up my hand, looking at it this way and that at the chunk of skin missing. "Not a bad job considering that you did it one-handed."

"Why thank you. So gallant of you to notice." I relaxed a little after he didn't remark on the butchered edges and had stopped smiling. I knew I hadn't done the best job ever but it had hurt like hell trying to slice skin off.

"Did you happen to borrow any of Bookie's salve while you were gathering supplies, or was that what the whiskey was for?" He raised an eyebrow, already guessing.

"Whiskey."

"Now that had to hurt like a bitch."

"It didn't tickle," I said as my palm started sweating in his hold. I tried to concentrate on the burning that still came from it as he wound the rag almost gently around it. I'd gotten used to being close to him on the bike, but standing here, face to face in my room, was a whole different ball of wax.

He tied off the end and then bent my elbow until my hand sat next to my ear. "Keep it above your shoulder until the bleeding stops, and come with me."

He stepped back and I was relieved I didn't have to worry about my breathing seeming normal or my palms sweating anymore.

"Where? We going on a run?"

He squinted. "No. You're not even done bleeding yet." He was still shaking his head as I followed him out of my room. He walked out the front door, across the yard and through the gate. We kept walking until we were near my assassin in the forest.

He stopped and leaned against the dead tree. "Go."

"Go where?" I asked, not following what he meant. There was no hint on his face. Expressionless Dax was back in action.

"Anywhere you want."

There had to be a catch. Had to. He didn't wait very long before telling me what it was, the explanation preceded by a smile. "But you're going empty-handed. I've got your explosives."

He was the only one smiling. He knew about my bombs. He had my stash.

"Not sure how you're going to blow anything up without those," he added, as if I couldn't have figured that out.

"They're mine." Those explosives were my only hope. I couldn't do anything without them and there weren't that many left behind in the bunker—if he hadn't already found them too. Bookie never would've said anything, but I was learning Dax had his ways.

"They'll be yours again after you do what I want." There might have been a smile on his face but it didn't match his eyes.

He had me. He'd won and I'd do what he wanted. I needed those bombs more than the risk of the Dark Walkers coming for me. But if I could deliver him some quick enough, I might be able to break my friends out before every Dark Walker in the area knew I was giving them up.

He wanted full disclosure? He was going to get it. "You want the truth? They're all over this godforsaken place. How's that for honesty? There's been at least one in every single place you've taken me. The Wilds are crawling with these monsters. How many you want? We'll be done in no time." I kicked some stones out of my way instead of walking over and nailing him with a solid blow like I wanted. "It's your death." Hopefully just his and not everyone else's as well.

I watched and waited for a reaction from him that didn't come. It hit me like a log to the side of my head. "You knew that they were all over this place, didn't you?"

He shook his head. "I suspected."

"Why?"

"Just a hunch." He didn't bother trying to act like he was telling the truth. It was bullshit. I was starting to believe there wasn't a single thing in the Wilds that he didn't have the pulse of.

"Don't try and play me again," he said, and

turned back toward the house.

"Seriously? You guard me like I'm the most precious thing ever and now you just walk away, not caring if you leave me in the woods?" I yelled after him. "What if I change my mind? Tell you to keep the bombs?"

He stopped and turned around. "Is that what you're saying? I should go throw a match on them?"

I started forward. "Sometimes I really don't like you."

"Why? Because I stole your toys?"

"For the record, they aren't toys. They are a means to an end. But yes, that is exactly why."

Chapter 27

I saw Tiffy heading my way dragging her feet, as I sat in between two rows of tomato plants. I was back to free rein again, but unfortunately, Bookie had to go help someone in the next settlement over, where they didn't have a doctor. I was stuck again, at least until tomorrow, but it was hard to complain about it while enjoying the scent of the plants.

"Bark's here," Tiffy said as she shuffled over to my side, all the joy sapped from her tone.

I'd heard the name come up during one of our dinners. Bark did some trading with Dax, coffee for fuel. I looked up and around, curious to meet the person who Tiffy clearly wasn't enthused by. A man with wiry gray hair and overalls strolled across the grounds toward the house and then changed direction toward us. He looked like a typical farmer—to a normal human, that is. Not to me. Dax was doing business with a Dark Walker.

A Dark Walker had just invaded the one safe place I thought I had. I wanted to grab the knife at my ankle and kill him right now.

"I thought I heard he didn't come by until the fall?" I asked, trying to remain calm in front of Tiffy even as I thirsted for his blood.

"He doesn't usually," she said as she watched him with a pout on her face. "I don't like Bark."

"Why? Because Dax is a little funny about him?" I remembered when the topic of Bark had come up, Dax hadn't seemed overly enthralled with the guy. It was as if he knew something was off with him but couldn't say for sure what it was. Boy, had he been right.

Tiffy let out a long, tired sigh that sounded like it came from a much older person. "My friends don't like him very much either. It could be tainting my opinion, but I don't believe so."

Her friends might have had one knock against them—being invisible and all—but they did seem to be good judges of character. "Tiffy, can you go to the back shed and get the special shovel for me? The one no one uses that you told me about."

"The shed all the way on the other side?" She pointed in the direction that led to the farthest corner of the grounds, as if I couldn't mean that one.

I nodded.

Her shoulders dropped. She looked at me, already exuding fake exhaustion, and said solemnly, "Only for you will I do this."

"Thank you," I replied, as if she were bestowing a great honor.

She skipped off a few minutes before Bark

got to me.

I grabbed a huge handful of weeds, grateful for the bandage around my hand and the mutilated skin beneath, which now replaced the brand.

Bark's toes came just shy of stepping on plants as he paused as close to me as he could.

"I'm Bark." He leaned forward, slightly bent at the waist with a hand extended, trying to reach me with the plants in between. I waved my handful of dirty weeds at him, not reaching over at all. "Sorry," I said. "Little dirty right now."

He dropped his hand and straightened. "You're the new girl, right? I've heard about you."

And boom, just like that, I was positive he'd heard I was Plaguer. It might've been paranoia, but my gut said he knew, and when my gut screamed like it was now, I listened.

I'd known it was only a matter of time before word got around about me. Most people talked. They couldn't help themselves. They just ran their mouths like a spigot turned permanently on, and having someone like me in their midst must have set the stream to full blast. I just hadn't expected there to be so many Dark Walkers for it to get around to.

I smiled and nodded. He smiled back. There was nothing friendly about the exchange. We were like two hyenas showing our teeth. He knew what I was. I knew what he was and there were no delusions past the surface layer of crap we were dishing out in each other's direction.

He tucked his hands in his *I'm a big fake farmer overalls* and rocked back on his heels. "So how'd you end up around here?"

Really? Were we actually going to play this out to the bitter end? "My community was taken out by a case of Bloody Death. All three thousand of them just keeled over in a day and dropped around me. It was horrible." Lie, lie, lie. Three thousand was an absurd number for a community out here. Everyone knew that, even me, but if we were going to play make-believe I might as well have a little fun with it.

He nodded and his hyena smile grew a little toothier. I knew he didn't believe a damn word I said and got the feeling he didn't like the game when he wasn't setting the rules.

"Dax around? We've got some business."

Dax wasn't there and I'd bet this jerk already knew he wasn't. Dax hadn't told me where he was going, but Fudge mentioned this morning that he wouldn't be back until late tonight. "Not sure. Maybe check up at the house," I said. "If he's not there, maybe try in the woods. He likes to kill wild pigs and then drain their blood and drink it while he performs ritual dances." It was the most ridiculous thing

I'd ever said, and Bark's eyes narrowed. He didn't like that I was amusing myself at his expense. Didn't matter. This wasn't going to end pretty no matter what was said.

Bark nodded, his hyena teeth hidden away now as he walked off. I imagined throwing a knife at his back as I watched him enter in the house. By no means did I believe that would be the last of him.

Now what? Did I leave? Make a run for it? Should I try and tell Dax? Dax had known this guy for a lot longer than me. What if he didn't believe me? No matter what he said or how much he didn't like Bark, I was still the crazy Plaguer and this was someone he'd done business with for years. Would he really take my word over his?

Bark was a Dark Walker. If he left here, I was doomed. The Dark Walkers wouldn't just leave someone out here, roaming free, that could ID them, and I wasn't going back to the previous hell I'd been living in willingly.

I yanked a couple more weeds while I figured out a plan of action. Offense or defense? Kill him or flee? If I fled, I'd be leaving the stash of explosives behind.

I'd have to kill him. In truth, it was what I wanted to do. I'd had to flee once and I didn't like the feel of it. But first I'd give Dax a chance to show his true colors.

He wanted a Dark Walker; I was going to deliver him one right up in his very backyard. Hopefully he'd believe me, because I wasn't sure what would happen if he didn't, and I hadn't done a whole lot to encourage trust.

***

I was watching Bark and Bark was watching me. We were doing a dance of sorts. No matter where I went, I made sure I knew his location. He did his part by never being far behind. I moved. He moved. If I was in the kitchen, he showed up in the dining room, pretending to wait for Dax to do business. He thought he was stalking me. I could've put his mind to ease. In this moment, I was the hunter. He couldn't have lost me if he wanted.

By the time dinner came around that night, I'd strapped my knife to my ankle and had borrowed another I wedged in between my belt and pants.

With or without Dax's cooperation or consent, I was going to have to kill Bark after Dax got what he wanted. Bark wouldn't leave this place and me in peace, and I was starting to realize how deeply the Dark Walkers were embedded in every aspect of this world.

I'd always thought that if I could get to the Wilds, I'd have the humans to deal with, but I would be free of the monsters. Now my suspicion that I might never be truly free was cemented, and it really pissed me off.

Bark was already there at the dinner table, waiting to eat, when the rest of us strolled in. Should've known he would be, considering Fudge's manners. The fact that he was sitting in Dax's spot, of all places, burned worse than if someone had ripped the bandage from my hand and dumped the entire contents of the saltshaker on it.

"To dinner?" Fudge asked, eyeing up both knives.

"Trying out a new look," I said.

She rolled her eyes but didn't say anything else.

Tiffy was on me like glue and was giving Bark a wide berth. She took in my new look and gave me a nod of approval. The kid was sharp.

Dinner was surprisingly normal, or would have been if I could've eaten. Every bite was forced as my adrenaline was trying to tell my stomach to go screw. So I chewed on delicious food that turned to sawdust in my mouth as I waited. I had to kill this monster before he left here. It was the only way I'd be safe.

Bark said he was going to leave at daybreak tomorrow morning if Dax wasn't back by then. It was bullshit. He wasn't leaving here without us having it out. I saw it in his eyes. He was going to try and kill me or take me with him before morning light. They'd all think I'd taken off on my own. Everyone knew the turmoil of my situation.

But I wasn't going to let that happen. I watched how the rest of the house had easy banter with Bark over dinner, just chatting it up with an old buddy, only me and Tiffy with watchful eyes for the monster. Even Bookie was laughing with him.

One of my favorite times of day—which was any time we ate—ruined by this goddamn interloping monster that shouldn't even be here. I went to my bedroom that night full but unsatisfied.

I lay upon my bed, fully clothed and awake, gripping my knife. Dax hadn't returned and Bark was supposedly sleeping on the couch below. The only question was: wait for him to come to me or take the initiative and figure out what to do with the body afterward?

The choice was taken from me as I heard my door open. The smell of him confirmed it wasn't one of Tiffy's nighttime visits.

He'd come for me. I wasn't upset. He'd saved me a trip. This wasn't anything like killing the human the other day. Not one part of me felt anything about killing Bark, a Dark Walker. I'd killed one at the early age of four and I'd been waiting for another chance ever since.

My hand tightened around the knife as I heard him close my door. I debated whether to wait and try and find out why he was here or be safe about it and just kill him quick.

I sat up, deciding I'd take the risk and try to get something out of him. It would be nice to know what these monsters were and why they were roaming the Wilds before I did the world a favor and got rid of one.

I didn't get the chance. The second the door clicked into place, he lunged for me. The knife released from my hand almost as if it had its own mind. It struck true in the middle of his chest and he fell to the floor, knocking into the dresser and banging it against the wall as he did.

That was loud. No way I was going to be able to sneak his dead body out of here now.

My feet had barely touched the floor when the door burst open, Dax standing in the entrance still in travel clothes. As he took in the scene, I knew it didn't look good. Bark was lying on the floor with my knife sticking out of his chest.

I didn't have time to explain before Bookie, Tank and Lucy were jostling to see who'd get through the door next. Lucy and Tank got in first and Bookie only had room to peek over their shoulders as they partially blocked the door. I heard Fudge in the hallway telling Tiffy to stay in bed, so I knew she was aware something was happening. Dax stayed standing where he was as Tank knelt by the body.

"Holy shit. You killed Bark?" Lucy asked, like someone else might have done it and fled the scene.

"Why'd you kill Bark?" Tank asked.

Lucy and Tank were both looking at me like maybe they didn't quite know who I was anymore. I could feel myself getting boxed in to giving them answers they weren't going to like. I knew whether I hung for this or not was going to come down to one man's decision, and he wasn't saying much of anything.

For as much as Dax wanted me to hunt him down Dark Walkers, would he really believe someone he'd known for years was one?

If Bark had just left tomorrow morning when he said he was going to, this could've been handled in the woods and no one would've linked his death back to me. They wouldn't have had a reason. But I'd known it wasn't going to happen like that.

I took a step forward, eyeing the knife in Bark's chest and missing the feel of it in my hand. I hoped I wouldn't need it again tonight.

"Why did you do that?" Tank asked again, looking at me as if I were a threat he hadn't realized. "*How* did you do it?"

I glanced at Bookie, who also looked

shocked.

I was saved from answering by Tiffy in the doorway, squeezing her head alongside Bookie's legs. "I'm glad he's gone."

"Tiffy, I told you to stay in our room," Fudge said from somewhere farther down the hall, trying to shield the young girl from seeing too much. I wish I could've told Fudge not to worry about it. That kid was tougher than all of us.

Tiffy smiled at me and gave me a thumbs-up before she left. She'd bought me some time. No one had wanted to pursue questioning in front of the little girl.

Dax pointed to my shoes, the only things I'd taken off when I'd gotten in bed. "Put your shoes on and come with me." Dax moved to where Lucy and Tank knelt by the body. "You two, move him to the back shed and lock the body in. Bookie, I want you to look it over."

"For what?"

"Anything strange."

Lucy looked from me to Bookie, obviously not liking her role. "Why do we have—"

"Lucy, shut the fuck up," Dax said, and Lucy's mouth shut. But only until he walked past her to the door and she mouthed to me, *You're gonna get it now*.

"Dal," Dax said, waiting outside the door.

I threw my shoes on as quickly as possible,

wanting to be prepared if I had to make a run for it. With no knife to defend myself, this could get ugly. Dax wasn't freaking out or screaming, but that meant nothing.

He moved quickly down the stairs and out the door, only pausing briefly to make sure I was behind him before entering the woods. The guy at the gate didn't say a word as we passed.

I let the gap between us grow gradually as we walked, building up a healthy space. He was bigger. I'd have to be faster.

He stopped and so did I, keeping the invisible boundary in place.

"What happened?" His arms were crossed, feet spread, expressionless.

There's two types of people in this world. Ones who know what they know, and are sure of it, whether it's true or not, and others willing to step beyond what their experiences are and see things for what might really be. Dax had known Bark as a normal guy he'd traded with. It was time to see what kind of person Dax was. "Bark was a Dark Walker."

"Bark was?"

"Yes," I responded, waiting for a crack in the cement to give me an idea whether I should be running for it or not. I waited, not knowing what would come. Would he try and kill me now? I scanned the landscape, wondering what would be the best escape route.

He let a disappointed sigh and all of a sudden a human being with emotions peeked through again. "I wanted one alive. Did you have to kill him so quickly?"

He believed me. I hadn't even tried to convince him. He'd just believed me. All the energy that had been building up inside me released in one sudden swish. Even with Margo and the girls, I'd had to win their trust over years. I'd never had someone just believe me before. He'd known Bark, done business with him. I'd lied to him and he still was willing to take me at my word.

"I have no control of where I hit. I just let it go," I said, my voice soft as my brain was still absorbing the shock of being believed. His body was relaxed. He really wasn't going to kill me?

"Next time, try and do better," he said, not even a little mad. I might have been wrong, but it almost sounded like he was partially joking about it.

"I'll do what I can?"

He shrugged and started back toward the house.

I had still identified a Dark Walker for him, though. He might have been dead, but Dax had never said anything about alive. "He still counts, right?"

"No. You killed him. Only live ones count."

"But you never said that. You can't

295

negotiate after the fact."

"Fine, I'll consider it a partial credit if it makes you feel better."

"Good. It does. And what took you so long? He might have been alive if you hadn't dallied."

His eyebrows shot up. "Let me guess, it's my fault you killed him?"

"Yes, exactly," I said as I realized Dax was actually kidding around with me. And I was joking right back, like two normal people, maybe even…friends?

Chapter 28

I got up in the morning and it was as if nothing had happened. The breakfast buffet had a line extending out to the living room. No one gave me a second glance as I joined the hungry. If the area rug hadn't been gone from my room, I might've thought it was a nightmare.

I heaped some favorites onto my plate, kind of digging the fact that I had favorites now, and made my way to the back porch.

Bookie squeezed into the seat next to me ten minutes later. "Dax told me to tell you to be ready in ten," he said, and then reached in his back pocket and handed me my knife.

"Thanks." I tucked it into my boot and waited to see if he was going to follow this up with anything having to do with me murdering the guy he was laughing with last night.

When he started scoping out the ears in the vicinity, I knew something was coming. I'd realized once I had a choice in the matter that I detested waiting, so I preempted the conversation I feared was coming.

"Are you pissed off I killed your friend?" I asked, not expecting a good answer. I mean, seriously, I had *killed* his *friend*.

His gaze swung back to me, startled. "I hated that dick."

The loud guffaws of last night rang in my head. "But you were laughing with him at dinner?"

"He's a dick, but a funny one." Bookie dug into a pile of eggs as a couple people walked by. As soon as they were down the stairs and partly across the lawn, he started talking again. "So what exactly was Bark?"

"Why do you ask?"

"He wasn't human. That shit was clear."

"Spill."

"Don't tell anyone I'm repeating this."

I rolled my eyes. "Duh."

"So I had him laid out on the table and was about to cut him open, per Dax's orders. He said he wanted my eyes only on the guy. By time I started, he was already turning to a pile of sludge. The skin was still there but everything inside was one big mixed-up mess. Couldn't find a bone or organ to save my life. Now you spill. You killed him. I know you know what he was."

"I don't know what they are. I only know what we call them, Dark Walkers."

"So they're real." He leaned back, plate resting on his lap and food forgotten. "That's some freaky shit."

"I know."

I heard the bike roar to life somewhere on the other side of the house and realized how much time had passed.

"Give it here," he said, motioning toward my plate.

"Thanks! I'll talk to you later," I said, and made my way to the front of the house, already in my work clothes and with the knife tucked in my boot. I'd gotten dressed that morning thinking anything could happen.

***

Dax and I were in the newest trader's hole and I was realizing why they were all called holes. This one was dumpier than the others, but it wasn't long before I spotted a Dark Walker. I'd seen one at every single place so far, so it wasn't a big shock, but how I wished it wasn't here. This had nothing to do with having to ID one either. It was the cold reality of how many were out here. There truly was no getting away from them. I'd thought that after I broke my friends out, I'd just have to get us to the Wilds. Now I wondered if I'd have to make it all the way to the Country of California, and that might not even be far enough. Maybe there was nowhere far enough.

Dax started walking toward a table not far from the Dark Walker until I tugged at his sleeve and pulled him to a different one close by. I might be willing to tell him but I wasn't looking to be overheard by the Dark Walker while I was dropping the dime on him.

I slumped into the seat and he sat down across from me, his eyes already intent. He was probably tipped off, because I'd never cared where we sat before. "The dingy guy in the shadows, wearing plaid." Damn, this was a realm I hadn't wanted to go, but I was still here. I leaned across the table, making sure he heard me. "And just for the record, I want nothing else to do with whatever it is that comes next. No part of it."

He scoffed. "Who invited you?"

I leaned back in my chair, seeing the amusement there. I watched Dax around people. When he got all cold, that was when they scattered, not knowing what to do or how to handle him. But this was the Dax that scared me. I liked this Dax. If I had slept with cold Dax and this one had shown up, things could've gotten really sticky in the emotions realm.

The amusement faded. "Don't leave this spot and don't talk to anyone."

"Sure," I said, surprised when he left abruptly after that. Was he really so used to people following his orders that he hadn't heard the sarcasm dripping off that one word?

I watched him walk across the room, pull out a chair and sit across the table from the Dark Walker. The Dark Walker looked as surprised as

I did. I couldn't imagine what he was saying. What could you say in these situations? *Hey, I know you're a monster but let's be best buds*?

Shit. I was so clueless about what Dax wanted, even after living in his house, that I couldn't even come up with a hypothetical conversation to mock him appropriately.

The two of them got up a minute later and walked out of the building together, but not before the Dark Walker shot a look at my hand, wrapped in rags. I caught a final glimpse of his face as the door was swinging shut. The expression I saw on it said I'd pay for this.

I'd had to do this, but that didn't mean I felt good about it. This could rain down a lot of heat on me, and if I didn't have other people I was worried about, I'd take it no problem. I kept my butt in the chair for ten minutes, and that felt like a huge accomplishment, but fifteen wasn't going to happen. That thing couldn't leave here with knowledge of me and who I was with. Invitation or not, I was joining the party.

Decision made, I couldn't get out of there quick enough. I pushed open the door and scanned the woods that surrounded the building, looking for Dax. He came strolling out of the woods a minute later, his eyes rolling as he saw me waiting. He walked toward the bike and I met him there.

"You don't listen well," he said as he got on

the bike.

"My hearing isn't the problem. Where is it?" I asked, not willing to go anywhere until that loose end was cut. I'd delivered one Dark Walker alive, but that didn't mean I was letting him leave that way.

"He's gone," he said right before he stomped on the bike to wake it up. "Get on."

"Where?" I asked. I raked my hands through my hair, making it messier than it already was as I scoured the forest with my eyes.

He leaned back on the bike to get a better view of me. "Gone as in *dead*."

"You killed it? I thought you wanted them alive?" Wasn't that the whole problem with Bark? That I'd killed him? Unless he'd gotten whatever he wanted, but if he had, it had been small, because it didn't look like he had anything new.

He hooked a finger behind him. "Get on."

I did as he asked, quite amicable now. "So what did you talk about before you killed it?"

"It was one of those things you had to be there for," he said, and then the bike was too loud to keep a conversation going. I didn't even care if he dodged my questions. The thing was dead, no Dark Walker to finger me. My plans were still in place with no one being the wiser.

Chapter 29

I'd lain in bed forever but my mind was still spinning with plans. One Dark Walker delivered, two Dark Walkers dead and I was still on track for bombing the hellhole to pieces. I hadn't gotten the bombs back yet, but Dax wouldn't renege on his end.

"Dax!" It was Bookie hollering in the hallway that had me sitting upright in my bed. I ran and opened the door just as he was getting to the second floor. Dax was already standing outside in the hallway.

"Lookout said they saw a beast close to the perimeter and it was hurt," Bookie said.

Dax nodded but I could see the immediate change in him, the urgency with which he moved.

"Stay here," he said to all of us, standing outside our doors in the hall. He took off down the stairs without putting on shoes. No one followed.

I looked about, and still no one moved. Why were they all standing there listening to him? I wasn't staying behind. "You're letting him go alone?" I asked, looking specifically at Tank and Lucy.

"He told us to," Tank said.

I shook my head but didn't verbalize the

word *losers*. I ducked back into my room but not to stay. I grabbed my knife and shoes, not quite so tough that I was willing to tear my feet up.

"Where you going?" Lucy asked as I ran back into the hallway and then past her.

"After him," I said as my feet hit the stairs.

"He said we should wait."

"And?" I asked like that was the stupidest reason I'd ever heard as I left her looking down from the top landing. Not one of my friends could have stopped me from going after them if I thought they might need me. I wasn't sure exactly what Dax and I were, but as I ran after him, I realized whatever blurry category he might have fallen into, it merited some sort of loyalty within me.

By time I got downstairs and out the front door he was ducking into the woods already. I ran after him. He was much quicker but I wasn't too far behind.

Sister-lover didn't hesitate when he saw me coming and had the gate open by the time I reached him. We'd come to an understanding, him and I. He didn't look at me like I was a freak anymore. He just didn't look at me. In return, I didn't taunt him or have to tell anyone what a freak he was. I thought we'd settled into a healthy place.

I could run a lot quicker than when I'd first gotten out—Fudge's cooking got partial credit there—but if he hadn't slowed down on his own, I would've lost him. As it was, I still lost sight of him for a few minutes. When I finally caught up, he was squatting beside a beast.

Even with it lying down, I could tell it was probably about seven feet tall and massive, covered in dark gray fur with a protruding jaw that had huge canines visible. I could see the moon reflect off places where the fur was wet, and there wasn't a rise in the chest area to indicate any breathing was going on. He must have just killed him.

I walked closer and Dax looked up as if surprised to see me, which was unusual for him, since he always seemed so alert to his surroundings.

He looked back down at the creature whose eyes were closed. "Go to the house and tell them it was a false alarm. There was no beast in the forest. Then when they go back to their rooms, get me a shovel out of the shed."

I didn't ask why as I turned to do as he asked.

When I brought the shovel back to him thirty minutes later, he was leaning against a tree, staring at the dead beast on the ground.

He took it without speaking to me and walked back to the beast. He knelt beside it and hoisted the massive creature over his shoulder. Holding the beast steady with one hand and the shovel in the other, he walked deeper into the forest.

I watched his back, not knowing whether to follow him or not. He was acting stranger than ever—or to be more accurate, colder. It was only a mere second or two before I headed after him.

I wasn't sure how many miles we walked for before we came to a clearing next to a small waterfall that bubbled along into a pond. In my mind I remarked on the beauty of the place, but I said nothing aloud.

He didn't seem to be paying much attention to me anyway as he laid the beast on the ground and began digging.

I sat down on a fallen tree, not far away.

He dug slowly and methodically and I wondered why he was burying the beast, but I knew instinctively he didn't want to speak. His wall was up thick and tall, and I wasn't sure if he wanted me there or not. He didn't acknowledge my presence in any way. He made fairly quick work of the hole and threw down the shovel beside it.

I took a tentative step forward to help lift the beast but he waved me off before I took a second. I went back to my seat wondering what was going on with him.

He lifted the beast and then jumped down into the hole with it. He didn't get out right away, and when he did, he seemed even heavier now without the burden. I sat and watched as he covered the creature with dirt, not understanding why this was so painful for him but knowing it was, wall or not.

He knelt beside the covered grave for a very long time until he finally stood.

"Come on," he said.

I got up and started walking along after him, wondering why he'd let me stay but afraid to ask.

He walked into the house and then to his room without saying anything.

Chapter 30

The first thing that came to my mind the next morning was Dax burying the beast. I'd dreamt of the creature when I went to sleep and now it looked like it wanted to carve out a piece of my waking hours, too. But it wasn't only the beast that threw me. It was Dax's reaction. He'd dropped to subzero temperatures pretty quickly, and I wasn't sure how long he was going to take to thaw out this time.

I got dressed with the assumption that I'd never really know what that had been about, just like I wouldn't know what the talk with the Dark Walker or the pile of other mysteries around here had been about. Good thing none of those were my problems anyway. It was time to get on with another day and move ahead with my own plans. I couldn't get sucked into the drama around here.

The noises from the buffet at breakfast were quieter then normal, people grabbing food and then getting out as quickly as they came in. I didn't think anything of it. Was in fact happy to not have to wait in line and was in the business of filling a plate when Lucy came up beside me.

"What's the deal?" she asked. "Do you know? You went after him last night."

"Nothing happened." I stopped with only

half the amount of bacon I wanted to find out what she was talking about, sensing it had something to do with the morose atmosphere of the breakfast hour. "Why do you think there's something wrong?"

Her eyes darted to the door and she went silent, going about her business of gathering breakfast food.

I looked up to see Dax. He wasn't glowering or screaming or acting angry, but there was that same feeling about him that he'd had last night. His cement wall was high and thick today and throwing off a chill that filled the room. He walked past us, not saying anything, and headed toward the front of the house.

"What happened last night?" she asked.

"I told you. Nothing." I grabbed some more bacon and went to go eat at my spot on the back porch.

Bookie came next, sitting beside me. "What the hell happened with Dax last night?"

"I don't know." Bookie was one of the only people here I really trusted, but if Dax didn't want to tell them about the beast, I wouldn't be the one speaking about it. "Can you go on a run later?"

"Yeah, I should be good. I found us a new spot, too," he said.

Dax was supposed to give me back all the explosives, but it would be nice to have a stash he wasn't aware of.

"I'll go handle what I need to and we can leave in an hour or so," he said, "if you're still here."

I waved him goodbye, having a feeling I would be.

I took another bite of eggs as I looked off into the forest that edged the grounds. Everywhere you looked in the Wilds was forest. I was meant to be here, in the Wilds. I'd miss this house once I left, but I'd build a new one where there would be room for all the girls from the compound.

The screen door squeaked open and then slammed shut with its familiar sound as people walked past with their meals. I'd have to remember to find me one of those doors, too.

I was on my second plate of food when Dax came and stood beside where I sat.

His hand lifted and pointed to the plate. "You done? We have to talk."

"Yeah, sure." I was more than a little curious what he wanted. Maybe I'd find out what was wrong with him. I put the plate on the railing and followed him down the stairs. I'd noticed this about him. He liked to walk when he talked.

"I need you to tell me some things about the institution," he said.

It was my least favorite subject, but I

nodded, curious where this was going. I'd been here for weeks. Why did he want to talk about the Cement Giant now? I'd thought he knew almost everything about the place anyway. What was left? "Shoot."

"How many Dark Walkers were there?"

"I know you've been in a bad mood but I'm not sure if a friendly stroll around the grounds talking about them is going to fix you." It certainly wasn't a topic I cared to discuss. I could've gotten frostbite on my eyes from the look I got. The Dax I could joke around with was gone.

"I need answers."

I was starting to understand why everyone was avoiding him. Deep down, I'd never been afraid of Dax, but I wasn't sure I knew the man walking beside me.

"There were five that were there somewhat regularly and others that came and went. Over the fourteen years I'd been there, I lost count."

"The others that came and went, who were they?"

"A lot of times they came as government workers, similar to how you did. Some seemed higher up, although I couldn't tell you their rank."

He was silent for a minute and I saw Bookie poking his head out of the barn. When he saw me walking with Dax he was probably trying to determine if we were still on. I gave him a thumbs-up when Dax looked the other way.

I could tell Dax was almost done with me. As distant as he seemed, and even though I'd asked a couple of times already, I still had to ask again. "You have any interest in hitting the place with me when I bomb it?"

He looked at me like he was talking to a stranger. "No," he said. "Go do your run. That's all I wanted."

What the hell? How did he know where I was going?

Chapter 31

I'd had more freedom in the last few days than I'd ever had in my life. Dax hadn't called me to go hunting for Dark Walkers once. When he wasn't scaring people away, he was nowhere to be found.

He didn't say anything or yell—that wasn't his way—nor did he need to. People just scrambled out of his way when they saw him coming. Something had changed inside him and I didn't know why. The only thing I knew was it had to be linked to the beast and what had happened that night.

Even today, when I'd strolled back in from a run to the library, arms piled up with books, he'd said nothing. I'd done it on purpose, hoping to find a crack, and he'd barely glanced at me. He wasn't at dinner again, like he hadn't been every other night. The craziest part was every day he was like this, I felt like it was chipping away at something within me. It was getting so I couldn't sleep at night, waking up from dreams where I felt like someone I'd cared for had just died.

I'd woken again from another dream tonight that I couldn't remember, but it had left me feeling just as empty as the last one. I dragged my tired body from bed when I knew sleep wasn't going to come back for a while, figuring the only fix for this mood might be food.

Dax was sitting in front of the fireplace with a glass in hand when I got downstairs. It was quiet, everyone sleeping, and I knew he must have heard the stairs creaking as I made my way down. Instead of heading toward the kitchen, I found myself walking toward him. I sat on the opposite chair from him and he didn't so much as look at me. I should've left but I didn't.

"I'm going to have enough bombs to hit the institution soon. How much longer do you think you'll need me?"

"You can leave whenever you're ready. I'll show you where I have the other explosives hidden tomorrow if you want." He took a sip from the glass he was holding.

It wasn't the answer I'd hoped for. No warning of impending doom and my imminent death. Just *go when you want*. I searched his eyes, looking for some flicker of the man I'd known before.

Even now, I could feel the cold coming off him, but it wasn't a kind that just left you chilled. I recognized this feeling. I'd felt this in others at the compound. I'd felt it creeping in myself at times. It was the type of cold that robbed you of all the warmth you've ever had. In my experience, it usually came when the person lost the last little piece of themselves, that small part they'd held on to that they couldn't afford to lose.

"What are you doing?" I asked, my voice hushed. He finally looked at me.

"Drinking," he said, holding up his glass and knowing that wasn't what my question had been about and still not looking at me.

I stood up, walked over and stopped right in front of him so he couldn't avoid seeing me. It pissed him off, and I was happy to have any emotion that wasn't the cold.

That tiny crack revealed a volcano buried beneath the surface. I could practically smell the danger coming off him, and I thought back to what Fudge had said to me about not poking the bear. But even all growly as he was looking right now, his teeth about to curl into a snarl, I couldn't seem to stop myself. All those years in the Cement Giant had done that to me. I'd take death by fire over a long, slow chill any day.

"I don't know what that was about in the forest and I won't ask. It's your business. But don't do this. Don't become this person," I said without thinking, desperate because of what I sensed he was losing, confused why I even cared so much. "I thought you were stronger than this."

"Dal." It was a warning—a yellow flag telling me to back up and leave him alone, mind my own business. I decided to ignore it.

"What? Too weak to handle the truth?" I said, taunting him right to the edge, where I wanted him to be. Anything but what he'd been lately, because as I stood before him my own truth hit me stronger than anything I'd said to him. I wanted him out of control because I wanted him, period. Out of control might be the only way I could get him.

"I think you should go to bed."

"I guess you're only good at dishing it out."

He was out of his chair and grabbing me by the shoulders, crushing me between him and the wall. His body was flush against mine and I tilted my head up, my lips parting without conscious effort.

"You want to be real? Stop looking at me the way you are. I'll never be that man, and you won't be the first wreckage I leave behind," he said.

"Maybe I don't have a heart either." It was a stupid thing to say, but at that moment, if that was what it took for him to take me, I wished it were true.

He smiled but it wasn't one filled with hope. This one held nothing but sorrow. "Don't change. Not for me." His fingers tightened on my shoulders. "What you're looking for doesn't exist here."

His hands dropped, and he left, leaving me sagging against the wall.

Chapter 32

"What are we looking for?" Bookie asked as we traipsed around the old library on our way back from emptying the last of the bombs from the shelter. We'd already found a pile of books on explosives, but I'd told him that there was one more book we needed.

I stepped cautiously over piles and overturned bookcases until I landed next to a pile of fiction. "It's hard to explain exactly, but in the Glory Years, they were called Urban Fantasies."

"What's that?" he asked, digging through a pile nearby.

"Best bet is to look for a cover with a woman who looks like they're going to beat someone up. Maybe skintight black clothes that are really shiny."

"That's weird. You like them?"

"Yes, because the main characters usually kick ass and don't get walked on."

"Can't imagine why that would appeal to you," he said. Bookie was allowed to mock me. He'd become one of my best friends.

I dug through my pile and I hit gold by my fourth book. "I got one!"

He looked at the cover. "That cover looks like the girl's going to a funeral. That's not what

I was supposed to look for," he said, sounding put out I'd found it first.

"This isn't the norm but it'll work."

"What did you need it for?"

"You have a pencil on you?" I asked, still kneeling by my pile as he made his way over.

"Don't I always?" he said, and pulled one out of his back pocket.

I flipped to the title page.

To Destiny,

May the moon shine bright and the breeze hit your face.

I scribbled out the author's name beneath it.

"That's the sign?" he said, reading over my shoulder.

"Yes. Once we figure out the exact date we're going to attack, I'll go through and underline page numbers. The first two will be the month, the next two will be the day and the last four will be the year, just to be thorough, since you never know what could happen.

"I know where the guard who sneaks the books to my one friend hangs out. He was going to find this one night and not think anything of it as he's giving it to her the next day. She'll know what to do when it happens." I hugged the book to my chest, thinking of Margo. *I'm coming soon, so you better not give up.* "I have to get it to her before we blow the place up."

"You planned this all while you were still in there?"

"Every little part. Let's just say I've had a lot of downtime."

I tucked the book in my pocket and we headed out. I was so close to getting my friends it almost seemed surreal. I tucked the book into the wagon we had hitched to the bike, reworking the straps over the tarp that covered everything. After a couple of trips, we'd gotten a bit more organized about the business. Plus, we'd also read up on some of the stuff we were carting and now knew how close we'd come to blowing ourselves up.

We were about ten miles from the compound when the bike hit something and came to a dead stop beneath us. Bookie and I kept moving. I flew over the handlebars and hit various things on my venture through the air—a couple of branches and then Bookie himself as I flew past. As I flew through the air, everything was sharp and clear. I heard the sounds of at least one of the explosives blowing. By time I landed, I'd lost the use of one arm, my head was wavering in and out of fuzziness and my ears were ringing.

"Bookie?" I yelled, hoping he'd survived the fall. I didn't know if he answered or not. I couldn't hear myself.

I rolled onto my stomach, trying to use the good arm to prop myself up when boots appeared in front of my face. I recognized those boots. They were part of the Newco guard uniform.

My hurt arm was wrenched roughly as the rags were torn from my attached hand. I couldn't hear what they were saying but I was quickly pulled to my feet. There were five of them that I saw as I was half dragged, half carried away. I didn't see Bookie, but I'd stopped calling for him. He was better off left here than where I was going.

They shoved me toward a truck not far away and the pain in my arm and head made me want to retch, but I passed out before I did.

**

When I woke up, I was lying on the floor in the back of their truck, and my hearing had returned. It had one of those canvas covers and the rear was wide open so I could see the night sky. Three guards sat on the bench next to me, their boots near my head along with the butts of their guns. Bookie wasn't there, and I hoped he wasn't dead. We'd been pretty close to home. Someone would've heard the explosion and hopefully was getting him help.

I was pretty sure I'd be on my own. If Bookie was alive, I doubted he was going to be up for a rescue mission. No one else would come. I was on my own and that was fine. I'd made it most of my life that way.

I lay there and took stock. The pain in my arm told me without moving it that it was damaged beyond use, every jostle of the truck shooting a new wave through my arm. Luckily for me, I was good with my left as well. My knife was still tucked into a boot, covered by my pants. They must not have bothered to check me. But I'd only be able to take out one of them, not three. My knife had one final throw, so I might as well make it count and land it in a worthy target. These guys weren't worthy enough.

When we finally stopped, I wasn't given privacy to go to the bathroom but forced to relieve myself in front of them or not at all.

The guards sitting in the back of the truck with me alternated. Other than bathroom stops, we kept moving. I was given a few ration bars a day and a canteen to drink from. No one spoke as we drove day and night.

My hope of escaping them dwindled more

each day, reaching a new low on day three when I saw the gates of Newco from the back. An hour later I felt worse as I heard the brakes squeal right before I watched as the Cement Giant swallowed us whole.

Inside I was screaming that I couldn't do this again, but there was no one to scream it to. There was no other choice. I was going to have to.

I was guided through the building and down the halls into a room I knew so well. They didn't bother putting me in the chair but dumped me on the floor. I didn't bother getting up, just slumped there and thought of Dax and how he'd been so cold. He'd told me that was how I'd need to be to survive. Maybe he was right, because all these emotions and desperation and a sadness that stretched so deep within me I couldn't see around it weren't going to help me survive. I wanted to shut them all down, wished I could.

Ms. Edith walked into the room, white jacket over her dark suit, hair slicked back. At the sight of her, I realized I had one emotion I could work with, and it was anger.

She walked over to her chair and sat down. "You really thought you could get away?"

I had. Now look at me. I couldn't run and I wasn't delusional enough to think Dax would be breaking me out a second time. I was going to die here. I had nothing good left to lose but rage to spare. My knife's final throw had found its target.

I forced myself into a sitting position with my back against the wall.

"What are you?" I asked, ready to lay it all out there.

Her head kinked sideways in the most unnatural movement I'd ever seen. "So, you admit that I look different to you?"

"You look like a monster that just crawled out of a swamp, you creepy fuck."

Her head twitched again, as if her natural movements weren't smooth at all. "I'm just a regular human, Dal."

"Kill me if you want, but for one time, let's just lay it on the table. You're not human. What kind of sick shit are you and your people?"

"I don't know what you're talking about." She leaned forward in a funny way again. "I wish I could tell you what you wanted to hear, no matter what it might do to your fragile sanity. But I'm human."

She wanted me to know she was something more. It was obvious by the way she moved, but she couldn't tell me. So she wasn't the top dog in charge. I'd heard that the Plaguers before me had said there were Dark Walkers in some very high places. So I wouldn't be killing the leader. It would still be worth it.

My opportunity came quicker than I'd imagined. The door opened to one of the guards I'd traveled with, several more standing behind him. She looked over for a mere second. That was all I needed. I drew my knife and threw it, watching as it flew true and nailed her in the middle of her chest.

There was shock on her face, and the guard who'd been in the middle of speaking and the ones behind him hadn't even realized something had happened yet.

They froze just long enough that I could hear her say with her last breath, "They'll never let you go. You're the key. You're doomed anyway."

She hadn't even gripped the knife, but accepted her fate. Her head lolled back and it finally jolted the guard into action as he ran in and the others behind him followed.

Her death would have to be enough satisfaction to last me the rest of my life, what little there would be left now.

Chaos erupted quickly as I stayed leaning against the wall, catching glimpses of my handiwork as they all filed in.

"Sir, what the hell—" I heard one guard say as he was staring down at Ms. Edith.

"Where did that knife come from? Didn't anyone check her?" he asked, pointing at me.

The other guard just stammered.

"Throw her in the hole until we figure out what to do about this."

"I think she's valuable, sir. They wanted her badly."

"The hole won't kill her."

They talked back and forth but I didn't care what they said anymore. She'd said they'd *never let me go.* Even if I somehow managed to get free again, I'd be on the run for the rest of my life. There would be no big house for me and my friends, no pretty curtains hanging over windows framing forests. I was doomed.

They grabbed me and dragged me out of the room, and I didn't fight. Not when I felt the air on my face or when I was dropped into the eight-foot ditch. I didn't cry when the lid was lowered over it—only a tiny hole, not even six inches wide, was left to see the world above.

The walls were stone; the ground under me packed dirt. I could scale the walls when I was in better condition, but not like this. It didn't matter, though, since the lid was too heavy for me to lift. I'd tried the last time I'd been thrown in here.

I would die here. And even if I didn't, there was nowhere left to go. The Dark Walkers were everywhere, the country and the Wilds. And they wanted me. I'd been on borrowed time all along, just waiting until word spread. All those Dark Walkers I'd seen would be hunting me for a reason I didn't even understand.

Chapter 33

Days blended together when you were in the hole, and the eight-foot square became your entire world. If you didn't make a mark on a stone or the ground, you lost track of how long you were there as the hours blended together. The guard had said "they wanted me," but "they" were taking a long time getting me.

Once a day they lowered in enough food and water to keep me alive. The thing about the human brain is it's meant to be stimulated, and if it doesn't get any of that stimuli from the outside, it will make up its own diversions. I wondered how long it would be until they broke my mind.

I'd lost count of how long I'd been there when I heard the explosions that night. At first, I thought I'd made them up in my mind—that I'd finally cracked.

It wasn't until I heard a familiar male voice that I started to consider that it might be real.

"Dal?"

"Dax?" I asked, my voice raspy from lack of water. You didn't get good catering in the hole.

"I'm getting you out. Hang on."

The lid lifted and a rope with a loop on the end was lowered, the sound of bombs exploding as it did. I climbed into it and he was pulling me up and out of the hole. For someone who normally lacked expressions, I must have looked pretty bad from the look of his face.

There he was, standing next to Tank. If I wasn't so stunned, I would've started crying full-fledged tears, but I'd have to believe it first.

He'd come for me. He'd actually come for me.

"Can she ride?" I heard Tank say.

"She has to."

"It's going to hurt," Tank said, looking at the way my arm was bent.

"It'll be death if we leave her here. Get the rope," Dax said, leading me over to the bike. I followed him and still couldn't believe he was here.

Dax got on his bike as mayhem was happening beside us, explosions still going off at the building. The last boom finally snapped reality like a band and brought me out of my shocked haze.

"My friends! I've got to get my friends!" I wasn't leaving them again. There'd be no getting them after this.

Dax grabbed my arm and dragged me back. "Bookie and Lucy are getting them. Bookie knows what to do. He should already have them. We have to go."

I'd told Bookie every step of the plan. He'd have it covered. I could count on Bookie. I knew it in my heart.

I nodded and Dax helped me balance to get on the bike behind him. Tank tied a rope snug around me to help me stay behind Dax, once we took off and I only had one hand to use.

"Why did you come back?" I asked before Dax started the bike up, still stunned he'd come for me.

I thought he'd tell me this wasn't the time for questions, but he turned his head so I could see his profile before he said, "Someone told me once not to be that person. I figured if I left you for dead I was a shoo-in for the role."

He was making a joke, but I knew what he'd risked coming here. "Thank you."

"You haven't experienced the ride home. Don't thank me yet."

I put my forehead to his back and wrapped my good arm around him. I was barely holding it together. Then I felt his own hand covering mine, as if he knew.

We took off and I heard bikes fall in behind us as we drove away from the chaos of explosions still going off and the Cement Giant being destroyed. I saw girls running from the building and knew that Bookie had made sure that the building was being bombed exactly the way I had wanted. That he'd gotten Margo the book so that everyone had been prepared. If the guards had looked in the cells that night, they might've wondered why everyone was sleeping underneath their bunks, the tables on their sides, set up like shields.

The bike ride was a rough one and I didn't see much after we got going, focusing on not retching on Dax's back as the pain shot through my arm with each bump. I heard the bikes roaring into place behind us as we took to the forest, but I didn't have the maneuverability to see them. This time, we didn't stop riding until we got to the pirates' bay.

I felt arms wrap around me before I got off the bike. Dax untied us from each other and then Margo was hugging me full force.

But only Margo. I looked over her shoulder and I saw Lucy and Bookie, and some other guy that I'd seen working guard duty at Dax's, but no Patty or Cindy.

"Where are they?" I asked, and I hoped that she'd say they got left behind somehow. It was better than what I feared.

Margo pulled back and she didn't have to say they were dead. It was there for me to see in the tears in her eyes. "Ms. Edith went nuts after you left. She thought we knew where you went. I think I only made it because of who my father is."

It took a minute for it to sink in. I kept looking for them, like they had to be with us somehow. It wasn't until I saw Bookie's expression that I really believed it. He'd never looked at me like that before, not once in the time I'd known him. His eyes dropped, as if he couldn't stand to see the realization in my own.

I fell to my knees and sobbed for the first time since I was four. Margo collapsed beside me. Everyone else gave us our space, except for a nudge when we had to get on the boat. We sat together on the deck as I told her everything that had happened, and she told me the rest of what had gone on there. By time we crossed the bay, I had no tears left within me.

The rest of the trip was a blur of pain and mourning. When my body wasn't in agony, my heart was.

Chapter 34

We got back to the house after two days and a really rough ride home. The pain of riding with my arm, even with the makeshift splint Bookie had given me, took a hard toll on my body. I had a blurry memory of Dax carrying me up the stairs to bed.

I slept for an entire day and didn't try and fight it, knowing the reality I'd wake to. I'd never avoided life before, but I wanted to now. When I woke up the next morning, though, I knew I was going to have to face the future. It was coming whether I wanted it to or not.

I inched along the hallway and made my way down the stairs in an effort to get to the breakfast buffet and get about the business of living.

Bookie was there waiting with a smile. He didn't say much but he made a pile of food on my plate while I held it, my other hand stuck in an unfortunate position attached to an arm that had been broken and recently set.

He walked outside with me and we both sat with our breakfast. We'd been eating for a few minutes before he started to talk. "I'm sorry. I wanted to save them. I wish I could've. Margo said they'd… It wasn't an option."

I didn't want to talk, and especially not

about them, but I'd do it for Bookie. He deserved that and more than I'd ever be able to give. "It wasn't your fault. I'll be forever grateful that you got Margo out. You did a good job."

He nodded and looked like he felt as inadequate as I did right now. But he cleared his throat and carried on. "So what are your plans now?"

"I've got to leave." I'd known it before I'd even gotten back here, but it still hurt to say the words.

"I was afraid you might say that. I want to go with you."

I dropped my fork onto the plate in my lap. I'd need my strength, but I couldn't force the food down any longer. "I can't take you from here."

"I know the Wilds as good as anyone and better than most. You need me more than they do. They've got a doctor. They'll be fine without me."

"I can't have you do that."

"I might not look like much now, but I can be the man you need."

"It's not that. I think you're one of the greatest people I'd ever met. But anyone that comes with me is getting a death sentence."

"I understand you have to do what you feel is right. But so do I. I won't let you do this alone." He shrugged.

I didn't have a chance to argue with him as I saw Margo coming. Bookie looked over at her and then to me, knowing the conversation that was going to happen, and got up, offering her his seat beside me.

She was eating but I couldn't swallow a thing.

I didn't know what had happened to me. I wasn't me anymore. I felt like I was living in some purgatory, perpetually on the brink of crying. I'd wanted to live life, but living it was a lot tougher than I'd thought it would be. I'd had this delusion that once I got out of the Giant, I could make everything right. Boy how wrong I'd been.

And this was going to be one of the toughest conversations I'd ever had.

"Dax said I need to get away from here. He found me a place to go nearby that he says will be safer if they come. I told him that we had to wait a little bit until your arm healed more if he didn't mind. He didn't say anything to that, though. If he thinks we're going to separate places he's crazy. Not that he said that, but he didn't seem to be including you, which was bizarre. Why wouldn't we go together? He's a little tightlipped, huh?"

I knew why he hadn't said anything. Even though Margo didn't see it yet, Dax knew I was the reason it was unsafe here.

"We aren't going there together." I looked down at the wood under my feet and dragged a toe across it. "They're going to come for me. They did this time and they're going to do it again."

"But I thought you killed Ms. Edith. Dax said she was dead."

"That might not be the end of things."

"I won't leave without you."

I shook my head. "I'm not giving you a choice. You've got a chance to live a peaceful life. I don't. I won't take that from you. If you force me, I'll go with you and then disappear, but you'll just be making it harder on me."

She put her plate down and stormed a couple feet away. "How come you can risk yourself for me and I'm not allowed to do the same?"

"I know it's not fair but I'm still not doing it. Margo, you've just gotten out, so maybe you don't realize how precious this chance is to really have a life, but I will not steal it from you just so that I don't have to be alone. And I don't want to be alone. Please, don't make this harder on me."

She looked at me like I was betraying her somehow, and it killed another piece of me. She got up and walked in the house as if she couldn't bear to speak to me anymore. Dax had been right about this too. I couldn't have emotions and survive.

Chapter 35

I was sitting outside on the front porch where not as many people came and went, a bag packed with all the things they'd given me plus a pile of food Fudge had shoved in. It was stashed in my room waiting for the dead of night, when Bookie would be asleep.

Not leaving this afternoon had nothing to do with having nowhere to go, even though I didn't. Bookie wasn't going to let me go alone and I wasn't going to let him come.

Bookie had tried to talk me out of my decision for the last day, not knowing he was just making me want to leave sooner. He didn't understand, just like Margo hadn't. I was doing this for them and nothing would sway that.

Footsteps hit the wood beside me and I realized how much I loved the sound of this place, the screen door swinging shut and wind chimes tinkling in the breeze.

Dax walked down the steps beside me and then out a few feet into the yard.

"Margo left this morning with Tank," he said.

I already knew this. I'd watched her leave from the upstairs bedroom window. She'd finally relented this morning and said goodbye then hugged me as she cried.

"He'll get her there in one piece. It'll be safe there. I know the people she's going to live with and they'll take good care of her, help her make a life."

"Thank you for that."

His back to me, he stared off at the forest. "I hear you're planning on leaving soon, too?"

"I can't stay here for the same reason I couldn't go with her." I took in the same view, trying to burn it into memory.

"Where you going to go?"

"I'm not sure yet. You know, you never really told me why you saved me."

He turned and walked back to the steps, sat down a foot away and rested his forearms on his legs. "You don't have to leave."

"That's not how I see it. They're going to come for me." I dropped my head in my hand. "I won't do any more damage. If I stay here, sooner or later, they'll destroy this place, Wilds or not. I'm not stupid enough to think I can beat them anymore. At least if I run, maybe I'll lead them far away from here."

"If you stay, I'll help you."

"Help me what? Get you all killed?"

"Help you become someone that they'll be scared of."

"How? Look at me. You were right—I was a

fool walking around with these grandiose ideas of who I was, thinking I could be like some stupid made-up character from a book."

"I *am* looking at you and I know exactly the person you could be."

I wanted so much to believe he was right but I wasn't that naive anymore. "I can't stay. I won't do that to the people here."

"They're going to come here anyway. It's why I sent Margo to the other settlement."

"Why would they?"

"They've been searching for me too. This place. They just haven't figured it out yet."

"What do you mean? That doesn't make any sense."

"It will. You up for a walk?"

"Sure."

I got up followed him through the gate and into the woods. We walked quietly together, and I realized as we did he was one of the biggest reasons I didn't want to leave this place. Yes, I'd miss Fudge and Tiffy. I'd miss my talks with Bookie. I'd even miss Lucy's misguided ways and Tank's gruffness. But whether I wanted to admit it or not, I'd miss Dax most.

He didn't stop until we got to the place where he'd buried the beast, the one we never spoke of.

He looked at the grave he'd made, just

starting to grow some greenery but still obviously fresh.

"I know you didn't understand why we stopped looking for Dark Walkers." He pointed to the grave. "That's why. I'd found what I was seeking."

"The beast? I don't understand." We'd seen a beast after the bounty hunters and still kept going.

He stayed staring at the grave as he talked. "There used to be a story about the beasts in the Wilds known only to a few people. It said the beasts were once human, born from the very first Plaguers ever to survive in the early years, after the Bloody Death first started leaving a few alive. It was said that the beasts were born human babies and grew up like any other child, until one day they would disappear into the forests, never to be seen again. At first, the villagers and people thought their missing children had been eaten by bears or other animals.

"Then more people started disappearing, but carcasses were left behind, proof a large predator had fed on them. The sightings of the beasts started right around then.

"Still, no one made the connection until a farmer saw his son walk into the forest one afternoon. No matter how many times the man called to him, the son kept walking. Of course he followed him, worried something was wrong. That's when he saw his son turn into a beast and they figured out what was happening. He tried to approach his son, now a beast, and it nearly killed him. It was completely wild. He never saw him again.

"That's when they knew the children of the Plaguers were doomed to become these creatures. No one knew for sure if these children didn't want to be human anymore or couldn't. Maybe once they turned into the beast, they forgot they were human to begin with, or just preferred the animal to the man."

Dax knelt down and grabbed a handful of dirt before letting it sift through his fingers. "The people who knew were scared of the world becoming filled with these beasts, so they started spreading rumors of how the sickness would never really go away and that all Plaguers should be killed.

"Then a woman from the village got sick. Her husband, afraid that the rest of the community would kill her, snuck her away in the middle of the night. She survived.

"They were afraid to return to their home after so many knew she had gotten sick, so he found them a grand old farmhouse to live in with plenty of land to work, and a cliff to help protect it. They didn't know the story about the boy that turned into the beast until after they'd already birthed twin boys. An old relative who knew where they were found out about the children and told them the story when the twins were five.

"Every day from then on, the two of them wept for fear that their sons would turn."

"Did they?" I asked, even as I tried to deny the pieces that were clicking into place—how many large farmhouses were there with cliffs behind them?

"They did, just past their eighteenth birthday. The forest seemed to call to them one day and they changed into beasts. The parents cried, even discussed hunting them down and killing them out of guilt for what they'd created, knowing the beasts would turn around and kill others."

I took a couple steps back from where Dax was kneeling, fearing where this was going.

He continued, oblivious to my alarm or not caring. "A week later, their sons returned, looking as human as they ever had."

He fell silent and I took a couple more steps away as the ramifications of everything he'd just told me sank in. The farmhouse, the brothers. He hadn't killed that beast in the woods; he'd mourned it. And the next day, he'd changed plans abruptly as if his search was no longer a priority. He'd thought that the Dark Walkers had taken his brother.

When I finally looked up I didn't see Dax anymore. A chill had spread out along my skin as I finally confronted what he had said. "How do you know all of this?" I asked, looking for him by the grave he was no longer kneeling by.

Then I heard a low growl a foot behind me.

"Dax?" My voice was soft as I sensed the beast right behind me. I had to be crazy for even thinking the thoughts in my head. I was afraid to turn around and see him with my own eyes.

Then a wet tongue ran up the back of my neck, exactly how it had that first time I'd come in contact with one.

Dax was right. I did understand. I didn't have to leave here because I wasn't the only thing the Dark Walkers were hunting in this place.

They wanted a beast that could turn human. They wanted Dax.

If you would like updates on new releases, follow Donna through one of these social media accounts:

https://twitter.com/DonnAugustine

https://www.facebook.com/Donnaaugustineboo ks?ref=bookmarks

www.donnaaugustine.com

Made in the USA
Lexington, KY
28 January 2016